About the Author

C.B. Moraveck worked in the private sector, city and county government for many years before retirement. While serving as an adjunct professor, she has written one textbook and several journal articles. This is her first romantic mystery novel. She has lived in Southern California all her life.

Mystery On Orange Street

C. B. Moraveck

Mystery On Orange Street

Vanguard Press

VANGUARD PAPERBACK

© Copyright 2024
C. B. Moraveck

The right of C. B. Moraveck to be identified as author of
this work has been asserted by her in accordance with the
Copyright, Designs and Patents Act 1988.

All Rights Reserved

No reproduction, copy or transmission of this publication
may be made without written permission.
No paragraph of this publication may be reproduced,
copied or transmitted save with the written permission of the
publisher, or in accordance with the provisions
of the Copyright Act 1956 (as amended).

Any person who commits any unauthorised act in relation to
this publication may be liable to criminal
prosecution and civil claims for damages.

A CIP catalogue record for this title is
available from the British Library.

ISBN 978 1 83794 015 8

This is a work of fiction. Names, characters, businesses, places, events and
incidents are either the product of the author's imagination or used in a
fictitious manner. Any resemblance to actual persons, living or dead, or actual
events is purely coincidental.

*Vanguard Press is an imprint of
Pegasus Elliot Mackenzie Publishers Ltd.*
www.pegasuspublishers.com

First Published in 2024

**Vanguard Press
Sheraton House Castle Park
Cambridge England**

Printed & Bound in Great Britain

For Joan

CHAPTER 1

SHADY GROVE

In the year 2008, the recession and foreclosure crisis began in the United States. Nearly 3.8 million families were forced out of their homes. Now, it's happening all over again. The atmosphere was toxic. Those who didn't move out willingly were soon evicted. Some moved in with relatives or found cheaper places to rent. Others ended up being homeless where the sky was their roof, and the ground was their bed. Foreclosures happen all the time but not of this large magnitude, and for Megan and her mom it would be devastating.

Megan kept going over and over it again in her mind, what kind of daughter would not go out of her way to help her mom?

If there was not enough money for the Orange Street house payments, the home would be foreclosed and taken by the mortgage company. Trying to finish college would be almost impossible. Dreams would be only dreams and nothing else.

Megan's day started with a knock on the front door. Her friend Ashley was sitting next to the kitchen table sipping on a cup of tea.

"Just a minute, Ashley, I need to see who's knocking."

Megan opened the door and there stood two tall sheriff deputies, one with a piece of paper in his hand. Both of them were no strangers to those who lived in the small town. He handed the paper to her.

"We have to move your mom's furniture out of the house. She's being evicted," he said almost apologetically.

"What?" Megan was stunned and looked at their serious faces. "What are you talking about?"

"She hadn't paid the mortgage and the guys standing behind me are here to move everything," he replied.

Ashley walked toward the door after hearing the conversation and was confused as to what was going on. Three robust young men dressed in jeans, cotton T-shirts, tennis shoes, and wearing work gloves stood there staring at Megan. "Good morning," one of them said, trying to be polite.

Megan was shaken and didn't know what to say, stepped back, and the men pushed their way past her inside the house. She stood there dumbfounded. They carried the sofa out through the front door and placed it on the lawn, then the coffee table, the dining room table and chairs, and next was the recliner chair, the lamps and anything else they could grab.

"This is crazy!" Ashley shouted, observing what was happening.

Not knowing what to do, Megan was overwhelmed, and tears ran down her cheeks. Just then she heard a loud noise from screeching car tires. Uncle James drove up in front of the house.

He got out of the car, walked quickly toward the door waving a piece of paper in his hand shouting, "Put everything back! The mortgage has been paid. My niece and her mom aren't going anywhere!"

The deputy read the paper then shouted, "Hey, guys, we're not doing this today so stop and put everything back in the house."

Megan stood there observing everything, still traumatized. Everything happened so rapidly. Her thoughts were still spinning. Uncle James came to the rescue. He didn't have a lot of money but somehow managed to negotiate with the mortgage company and paid the overdue house payments. She grabbed her uncle, hugged and kissed him, and thanked him for his generosity. After they talked briefly, he got in the car and drove away.

She and Ashley walked inside, sat there on the sofa still in shock then Megan mumbled, "I don't ever want to go through that again."

"Thank goodness for your uncle," Ashley said softly and hugged Megan. "Life can be brutal at times."

Several people in the neighborhood had lost their homes when they were foreclosed, while others had been swindled by investors who deceived the owners who thought they would make money if they sold their homes to them. Many later found out the riches they were promised ended up being in the hundreds of dollars instead of the thousands."

Megan's family didn't always live on Orange Street. Before, when she was a little girl, they lived on Morgan Street in Los Angeles, but the water pipes broke and flooded the floors, so they had to move. Afterwards, they lived on Tamarind Street and the heater never worked, so some nights they shivered from the freezing cold. They moved to Mission Street, thought they'd finally found a place to call home, but then they found out the neighbors were selling drugs, so they moved again and again, only able to afford rentals. But Megan's dad had always promised they would one day move into their very own house.

During that time, Megan's dreams had always been simple. She'd imagined living in a beautiful house when she was older, just like in the story books. It didn't have to be huge—a small house would be fine—and dressed like a princess, she would meet her Prince Charming, get married, and have a family.

Now, troubling thoughts were going through her mind. She clearly remembered how she felt when they first moved into their house long ago. Wearing her best Sunday dress, the one her mom had sewn with love poured into every stitch, Megan was excited to see her parents' new home. After driving for an hour on the freeway, her family pulled up in front of an old house in Shady Grove, fifty-five miles southeast of L.A. She got out of the car, elated beyond belief, but after staring at it for a long time, her heart felt as if it had sunk to her stomach.

The house was literally falling apart. Megan was in disbelief. She was so disappointed, wanted to cry and didn't. But she held back her tears and wondered, *How could this be? This couldn't possibly be our new home. Is this what it's like living outside of Los Angeles?* Her dad had made a terrible mistake.

The front door was reduced to warped and dilapidated wood with rusted hinges, a weak shield from the outside world. The old wooden siding was cracked and dry and there was peeling white paint, loose wooden boards, and broken and missing shingles on the roof. Expecting lush, green grass, she was confronted by a large front yard with dry, parched dirt covered with occasional clumps of coarse ragged-looking crabgrass, and ugly brown weeds and rocks—a real disaster. The mailbox was nearly hidden by tall, deep-rooted wild shrubs. The only beautiful thing she could see was the house was surrounded by hundreds of trees filled with orange blossoms and dark green leaves. The smell of sweet fruit filled the air, and it invigorated her to try and stay positive, but it was difficult.

They walked inside and she was even more disillusioned. Her first thought was *This place is awful!* There were ugly tattered and faded blinds on the windows. It was dark and stuffy with little lighting. It was like a cave until her mother opened the windows. There were creaking stairs and floorboards. When she opened the bathroom door, she had to immediately brush the filthy, gritty dirt off her hands. The inside was disgusting. The attic was dim and gloomy with one large window. It was not the house she had expected to see.

Being a dreamer, her father wanted to escape the inner city and give Megan and her brother a better life. He had imagined what the house could become, but repairing the house wasn't going to be easy. He and her mom started almost as soon as they'd moved in.

Often, she would wake up to the noise of her father already working on the house. There was the sound of hammering and drilling, and there always seemed to be the smell of fresh paint late at night as she tried to fall asleep.

Megan and her brother, Chris, helped where they could. During rainy days they had to place large buckets in one of the bedrooms and in the kitchen because of the leaks in the roof. The sound of dripping water, at first annoying, but soon becoming soothing as she got used to it. Many of the nights were freezing cold. Other nights they could hear the howling Santa Ana winds blowing constantly against the house and shuffling the leaves on the orange trees. Those early years in the house produced a whole slew of memories Megan could never forget.

Her parents had taken three long years to finish work on the house and, in the meantime, their lives had gotten much better. The house and the yard were transformed inch by inch into something welcoming and comfortable, and now there was green, lush grass surrounding it and colorful flowers. Her mom had a talent for making plants thrive. A narrow driveway ran along the side of the house to the backyard and ended at the garage. Beyond it, her dad had even built a large shed.

Ever since her father had passed away a few years ago, they always seemed to be struggling. She tried to smile a lot, but some days were difficult. There never seemed to be enough money, and Megan knew many families in the neighborhood had the same problem. Unfortunately for a twenty-two-year-old, her love life had hardly lived up to the fairytale she'd built in her head. She had dated her fair share of attractive, charming guys— maybe a few not so charming—but never the one she could imagine settling down with.

Megan had grown to appreciate living in the small town of Shady Grove. It was a picturesque community situated inland, surrounded by orange and lemon groves with windbreaks of eucalyptus or clusters of palm trees, and beautiful grape vineyards. The downtown had vintage shops, restaurants, a small shopping mall with a movie theater, parks and biking trails, and was close to the college. It was a relief not to worry about commuting in a large city with all the traffic, and she appreciated the close-knit community where everyone knew everyone. There was the feeling of belonging.

There were very few crimes reported in Shady Grove, but Megan knew it was far from perfect. The town was struggling, her family was struggling, and since her father died, there were only a few people in her life to truly rely upon.

On Wednesday night, an annoying noise woke her up. Someone was outside. The sound was like a truck's engine but soon faded away. She turned over and glanced at the clock next to her bed—a little past midnight. Maybe someone was trying to get into the house?

She didn't like late night sounds, especially when she was home alone. But at least it wasn't the strange sounds she sometimes heard in the attic. The door near the end of the long hallway outside her bedroom led up to it, but nobody had been up there in years. Her mother forbade it. The attic was a dark place, with a musty wood smell, old peeling wallpaper on one wall, and in need of fresh air.

Rubbing her eyes, not fully awake, Megan walked to the living room window in her bare feet. Carefully pushing the drapes back, she peered out of the window cautiously. A large truck was parked in front of the house across the street. Two men were walking around and talking softly. She had difficulty seeing because there was little moonlight in the night sky.

Something was wrong. It just didn't feel right. The Emerson family was moving out of their house in the middle of the night. They were carrying clothes, boxes and furniture, and loading them into the truck. What a strange time to be moving. *Perhaps they're hoping people are sleeping? Maybe they're worried about what the neighbors think.* It was probably less embarrassing—nobody asking questions.

They were moving quietly, trying not to make any noise. Megan tried watching every move from her window, but it was too dark. Mrs. Emerson had never said anything about moving. She never mentioned it at all, and they talked often.

She remembered the day when Mrs. Emerson's son Scott moved away to Los Angeles to attend college. He would come back home on holidays to visit. Scott had always had a habit of smiling and flirting with her, but just when Megan thought there was something there, he always said she had some growing up to do.

But she never got a chance to grow up for him, because he'd passed away in a car accident. She missed him. There was a deep hole inside her soul always there wondering if she would ever meet someone like Scott again. She forced herself not to think about it. That was the past. There was the present to worry about now.

Megan watched through the window a little longer. Still sleepy, she finally went back to bed wondering if she'd ever see the Emersons again.

The next morning, Megan peered out of the window and saw the neighbors going about their daily routine not knowing what had happened. Nothing seemed unusual or different. Just like the Nolte and Copperfield families before them, without the Emersons, life would go on in Shady Grove like nothing had ever happened. Children were walking to school and people were leaving for work in their cars. Like she did every morning, the neighbor next door, Mrs. Atkins, bent over and picked up her newspaper from the driveway before going back indoors.

She wiped away a few tears from her face and wondered where the Emerson family had moved to. Everything seemed to be changing, and she knew in a few days, everyone would notice something different about the Emerson house—no cars in the driveway, no lights shining from the windows.

People losing their homes and not finding affordable places to live was becoming an epidemic. Nobody knew who the next victim would be until the day it was visible to the entire neighborhood.

Now things were likely to get worse because of her mom's accident. If she couldn't work, she could lose everything, and there wouldn't be enough money for the house payments. Megan heard about people sleeping in their cars.

At the hospital yesterday, Megan found her mom had no discussion about being worried. In fact, she said her situation was temporary and would only keep her off work for a few weeks, maybe a little longer. Strangely, her mom appeared to believe everything would be fine, but Megan wasn't so sure about it.

Soon after graduating from high school, Megan had to earn a living and worked for a while in retail stores, but never made enough money to get her own apartment and pay all her bills. Megan and her mother agreed that going to college seemed the best option for getting a better job, but Megan knew all the uncertainty around her mother and the house payments could delay those dreams.

It was already eight a.m. Monday, so she got dressed quickly. After three weeks of winter break from college, Megan rushed to finish her breakfast and went to the campus. She had dreaded this day because she had decided there was no other option but to withdraw from her daytime classes.

The Santa Ana winds usually blow in January, but today there was just a gentle breeze. Megan, standing at five-feet seven-inches tall, gently pushed her shoulder length, chestnut brown, curly hair away from her face as she walked to the college admissions office. Her full sensuous mouth, intelligent face and sparkling light, brown eyes captured the attention of most people she met.

Being a fulltime student was a great feeling when she started back to college again this year, but she must change her plans, attend classes in the evening, and find a fulltime job.

Megan walked quickly to the admissions office before it became crowded with students and convinced herself to be positive even though things had changed dramatically for the worse.

"Hi, Mrs. Clark."

"Hi, Megan, what can I do for you today?"

Megan's eyes looked down from hers. "I have to drop my daytime classes."

"What?"

"I need to find a fulltime job." Megan handed her the forms she had completed the night before.

"I'm so sorry to hear that, Megan. I really hope things work out for you and your mother."

It seemed Mrs. Clark had heard about the problems Megan was going through.

"Thanks, Mrs. Clark." Megan smiled weakly.

Mrs. Clark processed the forms and handed Megan her copies. After folding the papers, putting them in her backpack, she slowly walked out of the office. With her eyes focused downward, Megan made her way to her car in the campus parking lot. Her mother's problems overwhelmed her.

She finished her errands early, arrived home, opened the front door, and threw her things on the sofa. It had been a long, stressful day so she made her way to the bedroom, sat down on the bed, and arranged the pillows. Sinking into them, she stared at the ceiling for a while wondering if her life would ever change. She had to make sure her mom kept the house.

She desperately needed a job, not just any job but a good one so her mom wouldn't have to worry about house payments or foreclosure. Megan had no delusions about being rich, but just wanted to be able to live comfortably. She wanted to stop struggling, be able to pay all her bills on time, and own a decent car that wouldn't break down all the time. Was that too much to ask?

Megan stood up, walked to the kitchen in her bare feet, poured herself a glass of iced tea, then headed back to her bedroom. She started to reflect on the memories of her dad.

By evening, she soon dozed off to sleep but then suddenly woke up when she heard a loud bang. Her eyes quickly focused straight up to the ceiling toward the attic. Huddled under the covers, she gripped the sheets, and took a deep breath. Something strange was going on. Maybe it was the house settling. One time, Uncle James said most houses made nighttime noise from hot and cold air. Perhaps that was the reason for the noise. An elderly man who used to live in the neighborhood once told her mom the house was haunted but she didn't believe him. Mom said he watched too many horror movies and laughed. Still, an uneasy feeling ran through her veins.

She was tired and needed her rest. Megan convinced herself it was nothing to be worried about, her guardian angel would protect her, and eventually went back to sleep.

CHAPTER 2

THE TRIP TO LOS ANGELES

After spending all week searching for a job, Megan failed to even land one interview. Life could be difficult, but she was determined not to get discouraged.

Still, it was Saturday, she had made plans and was patiently waiting for Ashley, Corey and Mark. They were coming over to hang out together and cheer her up. Glad they wanted to spend time with her, Megan quickly cleaned the living room. She didn't want to be stuck at home by herself on the weekend.

She valued her friends. They knew what it was like not having much money and struggling to finish school. Coming from hard-working families, they had a flaming desire in life to better themselves.

Soon Ashley and Mark arrived at Megan's house. They settled down in the living room and sunk into the sofa to relax. Corey's friend dropped him off, so he was late arriving.

"Happy New Year!" he said smiling, as he walked into the house and hugged Megan.

"Stop saying that. It was over weeks ago," Megan replied, knowing he was trying to be amusing.

Light streamed into the room through the sheer drapes hanging on the windows. They huddled around Megan as she told her story. It had been a few weeks since they'd all gotten together, and only Ashley knew what was happening with her.

"You definitely need to stay in college," Corey said. "You can't live here forever, Megan.

"Yeah, I know. I have no intentions of dropping out."

"Good! It's going to be hard but in the long run it'll be worth it."

Corey had to drop out of his last two years of high school to work and help his mother with the bills and to prevent a foreclosure, so he knew what he was talking about. He'd studied hard to pass his GED, finally got his high school diploma, and was admitted to college the next semester. He was the clown in the group. Corey was the kind of guy who thrived being the center of attention at every party, but whenever Megan needed him, Corey was there for her. Still, he always had something to say even when people didn't want him to express his opinions, but he got away with it with his gorgeous mop of thick, black hair.

Mark kicked off his shoes, leaned back on the sofa, and put his feet on the coffee table. Megan's mother always scolded him every time he put his shoes on her furniture. Mark, an avid reader and technically savvy, was always willing to help Megan and anyone else who needed his help.

"You know, Meg, you need to get your mind off your problems," Mark said. "You're not homeless yet. Things can change for the best."

"I know but I can't help it." She was feeling down.

"You know what you need?" Megan shook her head. "Let's take a trip!"

"What?"

"C'mon, you know you need it!"

"I don't want to go anywhere. I don't even want to go down the street. I just want to stay here at home. We can eat ice cream and watch a movie."

Totally ignoring what she had just said, he continued, "Why don't we go to this house party in Los Angeles?"

"That kinda sounds cool," Corey said, leaning in. "Do tell!"

"Well, the house is unbelievable, a mansion. It'll be fun. Everyone's going! My friend called me yesterday and told me about it."

"Thanks, guys, really. But I'm not in the mood for L.A. I have too much on my mind right now."

"Come on. It'll make you feel better," Ashley added. Megan glared at her. "It's not like you have a reason to be here. Your mom won't be out of the hospital for a few days, right? And Chris is still on his way here from Texas."

"Yeah," Corey replied. "There might be hot guys there. You need a love life!"

Megan glanced at Corey, irritated. Did he really have to say that? Why would she want to go to a party just to meet some jerk? She tried to remember the last time she had meaningful physical contact with another person—a warm, romantic embrace or a kiss that excited her whole body. She couldn't remember.

"Meg, you need to have a little fun," Ashley said, giving her a wink.

"I know you guys like L.A… but the smog, I just hate it. You know I don't like the city. Too many tall buildings, all the concrete, black asphalt, and the noise and traffic…"

Most days in Southern California were full of radiant sunshine, and during the nights the cities glimmered with twinkling colorful lights. But sometimes when there was no breeze blowing, the skies turned a brownish color through a haze of pollution, and even the surrounding mountains would disappear.

"There's a breeze! C'mon, Megan, there won't be smog. You can even see the mountains," Mark chimed in.

Megan hesitated then leaped to her feet to see for herself. She walked outside on the porch, looked up at the sky, and it was true—she had a clear view of the mountains in the distance. Soon, she discovered the air to be so clean and blue, and walked back into the house.

"If you insist… I guess I'll go," Megan said reluctantly. "I'm driving."

Corey looked straight into her eyes. "Fine by me. Anyway, you're the only one with a four-door."

"Mind if my cousin tags along?" Mark asked.

"More the merrier!" Corey said before Megan could reply. "Let's go!"

By the time they left the house, the sun had already started its lazing descent. The shadows lengthened, making the leaves on the trees look like gold. They picked up Mark's cousin, Robert, and hit the main drag to Los Angeles.

The traffic made the drive to LA seem incredibly long even though it was only sixty miles outside of Shady Grove. Megan drove while everyone else talked and enjoyed the scenery. The California freeways had a deluge of streaming vehicle lights beaming as they cut through areas of flat land, over hills, and over numerous overpasses with streets below, with scenic views from the foothills of the San Bernardino and San Gabriel mountains. There were road-level aqueducts and concrete bridges built over dry creek beds, shallow washes and canals below. As she drove, they glanced at the shopping centers, businesses and hotels surrounded by hundreds of apartments, condos and homes with prosperous lawns and beautiful landscapes.

She drove past neighborhoods with small, old homes in need of repair and paint, and through areas with rundown buildings built too close together, their backs toward the freeway. Beside them were old buildings with brown and rusted corrugated metal roofs in dire need of care and maintenance. The view had gone from beautiful to dreary in the space of a mile.

"We're getting closer to the inner city. Look at all this traffic," Corey said, as he leaned forward from the backseat to get a better view.

"Why don't you let me drive?" Robert asked. He'd grown up in LA and knew all the streets and neighborhoods.

At first, Megan, a sensible and caring person decided it was a bad idea. She hesitated for a moment, then decided it was probably fine since he was Mark's cousin. Anyway, she didn't like driving in heavy LA traffic.

"I know a shortcut. Hold on!"

Not long after Robert had taken the wheel, he turned onto the freeway exit ramp to the city streets, going far too fast for Megan's comfort.

"Slow down!" she almost screamed at him.

"Hey, don't sweat it! Now you guys just sit back. I'll get us to the party, pronto."

They had been driving for about thirty minutes when they suddenly noticed a car behind them with red and blue flashing lights. It was the police. Megan's heart fluttered like a trapped bird. She'd never been pulled over before.

The tall, muscular police officer cautiously walked up to the car from behind. Robert rolled down the window. "Your right rear brake light isn't working," the officer said, his hand on his gun. Megan nearly screamed.

"Sorry, Officer. I had no idea," Robert replied.

"Can I see your driver's license?" he asked in a strong, commanding tone.

Robert leaned and reached into the back pocket of his pants, pulled out his wallet, and handed his license to him.

"Can I see the car registration and insurance?"

"Sure." Robert turned and looked at Megan.

"I'll get it out of the glove box."

She started searching for it hurriedly, worried she'd upset the officer. After a few stressful moments, she reached in, found the papers, and handed them to him.

"Are you the owner of this vehicle?"

"Yes," Megan replied.

"Can I see your driver's license?" There was no kindness in his voice.

"It's in my handbag. Can I reach inside?"

The cop nodded. Megan reached in, pulled out her wallet and gave it to him.

"Would you please take it out of your wallet?" he asked with a stern looking expression.

"Oh, of course." She was nervous and her hands trembled slightly as she pulled her license out of the wallet and gave it to him. There were plenty of horror stories about innocent people getting shot and killed just because of a traffic violation.

The officer walked back to his patrol car. Megan knew he was doing a background check on both of them. She wasn't worried because she had never gotten into trouble with the law. Robert was an unknown and she hoped he wasn't a problem. She didn't need any more problems.

The officer glared at them from his car. Five minutes later, he got out, unsnapped his holster, and quickly whipped out his black gun. He cautiously walked back toward the car, shouting in a loud, belligerent tone, "Everyone, slowly get out of the car and put your hands up in the air!"

"What?" Corey said from the backseat. They were all shocked.

"Be quiet," the officer commanded. "No talking. Now get out!"

Everyone exited the vehicle, put their hands up into the air and walked to the back of the car. One by one, the cop grabbed their hands and placed them on the hood of the car.

"Do not move your hands. Not an inch. You understand?"

Without hesitation, everyone nodded approvingly. Then he went to Robert, pulled out his cuffs, grabbed both of his hands and bound his wrists. "You are being arrested for failing to appear in court for a misdemeanor and other violations. You have the right to remain silent. Anything you say can and will be used against you in a court of law."

"What?" Megan said, hands shaking, knees weak.

"This man has several warrants issued for his arrest because of unpaid traffic tickets and numerous other illegal activities. Miss, you should know who you let take the wheel of your car," the cop said.

"I'm sorry, Megan. I didn't know," Mark said, shaking his head.

The officer ordered Robert into the backseat of his patrol car. He assisted him with a slight push and closed the car door, then walked back toward Megan.

"I'm writing you a traffic citation for the faulty brake light. You have time to get it fixed before the date written on the citation."

"All right," Megan replied with a mix of relief and terror.

"You can get back in your car and leave. Goodnight."

They were clearly shaken, but Megan was relieved to get back into the relative safety of her car.

As they did, Mark hesitated. He turned around and asked, "What about my cousin Robert? Where are you taking him?"

"I'm taking him back to the police station. You can call the phone number printed on the citation."

"Be quiet, Mark," Megan whispered. "No more questions." It was best if they left as quickly as they could.

They carefully got back into the car and hoped the officer didn't find some other reason to arrest anyone. Mark climbed into the front passenger seat next to Megan, while Ashley and Corey got in the backseat. Even though they were able to leave, they were still overwhelmed and shaken by what has just happened.

Megan turned and looked at Mark. "Nice going," she said feeling frustrated.

"I know, I know. I'm sorry," he said. "Robert had problems as a kid, but I was sure he'd grown up. I messed up."

"Why didn't you tell us about him?" Megan snapped at him.

"I don't know everything about him! Do you know everything about your family?" he asked, looking at all of them.

Ashley reached from the back seat and gently put her hand on Mark's shoulder. "It's not all Mark's fault, you guys. Robert was old enough to know better." She turned and looked at Megan. "Don't be so hard on him."

Feeling exhausted over the entire incident, Megan was reluctant to say anything and buckled her seatbelt. After some brief discussions everybody agreed it was best to drive back home. It was already dark outside and driving to a party in LA wasn't what anyone wanted to do any more.

"This area gives me the creeps. It's a dangerous neighborhood," Megan said, putting the car into gear. None of them were familiar with the streets, and they spent the next thirty minutes lost, just driving around trying to find the freeway again.

"Where the hell are we?" Ashley asked.

"Wherever you go, there you are," Corey replied.

"Seriously?" Ashley said, looking at him. "This is not the time to be funny."

Megan was getting worried. They couldn't find a freeway entrance. It was dark outside with little moonlight. They could hear the noise of the fast-moving cars and trucks on the freeway and see the reflection of lights shining in both directions.

"I hate to break the bad news, but it looks like Robert took us into no-man's land." Mark said, with his phone in his hand as he examined Google Maps. "I'm gonna dropkick his butt the moment I see him. The map indicates the freeway entrance is supposed to be right there," he said, pointing at a dead-end.

"That's just great! So, we really don't know where we are or where we're going," Megan replied. "Look for another entrance, would you?"

"L.A. is just like any big city. You better know where you're going else you can end up in deep crap." Corey blurted.

Nobody said a word. Megan was driving cautiously and turned onto several dead-end streets next to the freeway. There were very few streetlights. Megan gripped the steering wheel tightly. The car's headlights were the only thing lighting up the streets in front of them. She was driving slowly, peering through the windshield, intensely focused on the streets ahead while glancing ever so often in the rearview mirror. The silence and darkness were frightening and made everybody feel uneasy. It was scary, like waiting for large, angry dinosaurs with big, sharp teeth to walk out of the darkness and try to eat them like in the movies.

They passed by old houses with peeling paint and dry, brown lawns, the plants and shrubbery in dire need of care. They passed by rundown two and three-story apartment buildings. Some of the old wood fences were sagging. Many were faded and warped with broken and missing boards and leaning fence posts ready to fall down with the slightest gust of wind. There were some houses with old, rusted chain link fences. The area might have been a fashionable neighborhood some thirty years ago, but now the homes were badly in need of repair and coats of fresh paint. They stood out darkly against the night sky.

The four of them soon reached an old, seedy part of the city with small businesses, stores and nightclubs. Most businesses were closed for the evening and others were boarded up and abandoned. There were neighborhood bars with people standing outside on the sidewalks talking to each other and drinking. Other people were lighting their cigarettes and smoking weed, taking deep breaths and exhaling. Some streets were full of homeless people. Most of them were sleeping in tents on the sidewalks, and some in parked vehicles and old RVs. Others were living on a few scattered, vacant lots between commercial buildings. The surroundings were unfamiliar, and Megan just wanted to get out of this part of the city.

Mark was tracking their every move on Google Maps. He was navigating, telling Megan which direction to turn. She just wanted to get back on the freeway and didn't want anyone to know she was afraid of being lost. The freeway somehow gave her a feeling of security. Most people believed a car was a safe place to be, but not in these unfamiliar surroundings.

After a couple of minutes, Megan turned and glared at Mark. "Hey, dude, where in the hell are we?"

"According to this, we're going in the right direction."

"We're lost!" Ashley shouted. "This part of the city is really scary."

"I don't trust Google Maps," Megan said.

"What? Mark replied. "It's reliable ninety-nine percent of the time."

"It's the other one percent I'm worried about," Megan said. "I read about a lady who used her GPS in Death Valley. She ended up stuck in the sand on some dirt road in the middle of nowhere in the scorching heat, far from the main highway. Three days later the ranger found them."

"What happened to them?" Ashley asked.

"The park ranger noticed the tire tracks in the sand and followed them. When he finally found them, their tires were buried in the sand. He thought they were dead, but they had passed out from dehydration. When they reached the hospital, the one lady died from a snakebite the ranger didn't even know she had."

"Holy freakin cow… What kind of snake was it?" Corey asked, leaning forward from the backseat of the car.

"I don't know. Guess the snake didn't leave a business card," she said, rolling her eyes.

"Kinda dumb for not having enough water," Corey responded.

Mark reacted with frustration. "Hey, you guys, this is LA, not Death Valley."

Megan took a deep breath and looked in the rearview mirror. "Yeah, this is worse."

"We shouldn't be in this part of LA, day or night," Ashley said.

"If we get a flat, we're really in trouble," Corey said nervously.

"You guys are seriously that worried? We'll be fine," Mark said, leaning back in his seat.

Megan glanced at the road in front of her and in her car's rearview mirror. "I'm turning the car round and driving back the direction we came," she said, then quickly made a U-turn in the middle of the street.

"Well, that's an idea I guess," Ashley responded, head in her hands. "We have no idea where we're going."

Mark didn't say anything. He was still looking at the map on his cell phone. He hadn't said a darn thing about directions in five minutes.

Megan frowned, annoyed and snatched the phone out of his hands. She threw it in the backseat of the car on Ashley's lap. "If you're not going to help, then maybe help me look out for pedestrians. You're irritating me."

"You did not just do that," he replied.

"Yeah, I did." They were lost and she'd had enough.

Mark rolled his eyes at her. "What's your problem, Megan?"

"Look outside the car, Mark! That's my problem." She pointed out of the car window to their surroundings.

Marked reached into the backseat and Ashley handed the phone to him. Megan stopped the car at a street intersection waiting for the red traffic light to turn green. It took a long time to change, and she spotted five men standing on the corner smoking.

"Make sure your doors are locked," Megan said, then suddenly, one of the men left the corner sidewalk and quickly walked over next to their car. She looked straight ahead, and a second later the man tried at the backseat passenger door.

"He's trying to get in the car!" Ashley shouted.

Megan reacted and quickly pressed her foot down on the gas pedal. The tires screeched. The car accelerated across the intersection through the red traffic light, and an oncoming vehicle blared its horn and slammed on the brakes, nearly T-boning them in the intersection.

The man behind them, apparently drunk, yelled something obscene. But Megan couldn't hear everything. Shaking, terrified, with her hands gripping the steering wheel she started to turn pale.

"Oh, crap..." Corey said in the backseat.

"Okay, this is getting scary," Mark said. Everyone was visibly nervous.

"We're going to die! We're going to die in LA!"

"Be quiet, Ashley!" Corey said. "Nobody is going to die."

Megan could see the fear in Ashley's eyes. She needed to calm down. "Stop shouting and try to find the freeway entrance signs," she said, loosening her grip on the steering wheel.

Be calm... be calm... be calm.

She turned the music up hoping it would distract everyone, and they drove around for a few more minutes when suddenly the red engine warning light came on her car's dashboard.

Megan didn't need any car problems—not now, not at night in the darkness of LA. No one else seemed to notice.

This wasn't the time to panic. She kept repeating in her mind to stay calm, the car engine was still running. Repeating those words over and over again helped some but she wasn't able to convince herself not to worry. It was like being on a small raft in a deep, gigantic ocean, not knowing what's under the surface.

She turned the music down, leaned over, and whispered softly, "Mark, get out the owner's manual in the glove compartment."

"What?" Mark asked.

"You know. The owner's book about the car."

"Why?"

"I need you to find something for me."

"Why?"

"Just do it... please," she snapped trying to whisper so the others couldn't hear her.

He fumbled through the glove compartment. "Okay, I found the manual. Now what?"

"Try to find the page about the engine warning symbols and codes."

"What?" he said loudly as his heart started pounding faster and eyes widened.

Mark leaned over and studied the dashboard. "You've got to be kidding! The red engine warning light is on!"

"What's going on?" Corey asked from the back seat.

"I can't believe it!" Ashley said.

"Ashley, you're not helping," Megan said, turning back to Mark. "See anything?"

Mark fumbled through the pages of the car manual. Megan turned off the music. He flipped the pages as fast as he could. "I'm trying. I'm trying." He finally found the page and read it out loud. "Okay, it reads, 'The possible reasons for the engine warning light can number in the thousands. Your car dealer can address the problem.' That's no help!"

"Is that book for real?" Ashley asked.

"It also has in fine print, 'A loose or missing gas cap will cause the warning light to come on'," Mark added.

"Okay, let's not panic," Megan said. "Listen you guys, as long as the engine is still running, we're okay."

"Oh, yeah? How long will that be?" Corey said, looking intently out the car window at the unfamiliar and depressed surroundings.

"Robert filled your car at the gas station before we left Shady Grove. Maybe he didn't put the gas cap on, right?" Ashley said.

"Well, I can always stop the car and one of you can get out and check to see if the gas cap is on correctly."

Corey's face flushed. "Are you crazy or what? Look at this neighborhood."

"Let's draw straws," Mark announced.

"We're not doing that!" Megan replied.

"I was kidding."

"Don't be ridiculous. Just keep looking for the freeway entrance signs." She took a deep breath and silently counted—one, two, three. It calmed her down.

After driving around for another fifteen minutes, they finally found the entrance to the freeway. Everyone immediately let out a deep sigh of relief. Their faces had previously been visibly shaken. Every fifteen minutes on the streets of LA seemed like an hour to Megan. As they entered the freeway, everybody was relieved to be on their way back to Shady Grove.

Megan stepped on the gas pedal and merged into the speeding traffic feeling happy to be going back home.

All of a sudden, Mark gasped and shouted, "We're going the wrong direction! We need to go east not west!"

"Oh, no! Tell me this isn't true!" Megan said loudly.

"I don't believe it! Corey shouted.

"Should I exit the freeway when we reach the next street exit ramp?" Megan asked, feeling nervous with her hands tightly gripping the steering wheel.

"Only, if you see an entrance ramp on the other side. We want to be able to get back on the freeway and go east," Mark replied.

"Yeah, we could end up back in a scary neighborhood again," Ashley blurted.

"Okay, you guys need to look. I can't drive and see everything too," Megan said as she focused on driving.

She drove another two miles. "How about this next exit?" She asked as she changed freeway lanes.

"No! No! Don't take this one!" everybody screamed. "There's no entrance ramp!"

"We'll get lost again!" Ashley shouted.

Megan quickly steered out of the exit lane and stayed on the freeway. She kept driving further and further into the city, away from Shady Grove. Mark, Corey and Ashley kept looking out the window to see which street they should exit on.

"Take this exit! Take this one!" Mark shouted. "There's a freeway entrance ramp on the other side."

"Okay, I hear you," she said loudly.

She drove onto the freeway exit ramp, went on the overpass street to the other side of the freeway, and got back onto the freeway going east.

Everybody screamed and cheered feeling happy and relieved.

"Thank goodness!" Corey said.

"Now we're headed the right direction back to Shady Grove." Mark smiled feeling much more relaxed than before.

Megan grinned and glanced at Mark. She wasn't nervous any more but felt calm as she stepped on the gas pedal and focused on the road ahead.

Mark turned up the volume on the music. Everyone was talking and feeling better as they headed back toward the small town.

After driving for more than an hour Megan started to feel tired and began yawning. Mark whispered softly, "Do you want me to drive?"

"No thanks. We don't have far to go."

She wasn't going to be foolish enough to let anyone drive her car again.

It was a relief to be near home, seeing familiar street signs, stores and buildings from the freeway.

Just half a mile away from the smoothly paved, freeway exit ramp, the rear tire of her car made a strange thumping noise. It started to feel like they were riding on a cobblestone road. One of the tires had a flat.

Megan had to slow down and pulled off the road onto the side of the freeway. She couldn't believe what had happened. "This is a nightmare from hell! I'm just glad this didn't happen in LA."

"We must have a guardian angel," Ashley replied.

"No kidding," Mark mumbled with a sigh of relief.

They got out of the car, and everyone stood there for a couple of minutes on the sandy soil next to the pavement. Megan wiped her forehead. Standing there was scary with all the fast-moving cars. The big rig trucks were passing by with their glaring bright headlights, and the road noise from the cars, buses and trucks was loud and intimidating. The smell of diesel and gasoline exhaust fumes permeated the air.

Mark and Corey quickly walked to the back of the car and opened the trunk. They reached in and pulled out the spare tire, wrench and jack, and worked on changing the tire. Twenty minutes later, after they finished, Mark tightened the gas cap. When she started the car the red warning light on the dashboard disappeared.

Megan let out a sigh of relief. "Thank goodness there's nothing wrong."

"Told you it was fine!" Corey replied, smiling at her. "Let's put an end to this night, shall we?"

"Couldn't agree more," Megan said, then took off toward the exit ramp.

Megan drove Ashley home first before going to her house. After arriving home, she parked the car in the driveway, and could see the orange glowing light from the lamp she left on in the living room window reflecting on the front yard lawn. Mark's car was parked next to the curb in front of her house.

They got out of the car and all hugged goodbye. Megan pulled her keys out of her pocket, unlocked the front door to the house, and walked inside. Mark and Corey made sure she was safely inside before they got into Mark's car and drove away.

She kicked off her shoes and could feel the warmth of the wooden floorboards and soft area rug under her bare feet. After throwing her handbag on the reclining chair, she turned on some music, and fell backwards onto the sofa, exhausted. Megan calmed herself by thinking she had been through enough misery for one day. The chances of meeting a handsome guy at a party in LA didn't happen… but the drive was far from boring.

Silence muted the previous sound of traffic on the freeway. Her breathing slowed, she closed her eyes, and was finally able to relax. She had forgotten what it was like being in Los Angeles with millions of people and a melting pot of different ethnic groups. The brief time Megan lived there she didn't even know her neighbors well, and she'd made no close friends and none of her family lived there.

It wasn't like living in Shady Grove. This was home, and she needed to make sure it stayed that way.

CHAPTER 3

GROWING PAINS

Barely getting enough sleep last night, Megan lay awake with thoughts about everything, turning it over and over in her mind thinking, the mortgage companies and even the banks didn't care about people struggling. All those executives in their expensive tailored suits and shirts didn't care. They didn't care if people lost their jobs, were sick, or just ran into bad luck. They didn't care if she or anybody else went to college or not. They just wanted the monthly payments. Nothing else mattered to them. Living for the moment was now consumed with having to find a good paying job.

Around eight a.m. the phone rang. It was Mark.

"Hi, Megan, are you awake?"

"Yeah, kind of." She laughed, rubbed her eyes, and yawned.

"You might want to know Robert was released from jail and has to show up in court in three weeks. He wouldn't tell me why he was arrested." Mark apologized for everything that had happened. He knew the trip was a total disappointment.

"It's okay. Not your fault. Bad things just happen sometimes."

"Is that an apology?"

"Yeah, it is," she said and laughed again.

"I accept your apology. Hey, do you want to go to the trampoline park and watch some of those adventurous people get hurt?"

"What?" She wasn't sure if he was serious or not.

"Just joking. I'll give you a call later in the week."

She turned to her side to go back to sleep and Heather called.

"Are you awake?"

"Not really," she whispered softly.

"Hey, my neighbor told me about a guy who recently moved into my neighborhood. You might be interested. She didn't know much about him but said if she were younger, she would try to get to know him."

"Yeah, sounds good but how am I supposed to meet this guy if both of you don't even know him?"

"Well, that would be kinda difficult."

"I really wanna go back to sleep," Megan replied. "Can I call you later?"

"Sure, no problem."

Megan formed a close bond with her friends and didn't mind them calling so early even though she wanted to sleep a little longer. Still in bed trying to relax, she got lost in her resolutions for the New Year. *Got to finish college and get a good job—a high paying one.*

More than anything, however, she longed to meet someone special—her own Prince Charming. One day, she told herself, she'd fall deeply in love—a true romance.

When Megan was in high school, she had gotten into heated debates with her mom. She said going to college was a luxury, and although Megan wanted to tell her she had dreams of her own, she decided it was pointless to say anything. Her mother would never listen.

She knew her mom didn't understand how much things had changed since she'd grown up in a small town not far from San Diego. Her mom's friends had to go to work after completing high school, and some got married, usually to the men in the nearby military base. But the world had changed, and her mother eventually changed her opinion about college.

Hugging her pillow, Megan had flashbacks about high school when she met Tony in the eleventh grade. He was handsome and smart. Megan thought she loved him. His parents bought him a new car and he picked Megan up every day for school, but Tony's parents told him he shouldn't be serious about any girl because they planned on him going away to college.

Rumors had spread at school that another girl was pursuing Tony when they were dating. It was Anita, a popular cheerleader who was spoiled with parents who catered to her every wish. Anita was the kind of girl most shy girls couldn't stand. For a long time, Megan wanted to be like Anita, but after the breakup, she remembered the overwhelming pain when she saw Tony walk by at school holding Anita's hand. Even worse, Anita smirked at Megan when they walked by, like she enjoyed the pain Megan was dealing with.

Megan had no desire to go to her graduation prom, knowing she would feel awkward and uncomfortable because Tony and Anita would be there too. But Mrs. Emerson's son, Scott, convinced her to go, and told her he would take her to the prom. He liked helping Megan and being there for her.

A few days later, Megan decided there was no way she would give Tony the satisfaction of knowing she was crushed, hurt and angry. Everybody at school would notice and be talking about her, so she went with Scott. But she was miserable the entire time and did her best not to show it, faking her smiles and laughing more than usual. It was a desperate attempt to heal her wounded heart.

Megan heard Anita had gotten pregnant and they eventually got married. His parents weren't happy about it, and Tony never attended college. He ended up working in his parents' restaurant, and while it should have made Megan feel better, it didn't. It took her a long time to heal, but she did, and she'd moved on.

After a long day of being excessively busy, Megan finally sat down on the soft recliner and listened to her favorite music. She started to unwind from a day of homework for her classes and trying to find work. Suddenly, there was a knock on the front door. She didn't feel like moving. It was six in the evening, and she wasn't up to someone dropping in. Someone knocked again so she reluctantly got up, peeked out the window, and opened the door. It was Zoe, her mother's best friend. She'd popped by to pick up some things to take to the hospital for her mother.

So much for quiet time, as she and Zoe went into the living room, Mrs. Atkin's cat had followed her into the house.

"Not again! The neighbor's cat likes it here for some reason," Megan said and walked over, gently picked him up, and carried him back outside.

"So, Megan, how's your love life? You haven't talked about anyone in a long time."

She looked up at her, took a deep breath, and tried to figure out a way to politely duck the question. "It's fine," Megan replied abruptly.

She thought it was rude to ask a single person that question. In fact, it wasn't polite to ask anyone that question. But maybe she was just being defensive.

Megan hadn't been involved with a guy for a long time. There was nobody she'd dated steadily, and while there were the occasional hookups, there was nothing she cared to remember. Her mother's friends, like Zoe, were always trying to match her up with somebody.

"You should really put yourself out there more. You can't spend all your nights here locked up in this house of yours. Don't you get lonely?"

Sure, she did get lonely, but Zoe didn't need to know it.

"No, I'm fine, Zoe, really."

"Well, I've been looking around for you, Megan. I wanted to introduce you to this guy I know but decided not to. Do you want to know why?" she asked.

"Is this a quick story?" She cringed, not really interested in what Zoe was about to tell her.

"I found out he has a drinking problem."

"I see…" Megan replied. "You know, I really appreciate it, but I'm fine."

She wanted to snap and be rude but didn't because Zoe was a good person. There was nothing she wouldn't do for her mother. It was just that she could be so opinionated at times. It irritated Megan.

"Okay, well can't say I didn't try!" She walked out of the door with a tote bag full of things and waved goodbye. Megan was glad she didn't stay long.

The house was quiet again, no phone calls and nobody ringing the doorbell. There alone with her mom in the hospital, she clicked on the TV and started flicking through all the channels, finally settling on Netflix. It was hard to stay awake, she went to sleep, but then woke up when she heard unusual sounds in the attic again. She was scared and could call 911 emergency services but what would she tell the police? Nobody was trying to break into the house. The house was older but just an ordinary house in a friendly neighborhood. She was glad they had a nice home after all the work her parents had done to restore it.

She managed to convince herself there was nothing alarming up there, just an overactive imagination and, like Zoe said, she was just a little lonely. But her eyes hardly left looking up at the ceiling so she slept on the couch until the next morning.

CHAPTER 4

TALKING IT OVER

Megan was relieved to have someone to talk to when she worried too much. Dr. Sharma helped her work through things. He donated some of his time several days a month to the free community clinic downtown. She couldn't afford a paid therapist, so she was grateful for him. Megan liked his voice. It was soft and low, confident and even soothing. Her mind felt at ease during their discussions.

When they first started speaking, they didn't talk about anything substantial. Eventually Dr. Sharma asked her what was troubling her, and if she had any panic attacks, insomnia, loss of appetite or took drugs. Megan told him she had none of those vices, at least not yet.

She arrived for her two p.m. appointment. The receptionist greeted her with a smile and told her the doctor was waiting in his office. As she walked down the narrow hall, she heard him open the door. He was sitting behind a wooden desk, talking on the phone to one of his patients in his smooth, calming voice which always put her instantly at ease, but waved her in and pointed to a chair.

In her mind, he was handsome in a mature way, and she could see how some women would find him attractive. A mature psychiatrist in his early forties, his parents came to the United States from India when he was a young boy, and he spoke with a slight accent. His full head of black hair was neatly trimmed, giving him a distinguished air, and he was always smartly dressed in a suit, dress shirt but no tie.

She often wondered whether he was married, as he never mentioned his personal life.

One time she asked him if he had a family. He stared at her for a moment with his no expression, therapist face. Then he said, "Megan, these counseling sessions are not about me, they're about you," and then continued with their discussion. She appreciated his professionalism, but still—she was curious.

He soon ended his conversation and put the phone down. "How are you, Megan?"

She took a deep breath and said, "To be truthful, I don't think things are going very well, Dr. Sharma."

"What's going on?" he asked, and leaned back in his soft, black leather office chair.

"Without Dad or Chris around to help, my mom's been doing a lot of the maintenance on the house. She had an accident and fell, a real disaster. Actually, she could have asked for help, but she's so stubborn. Uncle James has offered to do some minor repairs around the house, and even our neighbor, Mr. Thompson, offered to help."

"Why didn't she let them help?"

"Mom didn't want to bother them because she thinks Uncle James is too old and she thinks Mr. Thompson has the hots for her and didn't want to encourage him," she said, letting out a small laugh. "What he doesn't know is ever since my father died, she's never even considered going out with another man despite my encouragement."

He raised his head, looked up at her for a moment and asked, "What kind of accident?"

"It's a long story. Do you really want to hear it?"

"Yes, of course."

"A few weeks ago, Mom said she needed Mark and Corey to finish painting the outside trim on the house. They both had to study for their exams and told her they couldn't do it until the following weekend. No big deal, right?"

"So, what was the problem?"

"She didn't wait. Mom tried to finish painting the trim on the windows and fell off the ladder. Can you believe that? Mrs. Wilson was near, and she immediately ran to help and called the paramedics. Mom was lucky she saw her fall because I wasn't home at the time. The doctor said she broke her right leg, and injured her back, and needed to have surgery on her leg. He said she was lucky she didn't hit her head. My mom still thinks it's nothing. She's too tough for her own good."

"That is serious," he replied.

"Her doctor, concerned about the trauma from the fall, wanted her to stay longer. Mom refused at first, but now she's having severe back pain, and they want to keep her there for observation for a few days. Sometimes she gets depressed, and I worry about her."

"Maybe she needs to come and talk to me when she gets better."

Megan rolled her eyes. "She would never do that."

"Why not?" he responded with a puzzled look on his face.

"She doesn't believe in therapists."

"Do I look make believe?" he replied with a grin. "You should have her come in with you once she's better."

Megan shook her head. "Oh, trust me, I've tried. You can't convince her to do anything that isn't her idea, and now I'm sure it's gonna take a while for her recovery. She'll also have to go through physical therapy. What makes matters worse is Mom's employer previously reduced her work hours because the company was having financial difficulties. Her injuries from the accident have complicated everything."

"All you can do is be there for her, Megan. Don't take too much on your shoulders, or you'll be overwhelmed and no good to anyone, least of all yourself. Do you understand?"

Megan nodded, and though she knew he was right, she also knew she wouldn't have a choice if her mother remained any longer in the hospital. The bills were mounting, and the stress was piling up.

Suddenly she asked, "Do you know anything about haunted houses, Dr. Sharma?"

"Not much," he replied. "Why?"

"Oh, nothing, I was just wondering," she said, and held back telling him everything. It was the fear of judgement that she couldn't handle some of her own problems.

Still, after talking a little longer, Megan had to admit she was less tense and the throbbing headache she had been nursing all morning had finally subsided. When she arrived home, Megan decided to give her brother, Chris, a call. He hadn't called back to let her know when he would be arriving in Shady Grove from Texas.

"Hey, Meg."

"Hey, what's going on?" she asked.

"I'm still waiting for permission to leave for California. Hopefully, I'll be there in a couple of days," Chris replied. He had promised to be there to help her.

"Okay, I was really getting worried, maybe you weren't coming."

"I'll be there soon. Don't worry. So, what are you going to do now Mom can't work?" Chris asked.

"I don't know. I think I'm having a quarter-life crisis."

"Be serious."

"I don't have to think too hard about it. I have to find a full-time job. Mom doesn't have enough money saved up to pay the monthly house payment and all the other bills."

"I kinda figured as much. I should be able to send her some money, but it won't be enough to pay for everything."

"Thanks, Chris," Megan said, feeling a little more relieved. "Hopefully it's just temporary. When I finish college, I'll get a better paying job and help with the house payments."

"It sounds like a great idea. But you're not finished yet."

"I know. I need to find a job—like, right now," Megan said, worried about her neighborhood. About the Emerson family. "Chris, it's scary. Everyone is going into foreclosure. We can't let that happen to us."

Chris sighed on the other side of the line. "Yeah, I know, Megan. I'll do what I can. Any other ideas?"

That was all Megan had been doing the past few weeks. She did have some options.

"I wasn't going to say anything, but my friend Corey has an uncle who's a professional photographer. He freelances for several different magazine publishers. I remember, a couple of months ago, he asked me if I would be interested in a photo session to do some modeling. He gave me his business card and said I could make a lot of money."

"Are you serious?"

"Of course, I am. Corey's uncle is always telling Corey I would make a great model."

"Are you sure he's not some old guy just trying to seduce you?"

Megan cringed. "No, I don't think so. Corey said he's professional and all business."

"Well then what are you waiting for? You should check it out."

"You're right. It never occurred to me I could make some extra money doing something else instead of working an eight to five job," Megan said. "I have his business card right here." She pulled it out of her wallet and studied it for a moment.

"Just be careful, Sis. There are a lot of crazy people out there."

"Are you saying I shouldn't do it?"

"Not at all, just make sure you check this guy out and take a friend with you if you go for a photo session, okay?"

"Okay. It does sound good, but I need to consider all my options."

"What options? You don't have a lot of experience. Your part-time job at the college working in the library and office, and sometimes cleaning the neighbor's house isn't really going to land you anything spectacular. For now, you're just going to have to take what you can get."

"I know. I'm hoping the college courses I've completed will help me get a better job."

Chris hesitated for a moment then said, "Here's hoping. But if you get a fulltime job, someone has to take care of Mom when she gets out of the hospital."

Megan hadn't even thought of it. "I can ask Aunt Ruth and Uncle James if Mom can stay with them for a while until she gets better. Then I can work on trying to figure things out."

"Aunt and Uncle? Megan, they don't have a large house or much money."

"I know... but I don't know what else to do, Chris."

"Do you want to wait until I arrive in California? We can go over to Aunt and Uncle's house together and talk to them."

She paused then let out a deep breath. "Yes, sounds good to me".

"Okay. I'll see you soon."

Megan fell asleep at night but woke up around two a.m. sweating and shaking. She had a nightmare about being homeless and living in her car. Suddenly, she gasped and realized she didn't even know how to live in a car. It couldn't be easy. The space would be incredibly cramped. Megan tossed and turned for a while but was eventually able to go back to sleep.

On Saturday, Chris arrived from Texas. Megan picked him up from the airport and they headed to their aunt and uncle's place. After they caught up, they asked them if their mother could stay with them for a while, just until she got better, and it didn't take long for Aunt Ruth and Uncle James to agree it was a good idea. Megan was relieved, and so thankful.

In the afternoon, Megan and Chris walked into the hospital room and found their mom in bed, bruised and bandaged with her leg in a cast. They both smiled and grabbed her with a lot of hugs and kisses.

"How are you, Mom?" Megan asked.

"I'm doing a little better than yesterday. But the doctor said I'm going to need more surgery on my leg after the swelling goes down."

"Well, you certainly started the new year with a bang, didn't you?" Chris replied.

Megan turned and gave him a dirty look.

"I know, I know... it was dumb of me to get on a ladder and try to do everything myself."

"Why don't you stay at Aunt and Uncle's until you get better?" Chris asked.

"Your Aunt Ruth already called me a few minutes ago and told me to come and stay with them."

"Good," Megan replied, feeling relieved.

"I said yes, because I really do need someone to take care of me for a while, and Megan, you won't be at home all the time."

"That's true," Chris said. "Megan and I have been talking and she needs to find a fulltime job, even for a short time. We both plan on helping you cover the house payments... that's if Megan can make enough money. At least until you return to work."

Their mother sighed, then nodded. "Thank you both for helping me. I certainly need it right now."

Soon after they left the hospital, Megan said, "Aunt Ruth will take good care of Mom."

Growing up, they had experienced the kindness and generosity of Aunt Ruth and Uncle James. They had a modest sized older Spanish-style stucco house with a clay-tiled roof, three bedrooms and a large front yard covered in lush green grass and several sycamore trees. There was a long driveway and a detached two-car garage, though Uncle James spent most of his time out in the old tool shed in the backyard. He loved working outdoors, cutting the grass, trimming the trees and helping Aunt Ruth plant seeds in the garden.

Megan would never dare ask some of her other relatives for help. Most had their own problems, and nobody talked about them. Her Uncle Ray had lived in their garage for a year, then he was arrested for stealing merchandise and was sent to prison for a short time. Her parents said he was beyond help but she didn't agree with them.

Megan found him entertaining. He would always joke around and make people laugh. He just needed somebody to help him when times were difficult. After completing a job training program in prison, he was released from jail, and got a job doing landscaping and yard maintenance.

Her parents said he was never right in his thinking after prison, and often spoke to the trees and people who weren't there. They'd tried to get him help, but he wouldn't accept it. He often missed taking his medication. She thought her parents should have been more patient with him.

Megan was happy they had Uncle James and Aunt Ruth. They'd always been dependable and loving—a rarity in Megan's life, especially since her father's death.

Later in the week, Chris had to return to the military base in Texas, so she had to drop him off at the airport early in the morning.

"I really don't want to leave but I have no choice."

"I know. Don't worry about it. Love you." They hugged tightly and she kissed him goodbye.

Before he left, she promised Chris she'd call Corey's uncle, and after two days of no luck finding a job, she decided it was time.

"Hello?"

"Hello there! It's Megan, Corey's friend. Remember you gave me your card a while back? I want to take you up on modeling work."

"Oh, hi, Megan. I'm really sorry, but I don't have anything right now," he said. "It's been a while since we talked about it. But keep in touch! Something might come up."

She was sick to her stomach. She really needed this.

"Are you sure there's nothing?" she asked, her voice laced with disappointment.

He paused on the other end. "Hmm, wait a minute. I can give you the number of another photographer named Bruce. He might have something. I don't know him very well, so it'll be up to you to determine if he has something worth your time or not."

"Sounds great!" Megan replied, feeling anxious and excited at the same time.

She hung up and called Bruce immediately, introduced herself, then explained Corey's uncle had given her his number.

After a brief conversation he said, "Why don't you come to my photography studio so I can see you and we'll go from there?"

"Sure!"

"How about coming here tomorrow at four p.m.?"

"Works fine for me."

"Megan, don't forget to bring your best-looking bikinis so you can change into them for some of the photos."

"Okay, I will." She didn't have a bikini.

She said goodbye and immediately wondered if her friend Heather was home. Megan called her and she explained her situation.

"I don't have any bikinis. You know I never wear them." She didn't want to tell Heather she didn't have the money to buy one as she examined the hole in her jeans.

"Don't sweat it," Heather replied. "You can borrow mine. You should be able to find something for the photo session. Most of them I haven't worn in a long time."

"Thanks, Heather. At least I don't have to worry about shopping for something I'll never wear again."

"No problem! Coming over now?"

"Now? Um, sure!"

Megan hung up the phone and rushed over to Heather's apartment to pick them up. Then Megan asked Ashley to come over and help her select which bikini would look best on her. She loved Heather, but she didn't have that kind of relationship with her. Plus, Heather looked so good all the time, and she didn't want to be judged.

"I don't like wearing bikinis," Megan said to Ashley. "Remember the time I dove off the diving board into the pool? My top came off the second I hit the water. I had to swim to the side of the pool and yelled for you to bring me a towel."

"Yeah, I remember how embarrassed you were," Ashley replied, laughing. "The guys were whistling and yelling. They couldn't take their eyes off you."

"All those flawless pictures of models wearing perfectly fitting swimsuits. I never feel like I look like that."

"Welcome to the club," Ashley said.

"Shopping for swimming suits is a headache. It takes too long to try them on and find something I really like."

"You're lucky Heather has a lot of them," Ashley responded while pulling a skimpy bikini out of the bag.

Megan eyed the skimpy bikini uncomfortably. "Am I supposed to show that much skin? I'm so out of my comfort zone. I'm not that skinny."

"Neither am I." Ashley laughed.

"I'm not a fan of tiny bikinis... I like one-piece swimsuits with see-through fishnet fabric or cutouts. At least they stay on when you're diving or swimming."

"How many women do you know who actually go to the beach or pool to swim?" Ashley asked, looking somewhat amused.

"Probably very few," Megan replied, and they both start giggling like young girls.

Megan slipped off her shirt and jeans, walked to the bedroom to change, and emerged from the room each time after trying on several different bikinis. She studied herself in the full-length mirror. A couple of them flattered her figure, but most she didn't like.

She inspected the beautiful coral bikini which supported her in all the right places. It was a perfect fit. "I'll wear this one for the photos, and the yellow one."

"Yes, they both look great on you. Good choice," Ashley replied. "I guess you don't need me anymore. I'm gonna head off. See you later!"

Megan had the afternoon free to do whatever she wanted. The warmth of the sunshine from the window on her face and arms felt good. She picked up her novel, got comfortable on the sofa, and started reading.

The next day, Corey went with Megan to see the photographer. He had promised to go with her because it was safer that way; after all, she really didn't know anything about Bruce.

When they arrived at the studio, they carefully looked around. There was a plush, beautiful sofa, side tables, and several chairs in the waiting room. Hanging on the walls were several magazines covers with photos of men and women models.

Bruce, a tall, nice-looking guy, greeted them. He was much older, maybe in his late forties. He was distinguished looking with a well-trimmed beard and brown hair with grey on the sides, wearing a blue shirt, and a pair of casual grey pants. They talked for a while, and he told Megan he'd been a photographer for over twenty years and normally traveled to the larger cities. He talked about his condo at the beach and mentioned he liked to go there frequently. She wasn't sure why he was telling her all this.

Bruce studied her for a while. "Please turn to the back. Good. Now turn to the side."

He looked at her body from the front and back. He carefully studied her legs, her hands, feet and her neatly manicured fingernails.

"Okay, let's take a few photos to see how you look on camera because you need a portfolio. I have some extra outfits here you can put on."

He took several photos of her in his studio. Some photos were of her in the bikini.

"Do you have any modeling experience?"

"No, but... I learn fast!" She hesitated for a moment, realizing how cliché it sounded. Everybody probably said the same thing.

"Let me see if I can find something that would be a good fit for you, and I'll call you back when something comes up. Sound good?"

Megan gently bit the side of her lip. "I really could use some extra money right now."

"I see. Well, I usually tell everyone to sign up with a modeling agency, but I do have some of my own clients and hire models occasionally." He paused for a few moments. He had a strange look on his face she couldn't place. "But I'll see what I can do for you."

They talked a little longer. He was very professional, and Megan found she was surprisingly comfortable around him. But the time flew by, and it was late; she and Corey were famished. So, they said their goodbyes and headed for their favorite Italian restaurant for sliced pizza and salad.

"I'm not sure I'll even hear back from him. I really need this, Corey," Megan said, playing with her food.

"Gotta stay positive! It went really well, and... Megan?"

"What?"

"You looked really fine in those bikinis," he said, suppressing a smile. She punched him on the shoulder and they both laughed.

"Last time I invite you!"

CHAPTER 5

THE VISIT

Since her mom was staying with Aunt Ruth and Uncle James until she fully recovered, Megan was able to spend most of the morning at home on her computer looking for jobs. It was time consuming, but she was desperate for money. She applied for what seemed like hundreds of jobs, glanced down at her watch and it was already one p.m. Feeling tired and needing a break, Megan headed to her aunt and uncle's house to visit her mom.

After arriving at their place, she opened the door, removed her backpack, and threw her things down on the living room sofa. The exposed brown ceiling beams and the black Castilian wrought iron banister next to the stairs and arched doorways gave the house a warm, cozy feeling. Uncle James was sitting in his brown leather reclining chair in the family room reading his paper. His dog, Susie, was on his lap. He enjoyed reading or watching movies on a large flat screen TV which sat on a stand with two shelves. The shelves were filled with neatly stacked magazines and a few books.

"Hi, Uncle James," she said loudly, smiling at him.

"Hi, Meg, how was your day?"

"Fine, Uncle. I've been applying for different jobs. I hope to get hired soon."

"Good. Just keep trying. I'm sure someone will hire you. You're a bright, intelligent young lady."

"Thanks, Uncle," she said and smiled, thinking, of course he thought all those wonderful things, she was his niece.

Megan grabbed an orange from the table to eat and started peeling it. "Where's Mom?"

"She's in the bedroom sleeping. Her back has been hurting her a lot today."

"What about Aunt Ruth?"

"Who? What?" Megan sighed. Uncle James was elderly and hard of hearing, but he didn't want to 'waste' money on hearing aids. He said they cost too much money. Her aunt said he could afford it if he wanted them. When he watched television sometimes, he turned the volume up so high it was hard for anybody to talk.

"Aunt Ruth!" Megan yelled. "Where is she?"

"Oh! Probably outside digging in the garden. Your aunt is always out there, probably to get away from me," he said, chuckling. Aunt Ruth spent a lot of time outside working in the yard. She had a well-kept garden that ran thirty feet long and wide, and beyond it were the fruit trees and another smaller vegetable garden on their acre of land. There were always sweet oranges and bright yellow lemons in a fruit bowl from the trees in the backyard.

As she made her way toward the upstairs, the two resident dogs came running to greet her. "Hi, nosey, and hello there, Susie," Megan said smiling, crouching to gently pet the dogs before pulling them both into a tight hug. They licked her arms and looked up at her wagging their tails. She had a soft spot for dogs, especially these two. Megan walked upstairs and put her laptop computer on the desk in the guest bedroom. The dogs always followed her around.

Three years ago, Aunt Ruth had seen both of them walking around her yard. Both dogs were skinny, malnourished and dirty. They were thin and underweight due to neglect, or they had been homeless trying to survive. She immediately brought them in, fed them and gave them both a warm bath. They thoroughly enjoyed all of the attention, and they'd been a part of the family ever since.

Uncle James said somebody probably dumped them off in the neighborhood hoping someone like Aunt Ruth would adopt them. Aunt Ruth always had a weakness for taking in any poor, unclaimed dogs and cats, but always tried to find the owner and advertised in the newspaper. In Nosey and Susie's case, nobody claimed them, so she kept them.

They also had a cat who walked around like she owned the house. She didn't pay much attention to the dogs and loved it when people petted her. The cat had her own pink blanket and stuffed toy Megan bought her last year.

Aunt Ruth walked into the house from the backyard and called Megan downstairs for a chat.

"How is that young man, Drew, you used to date? I haven't seen him around town in a long time," Aunt Ruth asked, cleaning her soiled hands in the sink.

"Really, Auntie? We broke up a long time ago."

"He was a handsome young man."

"Sure, he was, but it just didn't work out," she said flippantly. She didn't want to go into any details about Drew.

It was better for Drew to remain a memory. They had made peace with each other, and both moved on, but even to this day, he would call her every time he split up with a girlfriend, asking to see her again because he couldn't get her out of his mind. Megan always said no.

"I hope you meet someone nice one day."

"Me too. But I'm not worrying about it."

Megan walked into the bedroom to see her mom. She gently kissed her on the forehead, and she woke up.

"Hey, Mom. How are you feeling?"

"Pretty good. I've been taking medication, but it just makes me so drowsy. Thank God for your Auntie Ruth. She does everything for me."

That couldn't have been easy for her mother. She was always used to doing everything herself, and she'd been independent from the moment Megan was born.

"I knew she would. Aunt wants you to get better without worrying about trying to get around all by yourself. Just rest. You deserve to be taken care of."

Her mother didn't like that. "I know you probably think I'm crazy, Megan, since I'm in bed and haven't moved for a few days, but I'm going to get better soon, and I'll be back to work before you know it."

Megan sighed. "Mom, you need to take this one day at a time. I know it's tough."

She steeled her jaw and let out a deep breath. "Megan, I appreciate everything you and Chris are doing. I know it's not easy, but I don't want to lose the house. I cherish my place."

"We're doing the best we can."

"I'm just afraid what will happen if I can't get back to work."

"That's not for you to worry about right now, Mom. It's our turn to take care of you for a while, okay?" Megan grabbed her and gave her a big hug.

"Thanks, honey, I needed that," she said, laughing.

Megan was worried, extremely worried but tried not to show it. She knew her mom loved her house and would be devastated if it was ever taken from her. She loved the sweet fragrance of white, orange blossoms that filled the spring air. Her mom would often sit outside sipping tea surrounded by orange trees with deep green leaves on branches soon to be weighed down by juicy, sweet oranges bursting with color.

As the weeks wore on, Megan was excited to get a few interviews, but every time she went to an interview, they would tell her she didn't have enough of the right kind of experience. How was she supposed to get experience?

In the evening, she called her mom in frustration, "How can I get the work experience I need unless someone hires me? I just need the opportunity to prove myself."

"I know, hon. You'll get hired. Just keep trying," her mom reassured her.

She did, applying for everything she could, until, after a long dry spell which lasted weeks had some good news.

Finally, she was offered a job working full-time—five days a week, eight to five like the rest of the world. And she was fine being just like everyone else because she was desperate, and their family needed this. She was glad to have a job that would pay enough money so she could help her mom.

Hired as a staff assistant for a computer software firm, the manager said she'd get a lower salary in comparison to more experienced workers. He said, after she got more work experience, her salary would increase. Excited, Megan called Ashley too to tell her the good news.

"Guess what?" she said, not waiting for an answer. "I finally got a job!"

"That's great news, Meg! I'm really happy for you."

"Right? I'll get the experience I need, and, in a few months, I should get a pay increase."

"Will it be enough to pay your bills and everything else?" Ashley asked.

"Yes, I hope so. And guess what else? The company I'll be working for is just two blocks from the social services agency where you work."

"We'll be able to meet for lunch!"

"Exactly! And I'll be able to start saving some money and help mom with the house payments. Maybe someday I'll be able to move into my own apartment?"

"Moving up in the world, girl!"

"Heck yes, I am! I gotta call Mom. Talk later!"

She immediately called her mom to tell her the news. Uncle James answered the phone.

"Hi, Uncle James, I got a job!" she said loudly for the benefit of his hearing. But apparently, it wasn't enough.

"What?"

"I got a job!" she shouted again.

"You got robbed?" he said.

"No, no. I got a job."

"What?"

"I got a freaking job!" and laughed with excitement.

"You want Rob?"

"No, I got a job!"

"Rob doesn't live here!" he said.

"No!" she said, trying not to show her frustration. "Get Mom!" she shouted.

"Oh, okay."

Megan's mom was delighted to hear her happy news. Things were definitely looking up.

CHAPTER 6

HOMES LOST

In the morning, Megan talked briefly with her mother. She seemed to be feeling better, but her back pain hadn't improved much. The physician had removed the cast on her leg, and she started her physical therapy sessions. The bad news was he had found out the reason for her back problem and said she needed surgery, which meant it didn't look like she'd be going back to work any time soon.

Over the last couple of months, there hadn't been enough money to cover all of the bills. Her mother had a lot of medical expenses. She'd missed another month's house payment, and even with her new job, a good portion of Megan's income was being evaporated by taxes.

After grabbing her mom's mail off the table, she opened one of the envelopes. It was another delinquent notice from the mortgage company. Megan started counting the money in the metal box in her closet to be used for emergencies. She was already stressed when the phone rang. It was a woman from the mortgage company. They'd called several times during the past two weeks.

"Hello, I regret to inform you that you didn't send us the full house payment for this month."

"I know, I know already. My mom didn't have the money," Megan said feeling frustrated and upset.

"We're very sorry but you have to send the full payment or your mom's house will go into foreclosure. That means she'll have to move out and the house will be put up for sale."

Megan leaned her head down and put her hand on her forehead. "Can I ask who this is?"

"It's Anita... Anita Brown. I knew you in high school, Megan."

"Anita Brown... Aren't you the one Tony married?"

"Yes, that's me."

Megan felt uneasy, her stomach started to feel queasy. She couldn't believe it. Anita, the same woman who hooked up with her ex-boyfriend in high school was on the phone. Being late with the house payments was stressful enough, but this was even worse. Anita just added to her feelings of frustration.

"We're doing the best we can," Megan replied, feeling totally awkward talking to her.

"I understand but these are the rules."

Her feelings of frustration turned into anger because Anita kept calling and leaving messages. Megan avoided answering the phone. It was frustrating at times and made her feel powerless because her mom's home had always been a safety net for her.

In the afternoon, she decided to go for a drive to clear her head, and as she did, she tried to convince herself not to look at the vacant, foreclosed houses. She couldn't resist and looked anyway. Seeing the homes on Orange Street, Lemon Street and Maple Avenue made her disheartened. The houses were painted inside and out, and the front yards re-landscaped. Most homes were on spacious lots. Some houses were large and others modest in size and all had mailboxes, lawns, orange trees, and long driveways with two-car garages. They were the same homes her neighbors used to own—the Smiths, the Garcia family, and the Carters. Different families live there now.

She wiped her eyes, and a single tear rolled down her cheek because seeing them brought back echoes of the past. Even the Emersons' vacated home had been painted a different color. The houses didn't look bad, but seeing the change struck a nerve, it was devastating. Would they do the same to her mom's house?

Upon arriving home, Megan sat down on the sofa, took a few minutes to relax and wondered what could happen to them. It would be a disaster if they didn't have a place to live or were forced to live in a much worse place. Rent prices were constantly increasing and moving was costly. It would be difficult to find a suitable place. It was a terrible thought. Maybe Aunt and Uncle would take them in, at least for a while, but it wouldn't be the same as living in the Orange Street house. She tried to sleep during the night but was restless going over everything in her head. She had bigger problems to worry about and thought about the previous conversations she'd had with her mom.

Her mom didn't want to live in the house alone. When Megan's father passed away, her mom was depressed for a long time but didn't feel alone because she had both Chris and Megan at home. When Chris went into the military and moved to Texas, Megan noticed how sad her mom became. Over time, her mother became even more depressed. It got even worse when Megan moved to LA with her cousin for a short period of time. Her mom told her she was lonely and called her almost every day.

Megan always told her, "You're not alone, Mom. If I move, it won't be far away. Anyway, you have Aunt Ruth and Uncle James, your friends, and our other relatives."

"It's not the same," her mom had told her.

Not knowing what else to say, Megan moved back home. They had the same conversation repeated over and over again whenever she was concerned Megan was going to move out. Sometimes, she could see the worry in her mom's eyes, an uneasiness she tried hard to hide.

Megan was tired and as she was finally falling asleep, she heard knocking on the roof. No, the attic. She pulled the covers over her face, just like she used to when she was a little girl. Years ago, her mother put a lock on the attic door at the top of the stairs. She and Chris were told never to go up there. Megan sometimes wondered why but had no desire to find out. The one thing she could remember vividly was the attic was an unknown, dark place and she found it really creepy. Was there a dark story to the house's history? A tragedy? Her imagination started to run wild.

The other door to the attic seemed to be out of place. Someone had built it as an emergency fire exit to the outside with narrow, wooden stairs down the back of the house. Megan thought it was odd. The door was always locked, and nobody used the old wooden stairway. The nightmares Megan sometimes experienced were the same thing, always about the attic, and while it scared her, she really didn't know what she was afraid of. Still, she was curious as to what could be up there that her mom was hiding. It was so unlike her mother. She turned up the volume up on her earbuds and her thoughts soon disappeared; she was exhausted and fell asleep, too tired to worry about her surroundings.

The next morning, Megan got up later than usual, and was busy cleaning. After she finished and had eaten lunch, she reached for her phone to call Chris, and it suddenly buzzed.

"Hey, Megan, this is Bruce."

"Hi, Bruce. What's up?"

"I looked through your photos and I like what I see. There are some modeling jobs available, but I need to talk to you about them. Why don't you come by my studio tomorrow briefly and I'll take some more photos?"

"Oh, that sounds great!" Megan replied, ecstatic.

Although she was desperate for money, she didn't know him and was cautious. Megan had read stories about photographers who seemed cool until you were alone with them. So, she was going to make sure Corey knew where she went for photoshoots.

Megan checked out his website on Flickr, and any other links she could find that displayed his works. The portfolios of models were made in good taste. It was a relief.

That afternoon, Megan had an appointment with Dr. Sharma. The receptionist sitting at her desk looked up at her. "You're late." She didn't smile at Megan.

"I know. I'm so sorry."

"I'll see if the doctor will see you. She picked up her phone and briefly talked to him. "Have a seat," she said. Megan glanced at her quickly and decided the receptionist must have had a rough day.

She waited for about fifteen minutes. Finally, she told Megan to go into his office and have a seat, then the receptionist was off to lunch.

He was talking to someone on the phone. He hung up, leaned back in his chair, looked at her and asked, "How are you, Megan?"

She sighed. Ever since her conversation with Anita on the phone, she'd had thoughts about dating again. It had been so long.

"I'm not really sure, Dr. Sharma… I get disappointed at times."

"About what?" he asked.

"There's a lot of things happening in my life right now, but it would be so nice to have someone special. Trying to meet somebody just takes too much time.

Anyway, I have more fun hanging out with my friends," she replied with a weak smile knowing it was untrue.

"Do you really mean that?" he asked with an inquisitive expression on his face and a raised eyebrow.

"Well, maybe not." She shrugged her shoulders.

"You have to put yourself out there, or you could miss out on the opportunity to meet someone."

Megan hesitated for a moment while picking the polish off her fingernails. "You're probably right. Maybe a handsome guy will suddenly appear in my life, and I'll fall in love with him."

"Does he really have to be handsome?" he asked.

She clenched her hands together for a moment. "No, he doesn't have to be handsome. Nice looking, not necessarily handsome. But I don't want him to look like Shrek." She laughed.

Dr. Sharma looked at her with his no expression therapist face. She couldn't tell if he had decided how she responded was something to be worried about.

"I want someone confident. I do like confidence. Someone who works hard who shares my interests. That's important, right?"

"Those are good qualities."

"He should be outgoing, truthful and trustworthy. He should be a thinker. Yes, he should be a real thinker."

"It sounds like you know what you want, Megan. Do what you need to do, pursue your dreams, use good judgement and be careful."

He had always given her insight to think sensibly for herself in the past, so she had no reason to doubt him. After all, he was a therapist.

The session with him flew by as it always did. They talked about several things bothering her and Megan headed home feeling more positive. She was glad to have Dr. Sharma.

During the middle of the week, Megan had driven home from her evening class. Feeling exhausted, she walked through the front door, tossed her keys on the table and sat down on the sofa to relax. Rushing to work, rushing home, to class and then back home again seemed to be the norm for her.

She climbed into the bathtub and relaxed by taking a long hot bath and listening to soft music. An hour later, she had gotten out of the tub and put on her soft, pink terrycloth robe. After pampering herself, she finally went to bed.

The next morning, Megan woke up tired because she had heard scratching noises during the night. Not fully awake, she walked to the kitchen to get a cup of coffee and found the hallway door with the stairs leading up to the attic slightly open. She had no idea how that happened. Megan reached for the doorknob and closed the door. Maybe Ashley or Corey opened the door when everybody was there hanging out together. No need to be afraid.

Her neighbor, Mrs. Atkins, told her some animals made that kind of sound in the attic, to clear out space for nesting, or maybe to bury food. Raccoons, rats, mice and squirrels. She was scared but tried to convince herself it was probably mice or some nocturnal animal because the noise was almost always at night. Still, the noise was haunting, and it was destroying her sleep. The first time she had heard the strange noise was nearly a year ago, but she felt it wasn't a big deal. She would hear it every now and then. Anyway, when she heard it, her mother didn't so Megan didn't worry too much about it.

After Megan had gotten dressed, her phone buzzed, and it was Mark. "Hi, Meg, how's it going?"

"I'm all right. Still struggling trying to pay bills, so that says a lot," she replied, and let out a deep sigh of frustration.

"At least you still have a nice home to live in."

"That's true. At least for right now." She sat down and leaned back in the chair.

"I know a guy who had to move out of his house because it was repossessed. I helped him move his stuff into one of those public storage units," Mark said.

"Seriously?"

"Yeah. They have metal garage doors with locks."

"That's sad. Where did he live?" Megan asked.

"He stayed with me a couple of weeks and slept on my sofa. It's not like he didn't go to work. He has a job and goes to work every day. He was actually doing couch surfing, staying with whoever would let him stay for a few nights until he could find a room to rent."

"That's difficult." She shook her head.

"Yeah, it is. The last time I talked to him, he was sleeping on the sofa in his storage unit until he got caught."

"He did? By whom?"

"The office manager. He told him that he couldn't sleep there. He felt bad about it, but it was company policy."

"Obviously, his home was everywhere. I hope that doesn't happen to me and mom." Megan sighed.

Ignoring her last comment, Mark said, "He was smart though."

"What do you mean?"

"He had a prepay cell phone, a car, one of those self-contained portable potties, and a five-gallon camping jug filled with drinking water. Sometimes he slept in his car."

"I guess that's better than nothing," Megan responded.

"Yes, and he joined a twenty-four-hour gym so he could take showers. At least he had some of the conveniences of home. He told me he was a vegan and didn't eat anything with eyebrows," Mark laughed, "so he didn't want the big fat, juicy hotdog I fixed him."

"Mark, that doesn't sound encouraging," Megan said, and pushed some of her hair back away from her face. She didn't enjoy his humor.

"Sorry, but don't worry. You can always sleep on my sofa if you have to."

"In your apartment with all your books, computers, and friends coming and going all the time?"

"Yes, of course," he replied.

"And your cat who walks all over me?" She laughed. "I don't think so."

After talking a little longer, Megan decided Mark's solution to everything was not the best, but he was her friend and was always trying to be helpful. She appreciated his enthusiasm.

During the week, Megan was busy and had a lot of things on her mind, so she called her brother to talk about their mom's lack of money.

"Hi, Chris. We need to talk."

She decided not to burden him with her fears of the attic. Chris couldn't help anyway. He was in Texas, and she was in California. There wasn't anything he could do.

"What's up?"

"I need some advice," Megan said.

"About what?"

"I'm getting worried. Mom gets these past due notices from the mortgage company all the time. They're constantly calling, and I don't have enough money to cover the full house payment and the other bills. The rent I normally pay Mom helps, but it doesn't pay for everything."

"What's she doing with the money I send to her?"

"She was using the money for the house payment, medical bills and other things. Mom had a hard time recovering and I really don't want to talk to her about it. You know she gets depressed sometimes."

"Slow down. Don't talk so fast."

"Aunt Ruth had Mom fill out paperwork yesterday."

"For what?"

"It's about getting some kind of disability income."

"That doesn't sound good... She probably won't be going back to work soon."

"Her employer said they can't keep her on the payroll any longer. It's not going to be enough money for her to live in her home, and I don't know if she'll even get it."

"Hmm. That's not good," he replied.

"I know and I'm worried. I don't want Mom to lose the house. So, I didn't say anything to her about it. I didn't want to add to her stress."

"I don't either, Megan." He was silent for a moment.

"My old nemesis, Anita, keeps calling about the mortgage. She called yesterday and said if I don't send the full payment amount it's a partial payment. Then they add a late fee too. It had to be paid for in full. If the payment is delinquent, it hurts Mom's credit, and the house will go through foreclosure if we don't do something. Then the company will take it."

"That's a real bummer."

"I feel lost trying to find solutions. What should we do?"

He was silent for a moment. "I'll see if I can get some more money to help you with the house payments until Mom goes back to work."

"Chris, I don't want you to go into debt over this whole thing."

"I know. But what else can we do?"

"I could have a couple of yard sales. Mom has so much stuff around the house. She should have gotten rid of some of her stuff years ago."

"That'll help some but you're not going to make a fortune on yard sales."

"I know. But every dollar counts. The last time I had one I made two hundred dollars."

"Listen, don't worry. I'll call you after I apply for a loan, and I'll send you some more money."

"You know what I wish I could do?"

"What?"

"I wish I could pack up everything and go to Fiji."

"Ha-ha, yeah, right!"

"Thanks, Chris. You're a good brother. I love you."

"Yeah, I love you too. Hang in there, Meg."

She was grateful to have a brother who was willing to help when the need arose. Megan hoped things would get better. *It'll just take a little more time.* She was trying to stay optimistic.

CHAPTER 7

DAY TRIPS

Early in the morning, Megan woke up under the soft covers staring at the ceiling, dreaming about happy times. She didn't always feel this way, down in the dumps. Sadness could get boring after a while, and nobody wanted to hang around a sad person. It was hard trying to be cheerful. Her dad had told her many times, the world was full of happiness and beauty, you just have to find it, and share it with others. Somehow, it wasn't that easy.

Megan yearned for the times when she went on day trips with Scott, exploring the surrounding area and just getting away from Shady Grove. She grabbed her diary and couldn't resist writing about her feelings. After turning over on her side, she put her diary back on the nightstand.

Her thoughts were going in circles, around and around, with memories of Scott. She longed for the days of being carefree talking about music, movies, sports or just nothing at all. Both she and Scott Emerson had been day trippers together after he had finished college in LA and moved back to Shady Grove.

Megan picked up her phone and called Ashley. They talked for a while then Megan started to reminisce. "I want to take road trips again. I want to walk in the woods and see the beautiful pine trees, hear the birds sing, and go riding my bicycle. I want to take long walks on the beach, feel the warm sand under my bare feet, and swim in the Pacific Ocean with Scott."

"I know," Ashley replied, "and he had a great smile and always tried to see the good side in everybody."

"Yes, he really did. Did you know on chilly mornings, Scott and I would leave Shady Grove with no destination in mind, but always somewhere different? Once in a while, we'd take short trips in his car to Big Bear Lake or to Lake Arrowhead in the mountains. Once time we even went to Palm Springs."

Ashley paused for a few seconds, not sure how to answer the question. She knew that like Megan, Scott was a dreamer, and they were best friends. But all that was over now.

"I miss him too, Meg," she replied. Ashley was careful how she responded because talking about Scott was a sensitive subject.

During the summer, when Megan was eighteen, she and Scott were going to go on a biking trip up the Pacific Coast. They had been planning the trip for three months, but he had a couple of things to take care of in the early morning. It was a perfect day outside. The sun was shining through the beautiful clouds and there was a crisp, fresh morning breeze.

Scott was coming to her house to pick her up, but he never made it that far. She waited for him, and he never came. After a while, she kept calling his cell phone and he never answered. Later in the day, she found out Scott had died in a car accident on Freeway 10, and her heart had broken into a hundred pieces like a shattered stained-glass window. Megan was devastated, and tears flowed for hours. Eventually, she wiped her eyes and gazed blankly out the window.

"There isn't a day that goes by I don't miss him. There were some days I couldn't stop the tears."

"I know but we all have a lot of good memories, Meg."

Megan had been happy with Scott. He was her friend, but he never did admit it was more than a friendship. But she didn't care because she was safe with him. He always did the right things, opening the doors, carrying her heavy bags, cheering her up when she was sad.

Scott was gone. No goodbyes, no phones calls, no more text messaging. There was a big hole in her life for a long time. His mother, Mrs. Emerson, never got over losing her oldest son. And now she too was gone, her house taken from her.

Months later, when his younger brother cleaned out his room, he found a small wooden box in Scott's closet. There was a note and a diamond ring inside.

The note said, 'For Megan when the time is right'.

It was his brother who told Megan that Scott loved her very much. He just didn't know if she cared about him the same way, so he never said anything. It broke her heart all over again, and in some ways, she'd still not recovered.

Megan remembered holding the beautiful ring in her hand and staring at it for a long time, unable to stop the tears. Mrs. Emerson had told her to keep it, but Megan had mixed emotions and didn't know what to say or do. They hugged and cried together. When Megan had gotten home, she had laid down in the bed, crawled under the duvet, and held the ring in her hand all night. She had cried herself to sleep listening to songs she and Scott both loved.

Before Scott passed away, they had carefully put together a map of all the places both of them wanted to go for day trips. They never had the chance to do it all. Sometime later, she rolled up the map, tied a beautiful, yellow ribbon around it, and put it on the top of her closet.

For months, sadness overwhelmed her because love was right next door to her the entire time, and she didn't even know it. She didn't know he cared so much about her. If only Scott had told her.

Megan had a hard time trying to deal with her emotions. She spent a lot of time unburdening her feelings in therapy sessions with Dr. Sharma, and if it wasn't for him, she wasn't sure what she would have done. After years with Dr. Sharma, she had finally been able to deal better with the sadness and grief she had experienced.

"Meg, I believe some day you're going to meet someone just like Scott again," Ashley said.

"I hope so. I really do."

CHAPTER 8

THE STRANGER

Megan's workdays at the software firm usually began with making coffee at eight a.m., then she did everything from answering phones, to opening the mail, coordinating meetings, preparing and updating the website, and filing documents for her supervisor. Work rules and procedures appeared to be lax. Nobody seemed to be concerned about her ability to manage her time. But it was a long, busy week and she needed a break from the stress, so she went to visit Ashley who conveniently lives near Heather.

As she walked toward the courtyard and glanced across the street, she saw him for the first time—the stranger. She couldn't help noticing him and she wondered if he was the guy their neighbor was talking about. There was an elderly man talking to him and they were deep in conversation. He was good looking in a mature, masculine kind of way, tall with a well-built body and thick, cinnamon-brown hair. She found it hard to take her eyes off him but turned her head and gazed in the opposite direction, trying not to be obvious.

She stared at him again and thought, *Maybe he lives in the new condos? Or is he just visiting someone?*

Her eyes were fixed on him for a few moments, studying the way he was gesturing with his hands and the clothes he was wearing—a tan sports jacket and casual pants. He had the appearance of confidence and sexiness at the same time.

Yes, the more she thought about it the more she was sure he was probably just visiting someone. There was a good chance she'd never see him again. But she had an immediate attraction to him, and it was hard to explain. She watched him walk to his car and he didn't see her staring at him. He got into a late model BMW, started the engine, and then drove away. It definitely appeared like he was doing well financially. Maybe one day she'd have the opportunity to see him again—maybe not.

Walking up the stairs to Ashley's apartment, Megan smiled and spoke to one of the neighbors. She'd gotten to know a few of them pretty well over the last year. One day, she hoped to get an apartment in the same building. The building itself was an attractive old hacienda structure but needed some restoration. The rent was reasonable, but the problem was people rarely moved out.

"How's the new job?" Ashley asked.

"Oh, you know, it's a job. But something interesting just happened…"

Ashley's eyes shone with enthusiasm and curiosity. "Go on… tell me!"

"I just saw a guy a while ago… a real eye-catcher!"

Ashley said with excitement, "What! Where was he?"

"Actually, he was just across the street. Maybe you've seen him before... cinnamon-brown hair, muscular... gorgeous."

"Hmm... I'm sure I'd have noticed somebody like that round here. Maybe he just moved in."

They talked for nearly an hour and Megan said, "I just wanted to stop by and say hi, but I should probably get going. We'll talk more tomorrow."

Megan had driven home in a good mood, thankful for having such good friends. But her mood was quickly ruined when, not twenty minutes after arriving home, there was a knock at her door. A man in his late thirties introduced himself.

"Hello, ma'am, I'm Austin Mitchell. I'm a friend of Anita Brown. I work for a real estate investment company looking at buying houses in your area that might be going through foreclosure." He handed her his business card. He was mysterious looking with dark brown hair and smiled frequently but it was like a forced grin, not sincere. His breath reeked of alcohol, as if he had been drinking too much.

She looked at him for a moment. "I'm not really interested. Anyway, it's my mom's house and it's not for sale." Megan didn't want anything to do with him, especially if he was Anita's friend.

"Well, you have my card. Call me any time."

She was curious, so she asked, "How's Anita and Tony doing now a days?"

"Oh, she's actually single now. They got divorced not long ago but she seems to be doing fine."

Megan wasn't shocked Anita and Tony's marriage didn't last, but she didn't say so.

"Oh, thanks," she said. "But I don't think I'll need your card."

Megan had heard about investors getting information on homeowners who were struggling to make their house payments. They would buy a person's house cheap, and, in the end, the homeowner would get practically nothing from the sale. The only person who benefited was the investor. Life was hard enough and there was no way her mother would want to give her house away to a stranger.

Frustrated with it all, she walked into the kitchen and reached inside the refrigerator for something to drink. Not much food to eat but eggs, milk, orange juice and two apples.

Megan yawned because it had been a long day and she had eventually fallen asleep on the sofa. Later, she forced herself to get up, walked to the bedroom, and got into bed. Not long afterwards, noise from the attic was interfering with her sleep.

The noise was more frequent than in the previous weeks. "Here we go again," she whispered. Megan wanted to tell her mom but decided it was not a good idea. *Maybe there's a creature from outer space or something else scary in the attic*. She had seen horror pictures about things like that but decided her imagination was overpowering rational thinking.

Although she was frightened, Megan came up with a well thought out plan. After searching the house, she found a can of pepper spray, her dad's taser gun that was stored in her mom's closet and had put them in the drawer next to her bed. It gave her a feeling of security. She tried to convince herself the unusual sounds at night were just mice and nothing else, was having a difficult time believing it, but she finally had fallen asleep.

The days started to flow by much faster than usual, but the weekends were too short. Chris sent money to help pay part of the monthly house payments, some of the medical bills and utility bills. There wasn't enough money between the both of them to pay for everything, so Megan called Chris again to talk to him.

"Okay," he said, "let's think about this situation." He cleared his throat. "I don't feel Mom has any other option than to rent the house on a lease."

"What? Rent Mom's house?" Megan said, not knowing if she heard him correctly.

"Yes. If you and Mom both live with Aunt and Uncle, she can rent the house on a yearly lease. Then she would have the money to pay the mortgage and maybe have some extra money for other things. At least the house won't go into foreclosure, right?"

Megan was silent for a moment. "What about me getting a roomer or listing it on Airbnb?"

"Would you want a perfect stranger living in the house with you?"

She mulled over it for a moment. "Probably not."

"Renting with a lease would be better."

"Yeah, you're probably right. But I don't know if Aunt and Uncle will have enough room for both of us. Would they even want us living with them? It can get kind of crowded. Anyway, it's sad Mom won't be able to live in her own home after all these years."

"Well, for now, moving is better than her losing the home to foreclosure. It's too bad she had the house refinanced more than once after Dad died. It made her house payments much higher."

"Mom said she needed the money back then to pay off some debts and pay the house payments every month until she could get a fulltime job."

"Yeah, I know." Chris fell silent.

"Are you still there?"

"Why don't you talk to Aunt Ruth and Uncle James, and if they're all right with it then talk to Mom about putting the house up for rent. Then you can think of options for finding some other sources of income."

"I'm not sure if I want to live there, Chris. But I really don't have a choice, do I?"

He was silent for a few seconds and didn't say anything, not knowing how to respond to her question.

"You know I don't have the money nor the time to be looking for my own place. Not right now," she revealed.

"I know but at least Mom will be able to keep the house until she goes back to work."

"Yeah, you're right." She paused for a moment. "Okay, I'll see what they say." Megan was reluctant but she knew it all made sense and her brother was right.

"On second thought, why don't you talk to Mom first and see how she feels about it?"

"Okay, I will tomorrow," Megan replied. "I don't want to worry her with more problems than she already has with her health and the medical bills. But I guess there's no other solution."

She hung up and made a quick trip to the grocery store. As she walked down one of the aisles, someone tapped her on the shoulder. It was Anita.

"Anita, what are you doing here?"

"Shopping just like you," she said.

"You startled me."

"Didn't mean to. Listen, I know your mom doesn't have enough money for the mortgage, so why don't you let my friend Austin buy your mom's house? Then you don't have to worry any more."

"And where are we supposed to live?" Megan asked.

"I don't know. You'll find a place."

"Over my dead body! No thanks, Anita. We'll manage just fine."

"Megan, I'm just trying to help you."

Megan knew she really wasn't and was more determined than ever to find a solution for her mother.

As soon as Megan got home from shopping, she changed into something more casual and forced herself to go talk to her mother about listing the Orange Street house as a rental.

"Mom, I had to go to the bank today to get some money out of the savings account so I could pay the house payment," she said, averting her eyes. She hated being in this position. "We just don't have enough money for the house payments and the medical bills."

Her mother sighed and tried to straighten her back. Megan saw her wince. "You know I expect to be back at work after I heal, Megan. I know it's tough right now, but I just need a little more time."

Megan was done with the uncertainty of her mother's situation. She had to step in and take control.

"Mom, there's nothing else we can do but rent out the house. You can't expect Chris to keep helping out."

"I'm going to pay him back. It's just a matter of time."

"I know, but it's not fair to Chris." And it wasn't fair to Megan either, but she wasn't about to say it to her mother who was already stressed.

"I need to think about it," she said reluctantly.

Megan frowned, flopped down on the chair in frustration. "Don't take too long because we have to do something, like soon."

Disappointed because of her mom's reluctance, she had another throbbing headache coming on, so when she got home Megan poured herself a glass of water and took a pill to eliminate the pain. She thought for a moment, *Maybe there's more to this? None of this makes sense!*

Then she worried about the attic. Perhaps, the locked door had something to do with her mother not wanting to rent the house.

Was her mom really trying to hide something?

Megan searched for the attic keys, and after nearly tearing the house apart, she finally found them. They were in the bottom drawer of her mom's chest of drawers. She called Ashley immediately.

"Hey, girl, guess what?"

"Sounds like something juicy already," Ashley replied.

"Yeah, it is," Megan said, laughing. "I found the keys to the attic."

"You did?"

"Yes! Mom needs to rent the house, so we need to see what's up there. Can you come over and we'll go up there together? I really need somebody to go with me," Megan said.

"Totally. There might be ghosts or maybe even something else scary up there," Ashley replied.

"Okay, that's creepy. I'll call Mark and see if he can come over and we can all go together."

"That sounds like a good idea."

Megan called Mark but he was sick in bed and Corey wasn't home. Too afraid to go up there without him, she called Ashley who said it would be best if they did it another time. It was disappointing but Megan shrugged it off as just one of the inconveniences that happen sometimes. Even so, she was glad to finally have the keys to the attic door. Her mom had hidden them for several years.

The next day, Megan was on her way out the door when her mother called and said she had talked everything over with Aunt Ruth and Uncle James.

"They're willing to help out as much as they can, and we can both live with them temporarily."

"All right," Megan replied, thought about it for a few seconds then said, "The furniture and household items have to be moved out of the house."

"I know," her mom responded.

There was a lot of work that had to be done. Suddenly the simple was not so simple. But what her mother said next was very strange.

"Megan, the renters can have access to most of the house but the door to the attic has to remain locked."

She wasn't sure what to think. "What? Don't you think they'll want to put things up there for storage?"

"Maybe, but just tell them I have a lot of things stored up there. Since they're renting, it shouldn't be a problem," she replied, sounding irritated.

"That's just really weird, Mom. Why?"

"It's my house and that's none of your business, Megan."

"Okay, whatever!" Megan said abruptly because she knew there were more serious problems to worry about.

The attic was the least of her concerns right now. It just wasn't worth getting into a dispute over it.

Unable to go to the house to help, Megan's mom made a list of things to keep and things to give away or sell. Over the next week, Megan sold some things and donated other items to a local non-profit organization. Ashley and Heather helped her clean out all the cabinets and drawers and neatly pack everything, while Mark and Corey came over and helped her paint the bedrooms.

Megan advertised the house as a rental. With Mark's help she decided to handle the background checks on potential renters and the leasing agreement herself to save some money.

The day arrived when most of their things were to be moved out. Two of her uncle's friends moved the heavy furniture. After moving the last two boxes from the house, she walked toward the front door. She took one last look at her childhood home, absorbing her surroundings for a couple of minutes. Megan wiped the sweat off her forehead then closed the front door.

Sadness overwhelmed her, and her eyes filled with tears, her mascara was smeared, as her bottom lip quivered. She felt as bad as she did the time her dog got lost for two days years ago. After slowly walking from the front porch past the flowers her mother had planted next to the sidewalk, she stared at the juvenile sycamore tree they had planted in remembrance of her father. She walked to her car parked in the driveway, got inside, and just sat there for a few minutes. Tears still streamed down her cheeks.

Her mind wandered way back, flashes of the past, reminiscing on the good. It didn't take her long to remember the backyard barbecues and the Sunday afternoon dinners. Family and friends would come over to eat. Her mother often made the traditional, crispy fried chicken dinner with mashed potatoes, gravy and fresh green beans from her aunt's garden. There were fresh rolls and butter on the table and peach cobbler. Aunt Ruth would sometimes bring a lemon meringue pie she made from the lemons picked from her tree.

Some Sundays, her mom cooked spaghetti, made garlic bread and a salad. The aroma from the food cooking filled the rooms and flowed outside to the front yard where Megan used to play with her friends. When dinner was over the older people sat on the backyard patio and talked for hours.

Megan missed those days and knew they would never happen again if their financial situation didn't change soon. Then she thought, at least they weren't losing the house. The solution to put the house up for rent was the only viable option.

It took nearly a month for Megan to get things organized and settled into living with her aunt and uncle. She had placed a few things in storage boxes in the garage, and other things she placed in a public storage unit. Now she was finally able to relax.

CHAPTER 9

ONE DAY AT A TIME

Thankfully, things hadn't gotten worse, but Megan still needed more money. Her car was not in the best condition so food delivery driver jobs to earn extra money weren't an option. The high cost of gas would further reduce her earnings. Getting a modeling job was becoming more and more important. She hadn't heard anything from Bruce, so she reached for her phone and called him.

"Hi, Bruce this is Megan."

"Hey, Megan."

"I'm wondering if we can discuss the details about the modeling job over the phone?"

"I'm sorry, but I don't do business over the phone. You need to come here to the studio."

Megan hesitated. She thought it was weird. But did she even have a choice? She needed the money.

"All right, Bruce, I'll be there shortly."

When she arrived, Bruce was already waiting for her in his back office. He sat behind his desk, and was flipping through fashion magazines when she walked in.

"Megan! Come sit down beside me and let's go through these so we can decide what we'll be working on together."

"Okay…" Megan walked to a seat behind his desk and sat down. He started flipping through the pages and pointed to photos as he spoke.

"What kind of modeling are you really interested in doing?" he asked, pointing to a particularly sultry photo of a woman in a skimpy two-piece bikini.

Megan was uncomfortable. "I'm fine with fashion clothing and maybe even bikinis, but I really don't think I would want to be seen in something like that," she said, referring to the picture he was pointing at. "And I don't want to model lingerie."

Bruce was disappointed. "I see. That's unfortunate, because I do have some jobs for lingerie models, but I guess I'll have to cross them off the list for you," he said, losing the magazine. Then he explained, "Megan, you need to realize when you first start out as a model there may be some jobs you have to take just to get into the industry. Besides, the pay is really good, and it'll get you noticed."

That was what she needed—to get noticed. But more than anything, she needed the money. "Well, I guess I'll see, but I'm pretty firm on not doing lingerie. I just feel really uncomfortable, Bruce. It's not my thing."

He sighed and then stood up from his chair. "Okay, but you're making my job a lot harder. I'll see what I can find for you."

"I'll hear from you soon then?" Megan asked.

"We'll see. I'm closing down for the night. I'll call you regardless."

Megan realized being busy on the weekend helped her to not dwell on how unhappy she was at work. She had been unhappy for a long time. Even though she liked the work, the pay was never enough, and it never would be. Not a good feeling to be underpaid, she concluded. It made her feel devalued and unappreciated. Fairness and appreciation were not in the company's vocabulary.

"Heather, this job isn't turning out the way it's supposed to be."

"What do you mean?"

"My employer had no intentions of me being anything else in the organization. They made promises of pay increases, but I hadn't gotten any since I started working there. Promises of a promotion were just promises. My manager did say the company was having a hard time, and once things got better, I would receive a raise."

"But you never got one?"

"Nope, and I can't continue to live on promises; nobody can."

"I agree, girl. You need to start looking for another job, like right now."

"You're right. I got to know this older girl in the next office. We go on coffee breaks together. You want to know what she told me?"

"Sure. Tell me."

"She found out the company was really in serious trouble financially, so they made sure the men were paid well but not the women."

"It's not a good place to work," Heather replied.

"Yeah. That's unfortunate. She told me I was young and had a lot to learn."

"Why did she say that?"

"She said some women lacked allies in top management and were often overlooked for promotions and pay raises. It wasn't uncommon."

"Hmm, that's discouraging," Heather said while frowning.

Unable to sleep that night, Megan's mind was spinning with feelings of no longer observing the world through foggy lenses. Things were getting clearer now. The topic was all too familiar, preferences for men over women at the workplace, the *old boys' club*. Her gut feelings told her to leave. There was no quick fix. It would be futile. She found comfort in knowing she was in control of where she *did not* want to work. Leaving was universal. Megan soon went to sleep feeling good about her decision to focus her energies elsewhere.

The next day while at home busy cleaning, the phone rang, and it was Austin Mitchell again. "Hi, Megan. Look, I have an offer on the table for your mom's home, and I think if you came down to my office, we could work something out for your family that would be amenable for all parties."

"You don't take 'no' for an answer, do you?"

He didn't say anything. She was wondering how he got her number.

"I told you before, she doesn't want to sell it," Megan said.

"I know you've been having a hard time, but once it's sold, you'll no longer have to worry about making payments. Think of the freedom, Megan."

"What about the time, work and thousands of dollars my mom and dad invested in it? Are you going to pay her what the house is really worth?"

"We would have to talk about it."

She knew he was lying. Uncle James had told her to watch out for people like him.

"I can come over and look at it and give you an estimate."

"No thank you." If she had to, she knew her mom would rather put it up for sale with a trustworthy realtor and get what it's worth.

"Okay, but I think you're making a big mistake. You'll regret it. You have my number if you reconsider."

Mega didn't like what he said. Why would she regret it? It was the right decision as far as she was concerned. *Who is this Austin guy anyway?* she thought. She had previously asked people around town about him, but nobody knew much of anything. There was something about him that was bewildering.

Megan wasn't getting much sleep because of all the things going on in her life. Chris called to see how she was doing. They talked about a lot of things, and she decided to bring up her concerns about the house.

"Chris, do you think houses can talk to you?"

"Talk to you? Of course not, why would you ask that?"

"I read this story once and the woman said that certain things were happening in her house. The house was actually trying to tell her that she needed to move."

"Move? But why?" Chris asked.

"Because her life would be better someplace else, in another city," Megan replied.

"I never heard of that, Meg. It's just a story."

"I know this sounds odd but when I was living in mom's house, I heard strange noises during the night. I had gotten frightened. Do you think there could have been something up there in the attic?"

"No, Meg. Your imagination was getting carried away. It was because you were there by yourself."

"Maybe." She mulled over it.

"Remember, Uncle James told us a long time ago most houses had noise coming from the water heater, pipes, walls, and heater? They could make rumbling, crackling, or popping noise."

"No. I probably wasn't paying attention."

"Yeah, he did."

"Exactly what did he say?" she asked.

"Uncle told us layers of sediment could build up inside the tank, trapping water underneath, and could make popping noises. The knocking or banging noise could come from the walls because air pressure had built up in the water pipes."

"Hmmm." She paused for a moment. "But Chris, it really did sound like the noise was coming from the attic. The hot water tank is in the basement. Maybe the house was trying to tell me something."

"Like I said before, it was your imagination." He laughed. "Houses can't talk."

She listened to him but wasn't totally convinced. "It was really scary when I was home alone.

"I know. You should have ignored it." He tried to make a joke of it. "Think about it. If something was going to grab you, it would have done it by now."

"It's easy for you to say, you weren't living there," she replied, not appreciating his humor.

The week was hectic but thankfully in just one evening, things had changed for the better. Megan finally had some good news to tell her mom. She was able to rent her house to a young couple: Glen, a firefighter, and his wife Jennifer, a stay-at-home mom. "They agreed on a twelve-month rental agreement. They have two young children."

The couple loved the house but said it was odd not to have the keys to the attic door. Megan almost agreed with them, but then told them her mother had a lot of boxes and things stored up there. She convinced herself it wasn't really a lie, more like a half-truth. They decided to rent it anyway. Even though she was relieved, Megan had mixed emotions about no longer living in the house where she and Chris had grown up. She knew it was going to be odd driving to the house each month to get the rent check. Maybe they could mail it to her? It would be easier emotionally. At least renting the house was a temporary fix to the foreclosure problem while her mom got better.

Megan had to clean the house before the renters moved in. She wanted to forget about the whole thing but who would do it if she didn't? She had no choice.

After she had been there for a while, Megan walked down the hallway and noticed the hallway door with the stairs that went up to the locked attic was open. She closed it on her way to the kitchen. Forty minutes later as she was getting ready to leave, the door was open again. She knew that she had just recently closed it.

She stood there staring at the door for a few seconds wondering what had happened because it was very strange, even bizarre. Maybe the door had loose hinges or something. She scratched her head, closed the door again, then locked up the house, left, and wasn't looking forward to coming back unless she really had to.

With the renter problem solved, Megan decided to go visit Heather. As she walked toward the apartment and glanced up, there he was again—the stranger across the street.

This time he had papers in his hands. She stared at him intensely. He was holding mail, looking at it and shuffling through papers and envelopes. He must actually live in the condos across the street from Ashley and Heather. It didn't look like he was visiting anyone. Hope and happiness flooded throughout her body.

Megan fixed her eyes on him for a few moments, trying not to be obvious. He was tall, handsome, and had a nice face, and looked like a professional. She watched him walk through the main gate and then disappear from sight. Could he be the right guy, her fairy tale prince? Hopefully, someday, she'll be able to meet him.

While visiting Heather, Megan sat on the sofa, leaned back and started to daydream about the story of Cinderella.

"Heather, did I ever tell you my mom read that story to me a lot when I was a little girl? I always wondered why the pictures didn't look like me or most of my friends."

"Yes, you did, many times," she replied and laughed. "Most of us don't even look like Cinderella. She should be a brunette with brown eyes and a golden suntan."

"I don't have blond hair like her either—it's long and thick with spiraling curls, and I love it just the way it is."

"I had to dye my hair dark, you're lucky," Heather replied.

"And another thing, I never had any glass slippers like Cinderella either. But I did have a pair of beautiful red stiletto designer shoes that were special to me. I saw them in the store window and couldn't afford them, but like a fairy godmother, five weeks later the store put them on sale, and I bought them. I felt like a princess when I wore them."

"It's a fairy tale. Little girls usually love hearing those kinds of stories. Even grown women like it," Heather replied.

Megan thought about the stranger: but life wasn't simple. Would it be possible to show up at his home in a beautiful dress and immediately fall in love? That would be wonderful.

No, life wasn't like a fairy tale—at least hers wasn't. But maybe someday things could change? Things had to eventually get better, didn't they?

CHAPTER 10

SISTER FRIEND

Megan's class assignments and tasks at work went by fast during the past two weeks and, on Thursday, she went to see Dr. Sharma. She arrived there on time, but the reception room was crowded so she had to wait longer than usual. After she walked into his office and sat down on the comfortable leather chair, they talked for a brief time before she brought up why she was there.

"You want to know what's really bothering me a lot this week?"

"This is on your time… yes, please tell me."

Megan hesitated for a moment because she didn't want to complain about her mom. She knew she had imperfections—everyone did. But Dr. Sharma was a psychiatrist. She trusted him. Anything she said was safe with him because of patient confidentiality. He wouldn't tell anybody else.

She reluctantly replied, "I keep thinking back over the years about my mom never wanting me to move out. Sometimes, I don't feel like I have control over my life. The house was comfortable, but it wasn't where I wanted to be. I was in the same room I slept in as a little girl, in the same bed where I used to accidentally wet the sheets after having nightmares from watching scary movies. Sometimes it was stressful for me.

Mom said she misses my dad all the time and things seemed different without Chris living at home. He joined the military when he graduated from high school and helps by sending some money home. I think she gets lonely and depressed at times."

"What you're going through is difficult. I suggest you let your mother know you appreciate everything she does for you but you're not a little girl any more. You have to make your own decisions in life. She should come and talk to me."

"Yes, I could tell her that," she replied, "but she won't make an appointment to see you."

"Keep asking her," Dr. Sharma said.

"All right, Megan replied. "Do you want to know something else?"

"What?" he asked.

"It was difficult trying to finish college when I was living at home. Well, now we're both living with my aunt and uncle. And who knows when that's going to end? I work most of the time, so I have to carefully manage my time."

Dr. Sharma suddenly stopped taking notes, looked up at her with his no expression therapist face again.

"You're living with your aunt and uncle too?" he asked as he leaned back on his chair.

"Yes, I forgot to mention that," she responded.

"Megan, you don't always tell me everything."

"I know. That's because there are some things, I don't think you can tell me that will help me fix the problem. I have to figure it out myself."

She could tell by the way he looked at her, he was concerned about what she had just said. Time had run out, he had to see the next patient but told her they needed to talk again during her next appointment.

When her session ended, Megan met Ashley at the neighborhood coffee shop. After ordering coffee, Ashley handed her a cup and they started talking about the latest movies at the theater and life in general. Megan was happy when she was with her friends. They were true, stick by you no matter what happens kind of friends. She didn't even have cousins like them but realized families can be complicated at times, too problematic to be around.

Ashley had no problem expressing her viewpoint on things. Most people assumed Ashley and Megan were sisters, because they liked the same music and some of the same food. Ashley worked for a social services agency and, like Megan, lived on a limited income. She understood what Megan was going through. But she got a lot of help from her family.

Ashley had got divorced recently but was coping well considering everything she had been through. Her husband started drinking after his mother died. Not long afterwards he was difficult to be around.

Ashley said, "He used terrible words blaming me for his unhappiness. He became an expert at making me feel bad. It was a job that required no real talent other than being a jerk. I didn't deserve feeling that way. I knew it was time to leave."

"I'm glad you left him. Nobody should be treated that way," Megan had said. In her mind, guys like him were like a large, open volcano spewing hot toxic gases and steam into the air. Nobody in their right mind would want to hang around waiting for it to erupt with flowing molten lava and smothering ash destroying everything in its path. Distance was the one thing to cherish under the circumstances.

He kept telling Ashley he could quit drinking any time he wanted to, but he was just fooling himself. She was angry at him for a long time. Then when the divorce was final, Ashley started working full-time.

Ashley's son, Parker, was a cute little boy who always stood hand in hand with his mother. His brown hair had a few curls on the back of his head, and he was smiling. He frequently had something cute to say and was loveable and full of hugs and kisses. Parker always gave Megan a big hug when he saw her. She loved children; they often did or said something which made her laugh.

The child support money Ashley received helped with paying the rent and other bills, but her ex-husband often missed payments, making it difficult for her to make ends meet. She was glad her mother and her older sister were there to help take care of Parker while she was at work.

When Ashley wanted to go out with friends, her family often gave her a weekend off by taking care of him.

Megan loved Ashley's family. When Megan's father had suddenly passed away from pneumonia when she was fourteen, her grieving mother had to work full time, so she wasn't able to take Megan and Chris on weekend campouts and summer vacations. But Ashley's family stepped in and took Megan and Chris on their camping trips. Megan even worked as a volunteer at the homeless shelter some afternoons with Ashley and her mom.

"I desperately need a job that pays good money, Ash. I keep thinking about it and can't get it off my mind. Sometimes, I just get frustrated. Maybe I should have gone into nursing or something else."

"I know what you mean. It's a struggle at times but I can't imagine you being a nurse. Don't even think about it."

CHAPTER 11

SECOND THOUGHTS

Three months had passed since Megan had moved in with her aunt and uncle. Her mom was still suffering from back problems, but she refused to have surgery. Going back to work any time soon didn't appear to be an option right now. Megan and Chris regularly deposited money directly into their mom's bank account to help her financially.

Adjusting to the living arrangements had been difficult for Megan. She knew having her own place would be great, but she didn't have the money to move, not right now. It was difficult living in a small house with three other adults, two spoiled dogs, and a cat who acted like she was the Queen of England.

Last week after she finished cleaning the kitchen, she heard her aunt talking to someone on the phone.

"Oh, you mean Megan?" Aunt Ruth said. "She's doing fine. She sleeps in the spare bedroom. It's my sewing room but I don't mind it being occupied. Megan is only going to be here until things get better, it won't be long. She's an ambitious girl."

Megan folded the kitchen towel, hung it up, and sipped her glass of water for fifteen minutes with thoughts about eventually moving to her own place. She just didn't have the money to do it right now but that could change one day.

The current living arrangements tested Megan's patience. She had her own space—a bedroom with a twin-size bed. There was a dresser, a small wooden desk and chair, and a soft reclining chair against the opposite side of the room. A sewing machine encased in a small, wooden cabinet was near the window. It was comfortable enough but there wasn't much space to move around. Still, it was better than trying to struggle to pay her mom's house payments. The Orange Street house seemed to always be in the back of her mind.

Megan tried to be patient but got upset when the dogs jumped on the bed, licking any available body parts they could. They would just lay there looking at her and wouldn't get down, even when she told them to. Eventually, she had to practically throw them off the bed.

But then, thirty minutes later, they would hop back on the bed again, staring at her. It was like a game and sometimes she laughed at them. The bed was comfortable, but it was too small for her, two dogs and a cat. They acted as if they owned the house, because Aunt Ruth let them do whatever they wanted to. Megan had to hang her clothes up after she got undressed or the dogs would lay on top of them. They forced her to be a neater person.

She turned her head and slowly looked at her surroundings and thought, *When did this room become so intolerably small?* Someday, she was going to have her own place. It would happen, she just didn't know when.

Frustrated, and after many attempts to remove the animals from her room, Megan grabbed the phone and called Heather. She needed to talk to somebody.

"Hi, girlfriend."

"Hey, Megan. How's everything?

"I don't know. Not so good, I guess."

"What's the matter?"

"There's a lot of stuff bothering me," she said while looking down and rubbing her forehead.

"Tell me about it. It'll make you feel better," Heather said.

"I don't like to complain but Aunt and Uncle won't let me pay rent. I want to but they insist I don't and keep the money to help mom. I help pay for other things, but I feel like a guest at their house. They want me to feel like it's my home but I'm still a guest. I stay in bed every Saturday morning trying to sleep, right?"

"Well, yes, if you say so," Heather replied.

"I can hear everybody in the kitchen. They get up too early, and I can smell the coffee and the aroma of eggs, bacon and hash browns cooking. Aunt Ruth always makes breakfast, and it smells so good, but she wakes me up to come to eat at the kitchen table with everyone. I'd rather have a glass of orange juice and go running. I don't want to hurt her feelings, so I get dressed and go downstairs for breakfast, but if I keep this up, I'll gain five pounds—maybe more. I long for the privacy of my own apartment someday. I know the arrangement here is temporary. I'll eventually move. It'll just take a little more time. Things will get better."

"I know what you mean. I wouldn't want to live with my relatives either."

"Don't get me wrong, Heather. I love them a lot but it's impossible to have friends over to visit and hang out together. You know what I miss the most?"

"What?"

"I miss taking long, hot baths in the evening before going to bed. I can't do that any more."

"Sorry, Meg." Heather replied. "You know you could stay with me if it wasn't for my brother. He always stays in my apartment when he comes to town on business trips. It would be difficult. My one bedroom apartment with a sofa sleeper doesn't provide a lot of options for guests."

"I know you would help me if you could," Megan said. "I just miss the silence sometimes. I like to turn off the sounds of the day and listen to peace and quiet, the breeze shuffling the leaves on the trees, soft music, nobody talking and no dogs barking."

"Yeah, it must be especially difficult because your uncle needs hearing aids."

"You're right. I have to shout all the time when I'm talking to him."

"Everything must be exhausting."

"I find myself shouting at everyone even when I'm talking to my coworkers on the job. They keep telling me I don't have to talk so loudly and to use my inside voice."

"It must be hard. Do you know you're shouting now?" Heather laughed. "How can you even study?"

"It's hard to concentrate. Sometimes after an hour of distractions from dogs barking and voices in the background, I go to the library. Other times I order a cup of hot coffee and just study at the coffee shop on First Street."

"How's your mom doing?"

"You know my mom. She cries sometimes and I try to comfort her and make sure she takes her meds, but it only helps for a while."

They talked for a little while longer and Megan soon went to bed, trying to clear her mind of everything.

The following day, Megan went to her appointment with Dr. Sharma. She had not seen him for a while. Sometimes he made her realize things weren't as bad as she thought they were after their discussions.

"My mom's Orange Street house has already been rented. Thank goodness. But you know what?"

"What?" he replied.

"I had this strange feeling of sadness after they moved in," she said.

Dr. Sharma stopped writing and looked up at her.

"Why?"

"I'm not really sure," she replied.

"You need to change how you view things. Why don't you think of the good things about them renting the house?"

"Yes, I guess I can." She paused for a moment. "I should be thankful the house won't be going through foreclosure. The renters are taking good care of the house."

"Yes, those are good things. What else?"

"They pay their monthly rent on the first of each month and are reliable tenants. So, I guess I should be thankful."

"There are a lot of things to be thankful for."

"You're right. Things will get better. I just have to give it some time," Megan responded, feeling somewhat better.

"True."

"I just hope they continue to pay the rent on time. I don't know what we'll do if they run into financial problems and can't pay."

Dr. Sharma glanced at her with a reassuring look. "Hopefully that won't happen. So, you shouldn't worry about it right now."

On her way home from work, Megan drove past her mother's house. Glancing at the sycamore tree in the front yard brought back memories of her father. Glen was getting out of his car parked in the driveway. The drapes were open in the dining room. The table had dishes arranged on it for dinner. Jennifer was standing at the front door holding their baby girl. The little boy ran to his father and gave him a big hug. They walked to the front door and Jennifer greeted Glen with a kiss. Megan felt something comforting about it. They reminded her of what it was like when her dad was alive.

After dinner she sat down on the bed, and accidentally knocked her diary off the lamp table onto the floor. When she grabbed it, the page opened up to what she had written last Thursday.

Therapists say most people suppress bad memories. Maybe that's why I don't remember much about the time we lived in Los Angeles and the day my dad passed away. It would probably be too painful.

I drive past my mom's house every day on my way to work and tell myself not to look, I shouldn't look. I really try not to, but can't help it. Don't know why I'm sad. There's nothing I want to see there but it brings back a lot of memories mingled with thoughts of how it was transformed into a really nice home.

Now, I look at the house and tell myself it's where we used to live. But at least mom still owns it.

Megan walked to the kitchen looking for comfort food. She poured herself a glass of milk and grabbed some chocolate chip cookies. Then she went upstairs, sat down on the bed, and reflected on all her feelings.

As long as she could remember, her mom was never happy about her wanting to move to her own place. It didn't matter what she said—not now. Megan had to make her own decisions.

CHAPTER 12

THE LETTER

Megan was asleep and her phone kept buzzing. Who would be calling her so late at night? It was 11:30 p.m. She finally grabbed the phone from the nightstand.

"Hello."

"Is this Megan?"

"Yes," she replied cautiously.

"This is Glen. I hate to tell you this but the shed in our backyard is on fire. I tried to put it out but had to call the fire department for help. Some of the trees and brush are burning."

"What?" She was absolutely horrified by what he had just said, and heat rushed throughout her entire body.

"The house and the garage didn't catch fire. At least not yet."

"I'll be right there!" she said, rising to her feet.

Megan, still not totally awake, quickly put on her sweats and rushed to the house. The shed was still burning. The fire engine and firemen were there hosing down the shed and even part of the garage which had caught fire.

"I can't believe it! How did this happen?" she asked.

"I don't know but it looks like arson."

"What? Somebody deliberately set the fire?"

"It looks that way, but we'll know better after an inspection."

Megan was bewildered and didn't know who would want to torch the shed. Maybe it was someone trying to get her mom to sell the house? She had a feeling it had something to do with Austin. Megan was really getting worried. She hoped Glen and Jennifer weren't scared and wanted to move out of the house.

"At least it was just the shed and part of the garage," he said, shaking his head. "Don't worry, Megan. We'll get to the bottom of this, and you can file a claim on your mom's homeowner's insurance policy. Maybe they'll cover the cost of having things rebuilt."

"Thanks, Glen. I hope so."

Megan was worried but didn't know what to do about it. Between the house payments and her mom having crying episodes when she was depressed life was difficult at times. Megan often studied her mom's eyes and could sense when there was something troubling deep inside. Megan convinced herself she was tough enough to handle all these challenges head on and not let anything stand in her way. Her mom needed help.

On Saturday morning, Megan, exhausted, picked up her mail and shuffled through the envelopes. There was a letter from the college. She quickly opened it not knowing what to expect. What was the college writing to her about? After reading the letter, she found the information hard to believe. Feeling excited, she jumped to her feet, and started screaming.

She was going to receive a large amount of financial assistance to help cover her living expenses. However, as she read on, there was one condition: she was required to live in her own place or on campus.

Her heart was racing and she started to breathe deeply. It was something she wanted to do. This was the one and only opportunity for her to move. She was so happy about it and called and told Heather and Ashley immediately.

Wanting to take control of her life, she made plans to see rentals. It would be nice to have her own space. She couldn't afford to spend a lot of money. Perhaps a cottage or small apartment would be affordable and within her budget?

After searching the internet for places for rent, she found a cute, one-bedroom, unfurnished cottage in the back of the main house. It was within her budget, so she called the phone number. The property manager answered and said he would show her that property and a few others.

The next day they were parked in front of the house. The two-story English style country home had grey stones on the front. There was lush lawn in the front yard, which was neatly edged and trimmed, as well as a sidewalk lined with flowerbeds with many different kinds of gazanias, hibiscus and marigold flowers. On one side of the house was a long driveway leading to the backyard with a detached garage.

In the distance, there was another building at the back of the house—light tan with medium brown trim. There were potted plants with colorful geraniums, and they walked through a tall, double barn door to go inside. Immediately she saw three stalls and a horse standing there in one of them.

She laughed loudly. "There's a horse over there!" She turned her head and stared again in disbelief.

"Yes. Just follow me," he said, not at all shocked as they walked by the horse to a door.

He unlocked the door and they walked into an apartment. The place was clean and freshly painted with tan tiles on the floors and a large area rug in the living room. But Megan didn't pay much attention to what he was saying because her thoughts were about the horse standing out there in the stall.

The property manager showed her the kitchen with a small refrigerator and a four-burner stove. There were butcher block counter tops with a sink and a few white cabinets. The bedroom was large with a small closet and the bathroom had a shower but no bathtub. Megan thought, *No bathtub, not good*. Taking a hot bath was her way of relaxing after a long day.

She said, "I can't believe there's a horse right outside the apartment..." and laughed again, and thought it was unusually funny.

"I know but the apartment is really nice."

"Maybe for a jockey," she replied with a smile. "It's not exactly what I am looking for. I don't want to walk by a horse every time I come home."

"I admit it might be a little strange, but they do own horses."

"What? You mean there's more?" she asked with a bewildered look.

"I think so," he said with very little to no expression on his face.

Megan found it hard not to laugh every time she looked at the horse, so she avoided glancing at the stall.

"Well, regardless of the horses, the apartment is nice but it's too far from where I work." She didn't want to tell him she didn't like it at all. "Do you have something closer to my job and the college?"

"Absolutely. If this doesn't work for you, let's go check out the others."

"Okay." She smiled trying to be polite and not laugh again.

He showed her another apartment in the backyard of a Tudor-style home. The house had a nice front yard with two large trees and dense green grass. They walked through a gate to the front porch. There was another sidewalk along the side of the house. She could see a separate building in the backyard with a bed of colorful flowers planted on each side of the front door.

They entered and there was one large room with mixed beige and brown tile floors. There was a kitchen along the back wall with dark cherry cabinets and faux granite countertops. The bathroom was the only room separated by permanent walls. After walking around, it occurred to Megan it was actually a studio apartment.

Megan turned around and the owner of the apartment walked in to meet her. She was a short, elderly lady neatly dressed in a knit top, skirt and black shoes with socks. It looked strange. The pink on her reading glasses matched the light pink tint on the tips of her gray hair. In her arms she carried a cute small dog with white fluffy hair. It leapt out of her arms and greeted Megan with a tail wag and a hand lick.

A few seconds later, a large fifty-pound golden retriever walked into the cottage and laid down near her. Then, as she was talking, another golden retriever walked into the room and laid down. Both were older dogs with mixed grey hair around their eyes, noses and on the top of their heads.

As they talked about the property, two more dogs, dachshunds, walked into the room and stood there staring at everyone and wagging their tails. The dogs started to jump all over Megan's shoes and pants. So, she crouched down to pet them, trying to calm them down. The bottoms of her pants were instantly covered with dog hair.

"How many dogs do you have?" Megan asked, smiling and trying not to laugh.

"I have five dogs and three cats. They're friendly dogs so you can walk through the gate to the cottage with no problem."

"Oh, okay."

Megan was curious and wondered how this elderly lady took care of five dogs. Who cleaned up the dog poop in the yard?

A few minutes later, the property manager and Megan said goodbye to the owner and walked out the door toward the front gate. As they were walking, he said, "So what do you think about this place?"

"Actually, it's nice but the rent is too high. It's more than I can afford to pay. I love animals but I don't think I want to be greeted by five dogs and three cats every time I walk in through the gate or leave."

"They're friendly dogs."

"Yes. I agree they are cute and friendly." She smiled and then laughed because as they were leaving, all five dogs and one cat followed them to the gate. "But this is like an animal shelter," she said, laughing again.

The property manager didn't laugh and clearly had no sense of humor. "Okay. Let me show you some of the other places I have on my list for rent."

They drove around during the afternoon looking at several apartments. Megan didn't see anything she liked apart from some she couldn't afford. Exhausted, she decided to head home and fix herself something to eat before falling asleep in her room listening to music.

The next morning, Glen called and said someone had in fact intentionally set the shed on fire. It was considered arson. So far, they haven't been able to find out who started it.

Megan was worried. Would Anita go so low as to have somebody burn the shed so the tenants would get scared and move out of the house? The more she thought about it, the more she was convinced the answer was yes.

CHAPTER 13

ANOTHER PLACE TO CALL HOME

In the middle of the week, Ashley called and told Megan a one-bedroom apartment was vacant in her building. There hadn't been a vacancy there in three years. Megan was excited because she really liked Ashley's apartment and had hoped to get one like it someday. The best thing was the rent was within her budget, so she arranged to see it.

"You'll like it even more now," Ashley said.

"Really?"

"Yes! Somebody bought the buildings not long ago and completed some major renovations. The separate three-story buildings surrounding the center courtyard now have a new three-tiered Spanish style water fountain. They even reseeded the grass and planted different shrubs and flowers lining the sidewalk."

"I've seen a lot of work going on but didn't know what they were doing. I really like the sidewalk near the street leading to the front archway entrance to the courtyard," Megan replied.

The next day she viewed the apartment hoping to rent it before someone else signed a rental agreement. Megan knew instantly she had to have this place. Before she even left the showing, she completed the paperwork, signed the lease agreement and planned on moving in two weeks. Just like that.

The day Megan got the keys to her apartment she just couldn't wait to open the door. Once inside, she walked around shoeless, feeling the warmth of the hardwood floorboards underfoot, relishing the space of all the empty rooms waiting to be filled with furniture. She carefully walked around studying the details, the round arched doors into the kitchen and bedroom, and the small balcony which overlooked the grass and three tall sycamore trees below. The apartment wasn't large or spacious, but it belonged to her.

Megan moved her things in with Corey and Mark's help. She thanked Aunt Ruth and Uncle James for letting her stay, but it was the right time to move; she was grateful and had no desire to overstay her welcome. Her mother wasn't happy, but Megan kissed her goodbye, and reminded her she was only moving four miles away. It wasn't like she was moving to New York or Washington, D.C. Megan knew her mother was getting the best of care, so she wasn't worried.

The next afternoon, Megan settled in, changed into a pair of shorts, and walked outside past the colorful flowers. She felt happy walking pass the yellow, orange and pink gazanias that accented the courtyard, but that wasn't what interested her today—she was hoping to get another glimpse of the stranger. She could smell the scent of the freshly cut grass and walked through the arched courtyard entrance. People passed her, walking their dogs, and some stopped to talk to her.

Later in the evening after returning from her walk, there he was, the stranger, walking toward his condo. Something about him reminded her of Scott Emerson. Feeling excited, Megan's heart started beating faster. But, disappointingly, he didn't even glance in her direction. It was like she was invisible.

She could only imagine what he was really like. She wondered what he was doing now. Maybe he was fixing dinner, watching a movie, or sitting in a soft recliner chair reading a good book. He probably has a girlfriend and could be talking to her on the phone right now. He could even have his arms around her, kissing her passionately. He wouldn't be alone—not a guy like him. But she hadn't seen him with a woman. Then again, he might be too busy to be in a relationship with someone.

The next day during her therapy session, Megan told Dr. Sharma about being attracted to her neighbor.

"So, you're attracted to a stranger even though you don't know anything about him?"

At first, she was reluctant to answer because it was difficult to read Dr. Sharma's expression.

"Yes," she replied. "I get excited when I see him and I keep wondering 'what if?', but he hasn't even noticed me. Maybe I'm not his type?"

"Why would you say that?"

"I'm not a flashy person. I don't drive a new car or wear designer clothes. Even if I had the money, I wouldn't buy designer clothes. The money could be better used for helping my friends or my family. But as it is, I'm just struggling to survive. I'm trying to finish college."

"Maybe he doesn't like flashy women? Have you ever thought of that?"

"I guess not…"

"You know nothing about him and now you're doubting yourself."

"I know."

"You're a strong and focused person, Megan, but it sounds like we have to work on your self-esteem. Let's talk about it some more. Tell me: what would you say are your strengths?"

"Let me think. I'm a very organized person, I guess. I'm a loyal friend. And I care about my family. I try to always be positive, even when I'm going through a tough time."

"Good… And what about your weaknesses?"

She paused for a moment. "I know I have flaws. Sometimes I guess I can be a bit self-centered, and I lack confidence—there are things I'd like to do but don't have confidence to do sometimes…" Megan trailed off.

"I think that's a very honest, accurate assessment of yourself, Megan. Plenty of young women lack confidence, and it's something we can definitely work on in your sessions." Dr. Sharma smiled reassuringly. "Let's talk about this more next time."

Megan glanced at the clock on his desk—the hour had flown past, as usual.

There were times when she envied those who seemed to have more than their share of happiness. After arriving home, she walked through the courtyard toward her apartment with pleasant thoughts of Scott. She missed him all the time. He was the big hole in her life, in the middle of her soul.

Megan stood there in the hallway staring at her front door for a moment, then turned the lock and opened the door to apartment number 205. From the hallway it looked like all the other apartments, but the inside was different, decorated and furnished just the way she liked it. She walked into her living room—it was such a good feeling being in her own home. The aroma of someone cooking permeated the entire building. It smelled so good, just like her mom's fried chicken. They were probably ready to eat dinner. Sitting on the overstuffed chair, she leaned back and relaxed, put her feet up on the ottoman, and studied her surroundings. She was glad there wasn't an attic.

Content and excited, Megan giggled. She had never lived alone before. Never had her own place. The more she thought about it, the more she loved it because dirty dishes could be piled high in the sink, and nobody was there to complain. The television could be on any time during the day or night, and nobody was there to care. Music could be on until midnight and nobody was there to get upset and turn it off. Her backpack or handbag could be on the sofa and the paper towel dispenser could be empty and nobody was there to care. Silence could mute the air and it would be so peaceful.

Suddenly, she heard the faint sound of someone's phone ringing in the distance. It was a cheerful ringtone and after four rings it stopped. They must have answered it. Sometimes, if she listened closely, she could hear keys dangling in the hallway or someone unlocking their front door. She could hear the sound of doors closing or the crinkling sound of brown paper bags from someone carrying their groceries. It was a good thing to have neighbors—a very good thing. Megan liked seeing familiar faces, people she recognized going or coming and they recognized her with a nod or greeting. It reminded her of elementary school when she saw the same teachers and children every day; some she had known very well and others she knew nothing about.

Last week she painted the walls of her apartment. The bedroom showed a strong, imaginative use of color. She indulged herself with a beautiful, matching comforter, bed skirt and pillows. On the bed was the stuffed teddy bear her father had given her for Christmas when she was five years old. In the living room, there was a small area rug on the floor and colorful prints of popular paintings on the walls from yard sales. She found attractive lamps from a discount store in town and put store bought slipcovers on the sofa and oversized chair, which updated the old, mismatched furniture that had once belonged to her mom.

The narrow, galley-style kitchen with a stackable washer and dryer had her personal touch, and the huge closet in the bedroom was filled with her clothes. There was a large, rectangle-shaped leather storage chest her mother gave to her. It was full of her books, papers, magazines and whatever else she could fit in inside. Two decorative serving trays sat on top of the chest she used as her coffee table.

She found four outdoor rattan chairs at a yard sale, painted them, and used them with her small dining room table. Next to the table were French doors which opened up to a small, narrow balcony.

It was her home, nobody else's, and she knew it was a part of building her self-confidence, just like Dr. Sharma said she needed to do.

The next morning, she needed to get her mail because she hadn't picked it up in three days. The mailman often complained her mailbox was too full. It was all the frustrating junk mail and she wished they would stop sending it but that would never happen.

Megan quickly brushed her hair because she didn't want the stranger to see her looking like she had just gotten out of bed. Every time she walked to the mailbox, she hoped to catch a glimpse of him again. Today, she glanced across the street and saw him walking toward his car as though he was in a rush. He finally turned and glanced in her direction but didn't even notice her. Then he got into his car and drove away.

He appeared to be a thinker, always preoccupied with whatever was on his mind. *Maybe he's an attorney.* She wondered what he did for a living. The stranger was handsome in a different kind of way. He was intriguing, and Megan was attracted to him in a way she couldn't even explain. Then she thought it would be so nice to meet someone she could love and trust with the same kind of interests, someone like Scott.

As she was walking back to her apartment, there were Austin and Anita standing in the courtyard talking.

"Oh, hello, Megan," Austin said. Anita didn't say a word.

"What are you two doing here?" Megan asked.

"Don't you know?" Anita replied.

"Know what?"

"Austin works for the investment company who bought the apartment building, and I live in the condos across street. I just moved in."

Megan felt sick to her stomach. She couldn't believe it. She couldn't get away from Anita no matter how hard she tried.

"Have a good day," she said, cutting the conversation short as she walked toward her apartment.

She was disappointed living so close to Anita, and it irritated her that Austin worked for the owner of the apartments. It was like every time she took a step forward, life seemed to push her two steps back.

But she had thoughts of perseverance. Things were getting better. She just had to keep reminding herself of that. Megan calmed herself by thinking of all the hurdles she had gotten through in the past, the incredible jerks and demeaning people in the world she had survived. She was a survivor, a title she was proud of.

During the afternoon while studying, Megan was alarmed to receive a call from Jennifer about her mother's Orange Street house.

"Megan, we really like living here but there's just one problem."

"Really? What is it?"

"Sometimes, we hear a strange noise at night and can't figure out where it's coming from, but we think it's coming from the attic. Could there be something up there?" Jennifer asked.

"Oh..." She paused for a moment. "No, of course not." Megan forced a laugh over the phone and tried to respond quickly. "I'm sure it's just the tree branches brushing up against the roof."

"You think so?" Jennifer replied. "Well, we don't hear it all the time."

"Don't worry. I'll talk to Mom about getting the trees trimmed."

"Thanks, It's just kind of creepy at times."

"I know, but it's nothing to worry about," Megan said.

Megan was nervous and clueless as to what to do next. Maybe there was something lurking behind the walls, maybe not. A mouse or a rat could get stuck in walls. There was no way she was going upstairs to the attic. Fortunately, this was the time of year when the strong Santa Ana winds blew strongly against the house making creaking sounds, which meant the winds would drown out most of the strange noise. After taking a deep breath, she decided the best thing to do was nothing unless Jennifer called again.

The dreams Megan sometimes had about the noise in the attic interrupted her sleep. She found herself still having nightmares even though she wasn't living in the Orange Street house. The nightmares were always the same. She was standing at the front door, knocking loudly, while locked outside in the freezing cold and trembling. Her fingers were numb, and the Santa Ana wind was whipping through the trees. She had no house keys and was shouting at the top of her voice for somebody to let her inside where it was warm and safe. But nobody came. All the while, there was a dim light shining from the window in the attic. What did it mean?

It was strange to still be scared but common sense told her something weird was going on. Still reluctant to share all her concerns with Dr. Sharma, she considered it minor compared to her other problems. Thankfully the insurance company had paid to rebuild the burnt shed and the damaged to the garage, so she felt fortunate.

Megan was busy throughout the week trying to accomplish everything she had written on her priority list, including visiting her mom and completing her class assignments.

Another week went by, and Jennifer called again. She said some guy was standing on the sidewalk in the front yard looking at the house and taking pictures.

"Was he tall, slender, dark hair, and wearing a suit and tie?" Megan asked.

"Yes, and he was writing something down," she replied.

"That's the guy who was interested in buying my mom's house before you moved into it. Just ignore him. But if it happens again let me know," Megan said calmly, but inside she was fuming.

"Okay," Jennifer replied. "It's really kind of weird."

Megan hung up her phone, shook her head and thought Austin hadn't given up believing he was going to buy her mom's house. Megan quickly searched for his business card, found it, and called him.

"You need to stop scaring the renters by standing in the front yard of my mom's house."

"I wasn't trying to scare them. I was just trying to figure out what we could offer your mom to buy the house. Anita told me you might be interested in selling it."

"She did? Anita was mistaken. I haven't even talked to her about it."

"Sorry, I didn't know that," he said.

Megan wasn't sure if he was lying or not.

"So, what figure did you come up with?" Megan asked because she was curious.

"I'll text it to you this afternoon," he replied.

"Okay."

Two hours later she received his text with the dollar amount. She was insulted and shook her head.

Megan texted him back and said, 'You've got to be kidding! It's worth much more. It's on an acre of land! That's ridiculous.'

As far as she was concerned, he was a snake in the grass waiting for someone naïve enough to accept his offer.

'Take it or leave it', he replied.

'We'll leave it.' She texted him, walked toward the bathroom medicine cabinet, and took a pill because she was stressed and getting another headache.

CHAPTER 14

THE NEIGHBORS

Megan loved being near Ashley and Heather who had their own separate apartments in the same building. As best friends they helped each other, laughed together, and even cried together. She had feelings of safety in the neighborhood with the neatly trimmed grass, beautiful trees and well-lit streetlights on every block. But everybody knew everyone else, which made it hard to keep secrets.

Megan had gotten to know several of the people in her building already. As she walked through the courtyard, there was John.

"Hi, John, how are you today?" she said smiling at him.

"I'm fine," he replied, "thanks for asking."

John lived in a first-floor apartment and had recently lost his wife. He lived on a limited monthly retirement income, but he always said it was enough to get by. And here was Ben who lived in a second-floor apartment down the hallway and was partially blind but had a small inheritance from his parents that provided him with the income he needed.

Then Megan walked by Mrs. Johnson. "Good morning."

"Good morning to you too, young lady," she said and grinned.

Mrs. Johnson, a sweet, elderly, grey-haired woman who lived in a large first floor apartment with her small dog. Originally from England, she liked to invite people over for tea served with finger sandwiches, crumpets and pastries. Sometimes she wore a wig and it always seemed to be a little lopsided on her head. But she was a colorful person and dressed just like a Christmas tree wearing bright red and forest green colors at the same time. Usually, she carried a fancy handbag with lots of gold or silver bling and left a strong trail of perfume after her when she walked down the hallway.

The stranger across the street lived in one of the newly built condos with a beautiful pool, clubhouse and exercise gym. She still knew nothing about him, and while she wanted to meet him, she didn't want to appear bold and just walk up to him and start a conversation. Instead, she decided it would be a good idea to get to know one of his neighbors and find out more about him. There was an elderly man who talked to the stranger often, so she decided she'd start there.

There was Sasha, a rude and snobbish woman in her late twenties with dyed, jet-black hair. She always wore designer clothes and flashy jewelry. Megan had repeatedly butted heads with her. She bothered Megan the most because of the way she talked down to people. She was good at making a person feel insignificant, and it didn't surprise Megan when she found out she was friends with Anita.

When Megan glanced at her in passing on the sidewalk, Sasha turned her head the other way, avoiding eye contact. Megan could see a detached coolness Sasha had toward her. It made Megan feel uncomfortable and she avoided any conversations with her. Ashley told her Sasha didn't like any woman who might prevent her from being the center of attention.

She lived in the building across from her in a second-floor, spacious, three-bedroom apartment, and frequently held dinner parties.

By noon, Megan was famished and was busy preparing lunch. It was a surprise when she answered the door and Sasha was standing there.

"What are you doing here, Sasha?"

"I normally wouldn't do this, but I have this letter that was in my mailbox, and it should have gone to you." She gave it to Megan while looking into the apartment.

"Thanks," Megan replied, suspicious about her visit, but then Sasha pushed past Megan and walked inside.

"Hmmm... looks like you need to paint and get some new furniture."

"I'm happy with everything the way it is," Megan replied.

"You sure?" she asked, and Megan nodded her head. "I guess some people are just happy with less."

Megan glared at her because she lacked diplomacy. Could she be more arrogant, inconsiderate and cold? She was the one with the problem. What a screwball, she thought.

"Anything nice to say?" Megan asked.

"No, but if I get your mail again, I'm giving it back to the mailman."

"Whatever. I really don't have time for this right now." Megan led her back to the door. "It's time for you to leave."

Megan slammed the door shut, thinking Sasha was a hot mess and her flashy jewelry was probably all faux diamonds instead of the real thing. Honestly, it would be great to Etch-A-Sketch people like her away. But it wasn't possible to merely shake a toy and erase someone. Life isn't that simple.

Later in the afternoon, Megan parked her car in front of her apartment building. Her face lit up because she saw him again—the stranger. She always looked to see if he was outside. Yesterday, she woke up with her head full of him, which was so unreal because she didn't know him at all.

Just by chance, she found out his name was Nathan during a chat with John last week. Being curious, she looked up the meaning of his name on the internet. His name meant gift from God. *Could he be?* she thought.

He could be a nice guy or a snob. *Maybe he likes to sip on a glass of wine at dinner gatherings, smile all the time, and have meaningless conversations about nothing?* This was something she had no interest in doing. He could have some serious flaws like some of the previous guys she'd dated.

She had seen Anita talking to Nathan one morning and wondered if she was interested in Nathan like she was with Tony when they were in high school. She hoped not because she didn't want any more problems with Anita. Sasha was already a handful.

Megan's mom told her all the time there were more men in Shady Grove to choose from now she was older. Megan told her most of the males were under ten and all the others were over fifty. Even though the town had grown from ten thousand people to over thirty thousand, the eligible male population was considerably smaller.

The next morning Megan walked to the mailbox to pick up her mail. She glanced across the street and there was Nathan looking at some papers in his hands as he was walking slowly to his car. He didn't seem to be in a rush which was unusual, then he suddenly turned and looked in her direction then actually smiled, then waved.

He'd finally noticed her. Megan smiled and waved back, totally enjoying the moment. There was a whirlwind of feelings going through her mind. After all this time he actually saw her. She was not the invisible person across the street any more. He actually knew she was his neighbor. Megan was thrilled.

It was seven p.m. when Ashley called. "Hey, Megan. Did you know we have neighborhood get together parties?"

"Yeah, Heather mentioned it to me."

"Some of the neighbors who live on our block have an annual barbecue. People bring drinks and other food. Everyone can invite family and friends if they want to," Ashley replied.

"Sounds like fun! I'm looking forward to going."

"Yes, it really is a lot of fun. Neighbors come and go throughout the day and catch up with the latest news and gossip. Maybe you'll be able to meet Nathan at one of the parties?"

"That would be great!" She was excited and pushed her beautiful hair away from her face.

During the week, Megan started to worry again about the noise in the attic at her mom's house. What would she do if Jennifer called again? Could the Orange Street house be haunted?

On a whim, she called Mark, told him everything, and asked for his help with trying to figure out what was going on. As a forensic student at the college, he always took pleasure in investigating different things for his friends.

"When did this all start, Meg?"

She rubbed her forehead and paused for two seconds, "Well, it was several months before mom's accident."

"Hmmm. That's strange because you've lived in the house for years."

"I know. That's true."

"Do you know the name of the previous owner?

"I have no idea. My parents bought the house years ago. It was old and needed a lot of renovation. My mom told me it had been empty for a long time."

"I read articles about people hearing strange noises in houses," Mark said. "Some people said they discovered small animals and mice in the attic. Others discovered problems with the pipes and plumbing. But for some people there was no explanation. They believed it was from ghosts."

She wasn't sure how to respond to what he said. "Ghost? But after all these years, why would there be ghosts in our attic?" Megan asked.

"Good question. I don't know but let me do some investigating. I need to find out who owned the house before your parents bought it."

"All right. Where do you start?"

"I'll look at the county land records first and go from there."

"Good."

"I'll get back with you when I get more info."

"Okay. Thanks, Mark."

CHAPTER 15

A DAY AT HOME

Megan took a day off work to unwind because she had enough leave time. At nine a.m., she opened the window slightly and a breeze of fresh air drifted into the room. She could feel the warmth of the sunlight as she sat on the sofa and took a sip from her cup of coffee mixed with her favorite creamer.

A few minutes later, Megan glanced at her monthly bills lying on the table. Tired of feeling the stress of bills and schoolwork, she read about how she could earn some extra money. Suddenly, her phone rang.

"Hey, Megan, it's Bruce! Can you come to the studio at five p.m. and model some really nice clothes for a photo shoot for a client?"

This was just what she needed. "Yes! I'll be by shortly. Do you need me to bring anything?"

"Just yourself, beautiful. See you in a bit."

Megan called Corey to see if he could go with her, but he wasn't home so she left a message telling him where she would be. Her inner feelings told her not to go alone. It wasn't a good idea. She knew it wasn't but went anyway.

After she arrived, Megan changed into several different outfits and Bruce took what seemed like hundreds of photos. Megan was nervous at first, but he was good with her and encouraged her to explore her creative side.

Then he said, "I think we really have some gold here, Megan. Why don't we take a break?"

She was glad about it. Megan was mentally and physically exhausted, and when she looked at her watch, she couldn't believe a few hours had already passed.

"Would you like a glass of red wine?" Bruce asked after they sat down.

"I guess one glass won't hurt."

He poured her more than she really wanted to drink and handed it to her.

"You know, Megan, this is going really well, but I don't think we're really seeing your true potential here," he said, taking a sip of his wine.

"What do you have in mind?"

"I saw some really nice clothes in the back we could experiment with?"

"Really?" she replied.

"I'm going to be honest with you, Megan. You have an incredible body, and I still have a lot of jobs for modeling lingerie. Why don't you try some of them on?" he asked. Megan was immediately uncomfortable, and Bruce noticed. "It's really not a big deal. A lot of models pose in lingerie."

"I told you, Bruce. I don't want to do lingerie." She was irritated because he wasn't listening to what she said. Her smile turned into a frown.

"Why not?"

"I just don't feel comfortable doing it."

"Comfort levels change all the time. You just need to loosen up! Here," he said, then he walked over and tried to top up her wine glass. She pulled it away.

"One glass is enough. Are you trying to get me drunk or something?"

"Only if doing so will change your mind," he said, grinning down at her mischievously. "Wow, you really are beautiful." He got closer, put his arms around her, and tried to kiss her.

Megan pushed him away angrily, violently. He tried again and she slapped him. She was yelling at him. "What the hell are you doing?" she shouted, stepping away from him.

He grabbed hold of her shoulders, his thumbs digging into her flesh, and told her to calm down. He shook her hard.

"Come on, don't be so goody, goody. Do you want to get into this industry or what?"

She pushed him away again. "This was a huge mistake."

Megan grabbed her things and rushed toward the door, almost falling, hoping he wouldn't try to stop her. A few of her things fell out of her handbag onto the floor. She bent down and scrambled quickly and picked them up, which made her even more nervous. She was really afraid and shaken. He grabbed her, she struggled, scratched him and pushed him back. He tripped and fell over the table in front of the sofa.

"Okay, fine, go!" he called after her. "But don't think you'll get another modeling job in this town. You really are screwing this up, Megan."

"If this is what I have to do, forget it! I don't care," she said, screaming at him. She burst out of the door, hopped into her car, and drove home angry.

It took her almost the entire drive home to calm herself and stop crying from disappointment. She really did need the money, but she wouldn't do that. Her fears all along were justified. What was she gonna do?

When Megan got home, she took off her ripped, knit top and examined the bruises on her arms, poured herself another glass of wine in the comfort of her own surroundings. She couldn't think of ways to describe how she really felt, still shaky, legs trembling as she sat there, like a bad dream. It took her a while to feel safe again.

She thought about reporting him to the police but it would be her word against his. Of course, Bruce would deny doing anything wrong and lie about everything. Men like him always did. She would be the victim again. The police would ask her, why did she go there alone? Why did she have a glass of wine? Was she drunk? Every woman gets labeled a party girl, a gold digger, promiscuous, or if she's lucky, naïve or innocent. Anyway, he had money, and she didn't. He could pay for a lawyer, and she couldn't.

Being twenty-two she had a lot to learn about the world and using good judgement. If only she had a mentor at a young age, but she lost that when her father passed away. Her mom did her best but couldn't take the place of her dad. He was wise, kind and honest. He wanted the best for her and Chris.

Unable to sleep well during the night, she recalled everything in her mind, over and over again, thinking, *Predators cared nothing about a person's dreams and preyed on innocence. They are always out there plotting for their next victim.* From now on, she was going to be more careful about the decisions she made when it came to trusting someone she didn't know very well.

The next morning, she got up early. Trying not to remember the horror of last night, she fixed herself a cup of coffee, toast, and relaxed while checking her text messages. Then she walked over to the window and looked outside. There was a man she had never seen before walking through the courtyard. He was wearing a baseball cap and walking fast like he was in a hurry. He looked up and saw Megan standing there. She didn't give it much thought and sat back down on the sofa, picked up her magazine, and started flipping through the pages.

Two hours later, someone knocked on her front door. She cautiously opened it, and two deputy sheriffs were standing there looking at her. Her first thoughts were maybe she had done something wrong and didn't know it.

"Hi, I'm Detective Lopez and this is Detective McCloud. We're investigating a theft in the neighborhood and would like to ask you a few questions." They were perfectly calm, even friendly.

"Okay," she replied. She immediately had an attraction to Detective McCloud. He was handsome, strong and protective looking with beautiful hazel eyes and a friendly smile. Detective Lopez had a light tan complexion and was nice looking with thick black hair and muscular arms. He appeared to be older than the other detective and asked most of the questions.

"Have you seen anyone unusual around the neighborhood today?"

She was silent for a few seconds trying to think. "Yes, I did see someone walking fast through the courtyard this morning."

He continued to ask her more questions about what he looked like, what time it happened, and if she knew anything else about the man.

"What happened?" asked Megan.

"Someone broke into Mrs. Johnson's apartment when she wasn't at home," Detective Lopez replied. "The person stole a lot of money, her diamond wedding ring, and some other expensive jewelry. Her small dog was found dead, and it appeared like he was given something to eat which was fatal."

Megan was shocked because this neighborhood was considered to be a safe place to live. "Poor Mrs. Johnson. She loved her dog."

"Would you be able to recognize the man you saw in the courtyard if you were to see him again?" he asked.

"I'm not sure because I didn't get a good look at him. He was wearing a baseball cap." She wondered if there were other witnesses who could possibly help identify him.

"Someone will contact you from the sheriff's department. Maybe you could help identify the suspect."

Detective McCloud kept staring at her, as though he wasn't listening to the conversation. Their eyes met, and Megan turned away and blushed. *He's really hot looking*, she thought.

The two detectives politely thanked her. They walked down the hallway, knocking on several doors in the apartment building.

Megan was feeling really sad about Mrs. Johnson's dog. It was small, couldn't see well and was not friendly. Mrs. Johnson warned people not to pet him because he might bite. Flashing back to her childhood, Megan glanced at the picture on the mantlepiece of her own small dog and cat. Pepper was a tan Chihuahua mix and Roxi was her grey and white cat. She loved her pets and would dress her cat in baby clothes with a cap. Sometimes, she would carry her around in a baby blanket. She had pampered her pets most of the time and often used her nurturing instincts as a little girl.

She remembered all those years ago on Thanksgiving, when her mother took the turkey out of the oven and put it on the dining room table, ready to be carved and served.

Megan was busy helping her in the kitchen and walked back to the dining room when she saw Pepper had jumped from the chair, onto the table, and had licked all the butter off the turkey. "Oh, no!" she said. "Pepper, get off the table. Bad dog! You're a bad girl!"

The dog had jumped off the table, ran down the hallway and disappeared. Megan didn't know what to do. She didn't want to tell her mother what had happened after all the work she had done cooking the meal. Her mother left the kitchen for a few minutes, so Megan carefully wiped the turkey with a wet paper towel, melted more butter, and poured it over it.

Her mom came back to the kitchen and Megan said, "Why don't you put the turkey back in the oven a little longer?" She figured the heat would help clean the turkey more.

"Why would I want to put the turkey back in the oven? I just took it out of the oven," her mother said.

"It could be browned a little more?"

"Don't be silly," she replied. "The turkey is just fine."

Everybody sat down at the dining room table to eat. Her father carved the turkey, and she took one slice but didn't eat it.

Megan's father glanced at her and asked, "Why aren't you eating your turkey?"

She was mumbling, "I don't know… I'm just not really hungry." She decided it was best to remain silent.

Megan's mother wasn't particularly fond of animals and always referred to their pets as the dog and the cat, and never called them by their names. She tolerated them only because Megan and Chris loved animals. Megan figured her mom didn't have any attachment to them because she didn't have any animals when she was growing up, but Megan loved her animals, especially Pepper.

Every day she had laid on the back of the sofa, looking out of the window waiting for Megan to come home from elementary school, then from middle school, and finally high school. She would get so excited when Megan opened the front door, walked inside, picked her up and hugged her, giving her lots of love and attention. She was such a sweet dog.

Pepper was fourteen years old when she got sick and had difficulty breathing, so Megan took her to the town veterinarian. Unfortunately, there was nothing the vet could do to help her.

"It's her time to go," he said. "She has been a good dog and she knows you love her."

Megan held and stroked Pepper gently. She kept talking to her with tears streaming down her cheeks. The doctor asked Megan if she was ready. She was all choked up inside and said, "Yes."

Megan kept saying, "You're such a good dog and I love you." She repeated it over and over again while she was petting her.

The doctor first gave Pepper an injection to put her into a deep sleep. Then, after the second injection, Pepper passed away peacefully in Megan's arms. It was one of the hardest things she had ever experienced. She cried herself to sleep. Later the same week, she received a sympathy card from the vet and remembered it to this day:

If tomorrow starts without me,
Don't think we're far apart,
For every time you think of me,
I'm right here in your heart.

Megan had regrets for not getting a good look at the robbery suspect. It was hard to believe how someone be so evil and hurt Mrs. Johnson's dog.

Perhaps someone else would be a better witness and could identify the guy who was walking through the courtyard. Her thoughts wandered for a few moments because she was attracted to the younger detective. He was handsome and there was something about him she liked. He appeared like a strong and protective, take-charge kind of guy. He wasn't wearing a wedding ring. *He could be single.* She dismissed the idea. *He's probably married with children.*

CHAPTER 16

THE DINNER

Megan felt it coming; the air was humid; it was going to rain soon. The grey clouds were gradually drifting toward Shady Grove. She loved the minty smell of the damp eucalyptus trees after the rain. They made the air smell fresh and clean. Driving home from work, Megan passed by the Bowmans' house. She slowed her car then stopped and studied the surroundings like the details in an expensive painting. They had moved out. There were trash bags outside. Maybe it was just another load of garbage? She looked closely and could see more items lying at the side of the house. There was a small broken table, two old lamps, an old rug, a pile of old shoes, and faded clothes in a large cardboard box. Perhaps nobody was around to put the trash on the curb side for garbage pickup today.

The once lush green lawn in front of the house had already turned brown with dry patches of grass. It didn't look like it had been watered for a while. The shrubs and flowers were wilting. The place was so desolate, and the longer Megan looked at it, the more she was sure it was another foreclosure. Another home lost and another family was forced to move from the neighborhood. She experienced the same feelings of abandonment, just like when one of her close friends moved away in elementary school. Nothing was going to change the fact her friend had to move, no matter how hard Megan cried and wished it wouldn't happen. She hated feeling that way.

Then, as she put the car gear into park outside the home, she saw Anita and Austin through the front window, looking over the property and walking through the house. She was sure he'd bought the house before it foreclosed for almost nothing, and now he'd fix it up, sell it at a top price, and make a huge profit. They were like vultures, feeding on the remnants of the small-town American Dream.

Thankfully, that evening, Heather knocked on her door.

"Hey, girlfriend! Want to go out to dinner this evening?" Heather asked, barging her way inside.

Megan placed her book on the end table and plopped back down onto the sofa. "You know, I'd really love to go... but I don't have any money. The bills and my mother's medical expenses really added up this month and—" Heather tried to interrupt her, but Megan put her finger up in the air to stop her, "and, as I was about to say, I don't want you paying for my meal. It doesn't feel right."

"Oh, come on, don't worry about it," Heather replied. "It's either I spend it on another pair of shoes I don't need, or I get to spend the evening with my best friend. So, what do you say? Let's enjoy ourselves and have a good time."

Megan hesitated. "All right, but I can't stay out late. I have a homework assignment I have to complete before the end of the week."

"We'll just be out for a couple of hours for dinner," Heather replied. "There's a friend of mine I've known for a while and he's bringing his friend with him. Just casual, don't have to get all dolled up," she said with a wink.

"This better not be a blind date. You know how I hate blind dates, Heather."

She laughed. "Nah, he's just Jason's friend. I'm not doing any matchmaking. Besides, you're already obsessed with that guy you've never even met," she said, sticking out her tongue. Megan blushed and turned away. "Oh, come on, I'm just kidding, Meg. This'll be fun! Pick you up at six-thirty?"

"Sounds good! See you in a little bit," she replied as Heather left out the front door. She closed it behind her, wondering how Heather always managed to convince her to go out, despite her better judgment.

As long as it's not a blind date.

The way she was currently feeling, Megan had no interest in meeting someone new through friends or relatives, especially on an arranged blind date. Every time she'd gone through with one of their ploys, it had turned out terrible.

But how else was she going to meet someone?

Online dating was an even bigger disaster. And who cared, anyway? She was busy with college, work and doing volunteer work at the homeless shelters. What was she even worried about? She was just going out with Heather for dinner with a couple of her friends.

They arrived at the restaurant on time and sat down at the table near the middle bar. Heather ordered two glasses of wine, and they chatted mindlessly, waiting for Heather's two friends, Jason and Travis, to arrive. Heather had known Jason for a long time and, at one point in time, he was interested in dating, but the relationship never went anywhere. As long as Megan had known her, Heather had never been interested in long-term commitment, so they'd decided to be friends.

After a few drinks, Jason and Travis entered the restaurant and sat down with Heather and Megan. Heather introduced them both, but Megan was shocked to find she already knew one of them. *Travis is Detective McCloud!*

Travis sat down at the table next to Megan and smiled. It was hard for Megan not to notice his gorgeous smile.

"You don't remember me, do you?" he asked.

"Of course, I do! You and the other detective came to my apartment and asked me questions about the theft at Mrs. Johnson's place."

"Right. But you don't remember me from before?"

She was silent for a few seconds but came up blank. "Can't say I do. Should I have?"

"Yes! We went to the same high school. You were a freshman when I was a senior in the twelfth grade."

Megan studied his face again for a moment and finally recognized him.

"I do remember now! I remember you didn't give me the time of day," she said, grinning at him. "But then again, I wasn't on anybody's radar as a freshman. But I do remember all the other girls were chasing after you."

He laughed. "You really believed the girls were chasing after me? I was kind of shy. I was focused on my schoolwork most of the time," he said, shrugging. "Anyway, you were young and skinny and a little bit snobbish. But you look really different now."

"I hope that's a compliment," Megan responded, not sure how to take it.

"Of course, it is. You're all grown up now and, I have to say, pretty mature looking."

She blushed, which was something she hadn't done in a very long time. He smiled, and then they all got to chatting.

All four of them talked for a while, but it seemed, just like at her condo, Travis's focus was all on Megan. The more they talked the more she was attracted to him. He said he had finished college at the sheriff's academy and was working on an administration of justice degree. "I won't be a detective for too much longer, but when the job calls me to come talk to someone like you, I thank the stars I'm at where I'm at," he said with a grin.

"Are you flirting with me?" Megan asked, feeling a little tipsy now.

"Well, it depends. Are you flirting with me?"

She laughed. "You're not supposed to answer a question with another question."

"Fair. Then the answer is a resounding yes," he said, and smiled.

As the night pressed on, they enjoyed their meal, cleared up their tab and hugged goodbye. But Megan was a little sour about the whole evening.

"Why didn't Travis ask me for my phone number? He said he was flirting with me!" Megan asked as Heather drove them home.

"Probably because you're a witness in the Johnson case. Law enforcement officers and deputy sheriffs can't get personally involved with anyone involved in the cases they're handling."

Megan shrugged, the wine getting to her head. "Whatever. I don't know anything about their department policies or rules."

"Patience. In time he'll be off the case, and I'm sure he'll call you. Anyway, all he has to do is ask me for your phone number and I'll give it to him," Heather said, squeezing Megan's shoulder.

"Well, in any case, I hope they identify a suspect and close the investigation soon. I had no idea how nice of a person he was. Isn't he nice?"

"He appeared to be," Heather replied, flashing her a wink as she parked the car and it started to rain.

After she said goodnight, Megan went to her room and immediately got ready for bed. She undressed slowly with thoughts about Travis, and after putting on her pink silky negligee with lace-trimmed panties, she laid down in her bed barefoot and closed her eyes wondering if Travis could be the kind of love she'd been longing for. The kind of romantic love with warm caresses like she'd always seen in the movies. She would cherish that kind of love, and her mind slipped back to her conversations with Travis, and the wonderful evening she had. She soon fell asleep, her school papers completely forgotten.

The next day, to her surprise, she got a call from the sheriff's department. They had a lineup ready for her, and they needed her there right away.

She drove to the sheriff's department with the hope of identifying the suspect in the Johnson case. Like they said on the phone, there was a lineup of suspects ready for her, and she was asked to identify the person she saw in the courtyard. After staring at each one closely, she asked if they could all wear a baseball cap, and so they did.

She let out a deep sigh. "I can't be sure, but maybe him?" Megan pointed to a thin man with sandy hair and deep eyes like the man who had walked through the courtyard of her apartment building.

"Okay, thank you, miss," Detective Lopez replied. "That'll be all. If we need anything more from you, we'll be sure to give you a call."

"Hey, Detective?" she asked before heading out. "Is the other detective here today? I wanted to speak with him."

Lopez raised an eyebrow. "Odd question. Why?"

She turned on her heel and tried to hide her embarrassment. "Um, no reason. Bye!"

CHAPTER 17

SOMEONE SPECIAL

Megan was busy at home studying when the phone rang. She really didn't feel like answering it, but she did.

"Hi, Megan, this is Travis. Do you remember me?"

Thrilled to hear from him, she replied, "Of course I remember you!" She didn't want to sound too excited.

"We had such a nice discussion when we were having dinner with Jason and Heather... I was wondering if you would like to go to out with me?"

She was glad he asked. "Sounds nice. What do you have in mind?"

"How about going out to dinner? Just you and I."

"Sure!"

"Saturday at six?"

"Great, I'll be expecting you."

Megan immediately called Heather. "I actually have a date!" she almost shouted.

"Okay, let me guess... Travis."

"You got it!" She laughed.

"Are you excited?"

"Of course, I am. This actually feels really good. I want to be in a relationship, and he seems so nice. It's been a long dry spell for me, and I want someone I care about and who wants to spend time with me. I want to fall in love."

"I certainly hope he's the right one for you."

"Me too!"

When Saturday finally arrived, Travis was called into work unexpectedly. He called Megan to tell her he'd be late and to meet him at the Roadhouse between seven and seven-thirty. She had a rule during dinner there would be no talking about work, nothing about the office or about anybody's aches or pains. She had heard enough of that from her mother and Uncle James over the past few months, and she needed a break.

Megan headed to the restaurant and sat at a table near the window patiently waiting for Travis. Forty minutes later he still hadn't arrived, and she was starving. Several people were staring at her. She felt awkward, so after five more minutes she ordered dinner—barbecue chicken, a baked potato with butter and sour cream on top, and coleslaw—comfort food. It was hard to believe he had stood her up on the first date. Nobody had done that to her before. He could have at least called her back again. She was totally disappointed and discouraged.

Her cell rang.

"Where are you?" Travis asked. Before she could respond he added, "I've been waiting for more than an hour."

"Hmmm… I'm here at the restaurant. Where are you?"

"Where? I don't see you."

"I'm sitting at the table on the right near the front entrance."

There was a long pause. "Wait a minute. Did you go to the Roadhouse on Oak Street?"

"Yes."

"Oh … I'm at the one on University Street."

"Oh no, I'm at the wrong restaurant!" she replied, laughing. She was embarrassed but relieved he hadn't stood her up.

Travis laughed. "I guess we have a communication problem, and we haven't even been on our first date. Stay there, I'm on my way."

"Okay, I'm not going anywhere!"

Travis arrived fifteen minutes later. She was sitting at the table, looked up, and smiled at him as he walked through the door. He sat down and she apologized for the mix-up. They talked for a while.

"Megan, what have you been doing the past few years?" he said and smiled at her.

"A lot. Mostly working and going to college. You know, things everybody else does."

"So, you never got married?"

"Nope. Just haven't found the right person yet."

"I think you should know I was hitched and me and my ex had a little girl. She's four, but the marriage didn't work out. I mean... obviously, or I wouldn't be sitting here," he said, grinning. "But I'm happy I am."

She wanted to ask what happened to his marriage, but she didn't want to seem too nosey. "I guess that happens to a lot of people nowadays."

"Unfortunately, yes," he said, shrugging. "So, why did you stay in Shady Grove? Most people I know from high school moved away."

"Oh, well, I tried living in LA for a year, but I just didn't like it. Too many cars, buildings and people, and it was always so noisy. I guess I'm just a small-town girl at heart," she said, smiling at him.

"Yeah, I hear you. I was going to apply to the LAPD but thought better of it. I really like Shady Grove, and I like actually knowing the people I'm serving," he said, winking at her. Megan blushed. "So, what about your family?

Oh boy... where to start, were her first thoughts.

"My dad passed away when I was young and my brother, Chris, went into the military after high school. So, it's just me and Mom living here now."

"I'm sorry to hear that. It must be difficult growing up without your father."

He had no idea... but she wasn't going to say it.

Just then the server walked up to the table. "Can I get you two something?"

Travis ordered dinner for himself because she had already eaten. They spent some more time talking and listening to music in the lounge.

"Wanna go with me to a fundraiser event for needy families next weekend?" he asked as he ate his meal. "It's going to be at one of the large indoor facilities at Fairmont Park."

"Yeah, sounds like fun!"

"Great. I was hoping you would say yes. They'll be selling all kinds of food, hot and cold drinks, and pastries. There'll be games, booths and other things for raising money to help families going through difficult times."

"It sounds like a worthy cause. Sure, I'd like to go."

"Fine, I'll pick you up on Saturday at eleven-thirty a.m."

"Sounds good," Megan replied. They made small talk for a few minutes and Travis walked her out to her car which was parked next to his.

"Wait here for a minute." He walked over to his car and pulled out a beautiful bouquet of spring flowers. The flowers were deep yellow, white, red, pink and purple, surrounded by delicate green leaves. He turned and handed them to her. "These are for you."

"Thank you, Travis. You're thoughtful. I love flowers." She smiled, took the spring bouquet and laid them on the backseat of her car.

"All right, guess I'll see you next Saturday!" He opened her car door, and after she sat down, Travis smiled at her, and they said their goodbyes. In truth, Megan really didn't want to leave.

When Megan arrived home, she searched for a glass vase, walked to the kitchen faucet, and filled it with running water. After arranging the flowers neatly, she put them on the narrow side table near her doorway. Perfect. Smiling to herself, she sat down and glanced at them for a while. It had been a long time since any guy had given her flowers. The date couldn't have gone any better.

When Saturday finally arrived, Megan found herself standing in front of her closet for the twentieth time trying to figure out what to wear. Nothing said, this is what Travis would like you to wear for the weekend outing.

Excited about seeing him again, she pulled out a pair of fitted jeans and a colorful top and decided simple was better.

She closed her eyes for a few seconds and tried to put it all in perspective. Maybe Travis was really the one for her? *Maybe all those thoughts around Nathan across the street are just silly fantasies?* Travis was real, and he was interested.

When they arrived at the event, Travis introduced her to some of his friends. Megan had a great time playing games, socializing with everyone and eating all different kinds of food.

After a while they sat down together and Megan said, "Travis, I'd like to ask you something."

"Sure, what's up?"

"Why did it take so long for you to call me?"

He had a serious look. "I had some unfinished business to take care of. I'll officially be leaving for another job in two weeks working in our neighboring county of Riverdale."

"What? Will you still be a detective?" Megan asked.

"Oh, yes, at least for a while. I've been taking more courses and I'm working toward moving up in the sheriff's department. Riverdale County government is larger, and I'll have more opportunities for promotions."

"That's great. Congratulations!"

"Thanks. And since I'm no longer on the Johnson case there was no conflict of interest with me asking you out on a date, so I called you right away," he said with a smile.

"Fine for me but I feel sorry for Mrs. Johnson," Megan replied.

"Don't worry. Her case is in good hands."

"I hope so," Megan said. "Who would want to hurt a little dog?"

"Don't you know?" Travis asked.

"Know what?" she replied.

"Her dog actually died from a heart attack from all the excitement. He wasn't poisoned," Travis replied.

"Oh! I didn't know. It's still sad her dog died."

"It is, and, regardless, whoever broke in is responsible. Who knows what he did to scare it?"

They continued talking and enjoying the afternoon, and by the end of the day he asked Megan if she had plans for the next week. She was hoping he would ask her and was happy he did.

As the week wore on, Megan's mind slipped back into thoughts about Travis whenever she was not too busy at work or attending a class. But Nathan was still on her mind too. As hard as she tried, she couldn't stop her thoughts about him.

Occasionally, she would see Nathan leaving the condo in the mornings. Other times, he walked his dog or talked to John, and each time she saw him, he became even more appealing.

He was probably just a dream. It'll never lead to anything, or will it?

She wondered what kinds of food he liked, his favorite movies or what he liked to do when he wasn't working. All she knew about him was he was the stranger across the street. Anyway, she was going out with Travis.

The following week, she invited Travis to dinner. He arrived a little early and came inside, studied the living room and the dining room, and carefully observed the surroundings.

"You have a nice place here," he said.

"Thanks. I tried to make it comfortable." She was so glad he noticed because she had worked so hard to fix it up.

They spent the evening together talking about this and that and binge-watching movies. When it was time for him to leave, he walked toward the door, then turned around slowly and reached for her hand. His gentle touch gave her butterflies.

He pulled her toward him and looked into her eyes. She was prepared because he gave her hair a gentle tug, enough to lift her mouth within a breath of his.

"Kiss me," Travis said in a commanding tone.

"What?" She was excited by what he just said.

"Kiss me." He put his arms around her, giving her a gentle and passionate slow kiss on her lips. She sank into his kiss. Slow and easy, his mouth tasted hers. His kiss was soft and warm. It was wonderful.

As they kissed, her whole body became aroused with excitement. Even as she started to pull back, he dragged Megan toward him again, diving into an even deeper kiss, and she surrendered to him. It was so passionate, and she loved feeling the closeness of his embrace and his touch. She wanted to know him better, to know what he liked and what he didn't like. Megan wanted to know what true love was.

Afterwards, he touched her face gently and stroked her cheek, nose, and forehead. He touched her lips and kissed her gently again.

"Goodnight, I had a wonderful time."

"Me too," Megan replied.

"I'll call you later in the week."

"Okay," she replied smiling at him. She gently closed the door with thoughts of how happy she was now Travis was in her life.

As the week wore on, she was busy at work, so the time went by quickly. Megan and Travis met for lunch several times and then they went out twice on the weekend. It was sexy and steamy, and though they didn't go all the way, she was enjoying every minute of it. She loved being with him.

Ashley popped in to say hello on the weekend. "Hey, Megan, how are things going?"

"Really great," she said with a smile.

"You and Travis must be hot and heavy! I never see you any more."

"I wouldn't say that." Megan blushed and smiled.

"Is that a hickey on your neck?" Megan grabbed her collar and covered it up. "Oh, my goodness, you have two hickeys on your neck!" Ashley laughed.

"Mind your own business." She blushed.

"You naughty girl."

"I like him a lot," Megan told her. "But even though it's going great, I have this strange feeling he's not being totally honest with me. He doesn't tell me much about his personal life or how he feels about me. He's mysterious at times."

"Sometimes it takes a while to get to know someone," Ashley replied.

"Yeah, I know, but it seems like my relationship with Travis is just going in circles and doesn't seem to be moving forward."

"Maybe he wants it to be that way?" Ashley asked.

"I don't know. But you're supposed to learn about the person you're dating, and we're just not getting there. It's frustrating."

"No kidding. Maybe he doesn't want you to find out more about him?"

Megan didn't say anything for a few seconds. "I hope that's not the case."

She held onto hope their relationship would progress into something more serious because spending time with him was so great.

Over the next few weeks, they had some late-night dates and sometimes they just met for coffee. She never really knew when Travis was going to call and ask her to meet him.

Megan had just finished eating dinner at her aunt and uncle's house. She was helping her mother and aunt clear the table and clean the kitchen.

"Why don't you bring Travis over for Sunday dinner so we can meet him?" her mom asked.

It was something she definitely didn't want to do.

"I really don't know, Mom. He's a busy person."

"I'm sure he can take time off just for dinner," Aunt Ruth insisted. "I'll even tell him you cooked it."

Megan laughed. "Okay, fine. I'll ask him, but I couldn't take credit for your cooking."

The following day she invited him to dinner. He said it would be nice to meet her family. Megan made a point to tell Uncle James she was bringing Travis so he would remember his name. Sometimes, his memory was not so good. She told him to remember the country and western singer Randy Travis. She told Travis her uncle was hard of hearing, and he had to speak loudly.

"Beware," she said, "my mom and aunt have the habit of telling ridiculous stories about me when I was little. I've heard them a million times, so don't mind me when you see my eyes rolling."

He laughed. "I think most parents do."

Aunt Ruth and her mother fixed a delicious Sunday dinner—a roast, mashed potatoes and gravy, salad, freshly baked dinner rolls, and a peach pie. When Megan and Travis arrived at the house, she introduced him to everybody including her mother's friend, Zoe. They walked into the family room to meet Uncle James.

"Hi, Uncle James, I'd like you to meet Travis."

"Who?"

"This is Travis," she said loudly so he could hear.

"Randy?"

"No, Travis," she said slowly.

"Oh, yes. I remember now. You're Randy Travis?"

"No, Uncle, his first name is Travis."

"It's nice to meet you," Uncle James said.

"It's a pleasure meeting you too," Travis replied and smiled.

Everybody sat down at the dining room table and talked while they filled their plates. Her mother told Travis about Megan when she was three years old. She would run around the house naked after she got out of the bathtub. She explained how she had to run and catch Megan and dry her off with the bath towel while she was giggling. Then she said Megan liked going barefoot and didn't like to wear her shoes, and just so she could prove all the stories, she pulled out the family photo album and showed him her baby photos.

Megan sighed. "Aren't there any secrets around here?"

While she sat there toying with her food, Travis just smiled and took it all in, still being polite. They asked questions about his job even though Megan had previously told them he was a detective in the sheriff's department and to not drill him with questions. She hated talking about work during dinner.

"So, Travis, have you ever shot anyone?" her mom's friend, Zoe, asked.

"Oh, Zoe, please!" Megan said.

"Not unless I have to," he replied. "I really don't want to hurt anyone."

"Let's talk about something else," Megan said and quickly changed the subject.

Travis just smiled. When dinner was over Megan and her mom dutifully cleared the table and stacked the dishes in the sink. Everyone sat in the living room and talked for a while. Sensing her family might be telling more stories about her childhood she rushed Travis into saying goodbye to everyone and they left the house.

"Thanks for being so polite and understanding. Now you know more about me than you ever wanted to know."

He laughed. "I had a good time. Your family is really nice. I enjoyed meeting them."

They drove to her place and decided to watch a movie. She fixed popcorn and got a couple of sodas from the refrigerator. They sat down and relaxed on the sofa, and he put his arms around her. She was happy just being with him, comfortable in his arms, and didn't want the night to end.

The next day, she woke up and the wind was blowing hard. It was cold outside. Megan got her short winter coat from her storage boxes under the bed. She hung it up in her closet and then called Ashley, wanting to talk.

"I'm still having a hard time paying my bills," Megan said after she told her all about the previous night with Travis.

"Join the crowd," Ashley responded. "But enough about that. We're always talking about money. I've been thinking a lot about something lately."

"About what?" Megan asked.

"I was watching this scary movie the other night. There was a lady who was going to buy this two-story house. She wanted to know what the attic was like. The realtor said she hadn't been up there yet, so they both went up there together. She slowly opened the door, and discovered the attic was full of boxes, and weird, creepy things. There were paintings of strange people hanging on the walls, faded with age. And there were four creepy looking manikins sitting around a table, one with an eye poked out, another dressed in black, and they were—"

"What?" Megan interrupted, squeezing the phone.

"You know... manikins? Like the dummies you see in the clothing store windows all dressed up?"

"I know what manikins are!"

"They were all bald headed and had—"

"Good grief, Ashley! I don't think I want to know where you're going with this story. It can't be anything good," she said and laughed.

"Yeah, it was really scary. But it reminded me of the attic in your house. You know, the one your mom never let us go inside?"

"I really don't want to think about that right now."

"I just thought you might be interested in the movie," Ashley replied.

"You can tell me the story after we move everything out of the attic."

"Fine."

"It's like when someone is going in for surgery and you tell them about how many people you know or read about who died on the operating table," Megan said.

"You're right," Ashley said, laughing. "Sorry about that."

CHAPTER 18

STRANGE THINGS HAPPEN

After work, Megan went home, grabbed something to eat, and then went to her evening class. When class was over at nine p.m. and even though she was seeing Travis, she couldn't get her thoughts about Nathan out of her mind. She quickly changed her focus on going home to relax, walked to her car, and noticed immediately her front right tire was completely flat.

"I can't believe this," she mumbled. She had just bought new tires three months ago.

It was scary and dark in the parking lot. Most of the students were getting into their cars and leaving the campus. She was uneasy being in the parking lot at night all by herself.

Her brother had taught her how to change a tire. He said all girls should know how to do it in case they got stuck someplace. But she was reluctant to do it because of her office clothes and high heeled shoes. She had forgotten to put her casual shoes in the car, so she called for roadside assistance. The dispatcher said someone would be there to help her in about thirty minutes, and she was supposed to stay in her car and lock the doors.

Sitting there in her car, uncomfortable with only a few cars in the lot, she looked around. Most of the students had gotten into their cars and left. She locked the doors, turned on the music, and tried to remain calm.

In the distance, she suddenly saw a man walking fast, straight toward her car. He was getting closer, and she was anxious but tried not to panic.

"Oh, no!" She was hoping he was another student.

Feeling rattled, she then imagined what if he wanted her to roll down the window? She remembered reading to lower it only one inch to speak through it if somebody wanted to talk. What if he was a criminal? If he got too close to the car, it would be easy to take a photo of him with the phone and send it to Ashley. At least the police would see his face. *What if he breaks the car window?* She cringed and tightly held her phone.

Suddenly, the headlights from a vehicle in the distance were approaching. As it got closer, she recognized the SUV as campus security. She was relieved to see him, turned her head, and saw the guy walking past her before getting into his own car.

The security officer pulled up next to her car and got out of his vehicle.

"Are you all right?" he asked smiling at her.

"Yes, and I'm really glad to see you. I'm waiting for roadside assistance to come and change my tire."

"Okay. I'll park beside your car and wait for him to arrive. Always willing to help a pretty girl."

"Thanks." She smiled and said, "I really appreciate it."

"No problem." He started talking to someone on his phone.

Fifteen minutes later, a large tow truck pulled up, the driver got out, and he changed her flat tire in only a few minutes. Then he said something really strange. "It looks like the tire has been cut somehow."

"Are you sure?" she asked, stunned.

"No doubt about it," he replied, showing her the cut mark. "Stay safe, miss."

Megan thanked both men for their help and quickly drove home. Tired from work and class, she was relieved to be back home, but couldn't stop worrying about her incident at the campus. Who would pop her tire? Why? She slowly sipped on a hot cup of chocolate.

"Did it have something to do with being a witness in the Johnson case?" Megan mumbled. "Or maybe I'm just being paranoid?"

Not knowing who would do it, she called the college security office and asked if they could look at the security camera to see if they could see who cut her car tire. They said it may take a while, but they'd review it for her even though it was likely they wouldn't find anything.

On the weekend, while she was home washing clothes and listening to music, Megan was feeling the moment, knowing how nice it was to live in her very own place. Just then, Mark knocked on the door. She was always happy to see him and hugged him tightly. He sat down on the overstuffed chair.

"Want something to drink?"

"No thanks. I can't stay long. I'm on my way to see my aunt."

"Okay, that's fine," she replied.

"I do have some more information about your mom's house."

"Oh, good. I was wondering how things were going."

"Believe it or not, I found out the house was built over one hundred years ago by a family named Woods. The mother and father died from elderly health problems."

"Really?"

"Yes, and their married son inherited the home. The land was covered with orange trees at one time. He bulldozed down some of the trees to expand the yard. He and his wife had two kids, a boy and a girl. The boy got sick and died at the age of fourteen."

"That's sad. It must have been difficult for the family. Do you know what he died from?" Megan asked.

"It was some kind of flu or something going around."

"Poor kid."

"Yeah, that was sad. The family moved to Rancho Cucamonga and put the house up for sale, but it sat empty for a long time. There's something else you need to know."

"What?" she asked.

"Afterwards, I read a lot of articles about haunted houses and found out most people believed houses were usually haunted because of some sort of violent crimes committed in the homes."

"Crimes? What kind of crimes?"

"You know. Crimes like murder, homicide, suicide, and even abuse or torture. It's strange because I can't find anything that shows anything sinister happening in the house before your parents bought it."

"Well, that's good in a way," Megan replied. "I wouldn't feel comfortable knowing there was a crime committed in the house."

"But it was empty for a while. Anything can happen in a vacant house. I'll do some more investigating. I'm not done yet."

"All right. At least I know a little more about the house."

"Gotta go, talk to you later." He gave her a big hug and rushed out of the door.

Megan scratched her head and sighed, hoping Mark wouldn't discover anything creepy or weird about the house. The thought of it made her shiver thinking, *Why does fear make people behave so strangely and others courageously?* Last year, someone broke into the neighbor's house; he beat the intruder with his walking stick, and he ran away. One time, Mom's friend Hannah had a panic attack and couldn't catch her breath, her heart was racing, and she felt sick. The adrenaline took over and she almost fainted. What did Hannah fear?

Although Megan had been frightened by the weird sounds in the house, she never had panic attacks. Hopefully, that would never happen. Even if it did, there was no one she would want to see other than Dr. Sharma. He would help her.

CHAPTER 19

TROUBLE IN PARADISE

Without a doubt, Megan was enjoying spending her weekends with Travis, but this weekend was different. On Saturday morning she didn't hear from him. In the evening, she called him but there was no answer, so she left a message for him to call her back.

She hadn't heard from him for several hours and began to worry. He would always call her back—not always right away, but he did call back—and when she sent him a text message, he always read his messages. Not today.

Megan called Heather. "I don't have a good feeling about all of this. Something has happened to him. Maybe he was in an accident?"

"Jason would have let us know," Heather replied. "Don't worry so much."

"Ugh, you're right. I hope he gets back to me soon."

But an entire week went by with no response. He'd just disappeared and dropped off the face of the earth. Something was wrong, so she decided to call him at work but was told they weren't allowed to give out any information. Megan wasn't surprised but it was worth a try.

Was he avoiding her? She called Heather again.

"Hey, Megan, Jason told me Travis does that sometimes. He just disappears. But from what he told me, this time his ex-wife contacted him. She was having some health problems and is in the hospital, so Travis had to fly to Sacramento to see their four-year-old daughter who's staying with her grandparents."

"That's weird. Why hasn't he called me to let me know what's going on? Why did he just leave without telling me anything?" Megan asked.

"I don't know," Heather said. "You know him better than I do."

"Obviously I don't know him as well. I really believed we had something good between us. I just don't understand."

"If he cared, he would've called you by now."

"I trusted him, Heather. He probably met someone else."

"Don't jump to conclusions, Megan. You're emotional and upset right now."

"Dating is so complicated," Megan said, feeling a bit down and trying not to listen to the negative thoughts in her head.

"I don't know what to tell you. If he hasn't called you yet, you need to forget about him, Megan. He really doesn't appreciate you, and I don't think it's worth spending your time thinking about him."

"I know you're right. But it's hard. I really believed we had something," she said, trying not to cry but the tears came anyway.

"I'm sorry, Meg. I wish I could be there with you right now, but I'm in New York for a few more days. I'll see you when I get back, okay?"

They talked a bit longer and then Heather had to go. Megan was lonely.

Heather never seemed to have problems with guys. Maybe it was because she didn't want to be in a long-term relationship? Could she be like Heather? Just shop around, meet different guys and have fun? Her instincts said, no.

It sounded so appealing because Heather seemed to have it all together. She traveled as a flight attendant and was always treated like a princess by the guys she dated even though she didn't want to be in a committed relationship and was normally the one to end it when a guy got too serious.

When morning came, she examined her phone again. No text messages, no missed calls—nothing, nothing at all. Every time she looked at her phone it was like a slap in the face, and it made her angry.

She closed her eyes for a few seconds and tried to put it all in perspective as to why she got involved with Travis. If the relationship was over, he didn't even have the courage to tell her why. He chose the easy way out. He had no consideration for her feelings. There had always been some signs of trouble or dissatisfaction when parting with her ex-boyfriends—not so with Travis.

She'd never been dumped before—at least not without some discussion. It was a terrible feeling, rejection. If there was no explanation, then the hours they had spent together were forgotten moments in time, like an entire chapter missing from a book. There would be a gap in the story. Megan sighed and thought, *There must be a lot of people with gaps in their stories. A lover who had disappeared was probably more common than most people ever wanted to admit.* The fear of judgement could make it worse. People often gossiped and no good would become of it.

She wasn't going to sit at home feeling sorry for herself. She had to do something to make herself feel better.

Megan decided to go out of town to one of the largest shopping malls in Orange County. She wanted to treat herself to something nice because she deserved it. Even though she didn't have a lot of money, she was going to buy herself a new, beautiful and brightly colored dress with splashes of pink and yellow flowers on white, satiny cotton using the money she'd saved for emergencies. Something with beautifully printed fabric. Then she'd buy a delicious chocolate ice cream cone with a double scoop.

Inside the mall she walked into several stores and strolled around and saw some gorgeous dresses, but then one in particular caught her eye in the window at Macy's department store. She went inside and first dug through the clothing racks trying to find it.

She glanced at another rack of dresses but nothing on the rack so far spoke to her saying, young woman with a burst of sunshine. After looking up for a split second, she was shocked. There was Travis in the ladies' department just a few feet away.

How could this be? She never imagined running into him.

He didn't see her. Megan couldn't breathe or stop her mind from racing. *What's he doing standing there all by himself?* She hesitated for a moment. Maybe she should go over and say something to him?

Suddenly, a tall, attractive redhead in slender jeans and a stone-gray jacket walked out of the fitting room showing Travis her outfit. She asked for his opinion, and he responded, "You look great."

Megan's jaw dropped and the color drained from her face. Her heart was heavy with a sinking feeling in her stomach. She was glad she hadn't approached him in the store. It would have been totally embarrassing.

The other woman was attractive and appeared to be around Megan's age. Megan felt a lump in her throat and found it hard to swallow. Her lips were dry; she couldn't even talk. Deep down inside she experienced the hurt and pain of rejection, and feelings of betrayal.

She quickly ducked behind the dresses. The woman walked back into the fitting room. Megan took a deep breath and slowly counted, one, two, three. She didn't want him to see her. She wanted to run away and hide but where to?

Just then a voice from behind her said, "Can I help you find something?"

She turned around and a sales associate was looking at her—a woman in her mid-thirties.

"No. I'm just looking," Megan whispered and forced a smile.

"Let me know if you need help finding something."

"Okay. Thank you," Megan whispered again. She stepped back behind the rack of clothes trying to hide. The sales associate stared at her for a moment wondering why she was acting strangely, then shrugged her shoulders and walked away.

Five minutes later, the other woman walked out of the fitting room. She and Travis both walked over to the cashier counter together. He reached into the pocket of his pants, pulled out his wallet, and paid for everything.

Trying to dismiss her feelings, Megan was crushed, and resentment tightened her entire body. She recalled her version of their conversations and now knew why he hadn't called. She turned away and hesitated for just a moment.

Maybe that woman was his sister?

Megan had never met her, and he had talked about her before. She shouldn't be jumping to conclusions and getting upset over nothing—not yet. After all, Travis wasn't holding her hand or anything.

Not wanting to be seen, she peeked through the rack of dresses again. The store employee handed the young woman a small shopping bag and Travis put his wallet back in his pocket. He turned and smiled at the young woman then reached for her hand. They walked away holding hands. Megan fumed, barely able to control her feelings. She knew when she first saw them, he had found someone else, but she just ignored her gut feelings.

Megan succumbed to a wave of mixed emotions—shock, hurt, betrayal, anger. Then she got furious and gazed into the distance, lost in a world of her jumbled feelings. She didn't care if she ever saw Travis again and just wanted to get back to Shady Grove. She left the shopping mall and went straight home.

When she arrived home, Megan slammed the door shut and leaned on it, feeling hurt and angry. Her breathing slowed as she walked to the bedroom, took off her shoes, and laid down on the bed. After turning on some music, she pulled her soft and cozy comforter up over her shoulders and the warmth of it was relaxing. She hugged her fuzzy teddy bear and didn't want to remember what had just happened. An hour had passed then she got up and poured herself a glass of wine.

She picked up her diary and, feeling emotionally drained, started writing.

The other woman with Travis didn't look that good—not in my opinion. It's not that she was ugly... but she was no raving beauty either.

I have these thoughts because I'm angry, critical, maybe even vengeful. It makes me feel better, at least for a while. I guess I'm just critical because I feel jealous someone else has stolen Travis' affections away from me. But it's not the other woman's fault. It's Travis. It's his fault. He picked someone else willingly and I feel hurt. Maybe, it's more about my pride over being rejected than about love. Nobody likes rejection.

The next couple of days, she had difficulty sleeping. She tried to avoid her thoughts about him. An entire week went by before Travis finally called her.

"Hi, Megan. It's Travis."

"I know who you are." She was abrupt.

"Sorry for not calling you sooner. I had to go to Sacramento. My ex-wife had to have surgery. Her parents are taking care of my daughter Samantha."

Megan was silent and said nothing.

"Are you listening?" he asked.

"Yes, I'm here," she replied trying to hold back from saying something she would regret.

"Look, I'm sorry for not calling. It was unexpected and crazy, and the time just kinda flew by," Travis said.

Megan was silent. Perhaps part of what he was telling her was true?

"Listen, just answer this one question," she said firmly. "Why didn't you call or text me and let me know what was happening?"

"There was just too much going on too fast."

"That's definitely not a good answer, Travis," she said, with a clenched jaw. "It's certainly not difficult to pick up the cell phone."

She wanted to hear what he had to say. She knew he had someone else in his life. Was he going to lie about it? Her dad once told her, a person's facial expression was worth a thousand words. The eyes always give a person away. Megan couldn't see his face, but she knew his words were shallow and empty.

"Okay, well like I said, I'm sorry. I'll call you again when things settle down."

Megan knew he was lying. He was just trying to delay calling off their relationship. Did he have any idea what she was going through? He obviously didn't care.

"Okay, Travis, do whatever you have to do. I guess I'll see you whenever."

"I don't want you to be upset with me."

After a moment of silence, she said bluntly, "You know what? This isn't working anyway. You know it's over, so goodbye, Travis." Megan then hung up the phone. She didn't like to lose and didn't like being rejected.

She found some comfort in what she had just done, to hang up, to be the person to end the conversation on the phone. It was better that way. Nobody liked being dumped. Being able to hang up on him gave her some pleasure, at least a little bit.

The phone rang again, several times. Travis was calling her back. Megan braced herself, had difficulty breathing, and her heart was racing. She ignored him and turned her phone off. She was done talking to him.

She sat there on the sofa for five minutes then turned her phone back on and called Heather to tell her what happened.

"Why didn't you tell Travis you saw him with someone else?" Heather asked.

"I didn't tell him because I wanted him to be truthful and tell me," Megan replied.

"Well, how did that work for you?" Heather asked.

She paused for a few seconds. "Not good. Not good at all. He wasn't truthful. There was no point in him lying."

"I didn't think Travis was the right person for you anyway. He's a self-centered jackass and too full of himself. You're too good for him, Megan. Just forget about him."

"I wish it was that easy."

"I know you're feeling down in the dumps right now."

Megan was, but she had been so much worse off before. Travis would be just a blip on her dating radar and knowing that made her feel a bit better.

"Heather, I often wonder what life would be like if Scott were alive. I probably wouldn't have even dated Travis or anyone else. My life would have been so different."

"I'm sorry," Heather said. "I'm so sorry about Scott but I'm here for you and so is Ashley. Scott would have wanted you to move on with your life."

"Scott would have never treated me the way Travis treated me."

They talked a little longer and Heather had to go to the airport for another flight out of town. Megan tried not to, but she couldn't resist playing Travis's old voice messages over and over again, listening to the kindness in his voice before the breakup, and the tears came. Going out with Travis was a mistake. He was not the kind of person she thought he was. Life was full of mistakes. She had to move on. But how?

The next afternoon Megan had to talk to someone, so she went to see Dr. Sharma. She sat down on the soft, leather sofa in his office and talked about Travis.

"I was actually starting to feel we had a future together. It wasn't love at first sight, but I did think our relationship was slowly developing to a deeper level," Megan said. "When we broke up, I started to reflect on some of the things he said and did."

"What things?" Dr. Sharma asked.

"Well," she thought for a moment and said, "after coming home from a date with Travis, he always had a habit of saying he would call me later. When we first started dating, he let me know when he would be calling me. But after we dated for a while, he said, 'See you later.' He never made promises."

"Why do you think he did that?"

"That's a good question. I had to think about it for a while."

"And what did you decide?"

"If he didn't make promises then he didn't have to worry about breaking them."

"You're probably right. You don't want to be in a relationship with someone like him, do you?"

"No, I don't. He wasn't the kind of guy who told me what was on his mind. I never knew how he felt about me. It's exhausting not knowing."

"Did he ever tell you that he missed you?"

"Sometimes," Megan said softly, looking down at her hands.

"You're young. You still have your whole life ahead of you, and it sounds like Travis is not the kind of person you want to spend your future with anyway."

"I know. It's still painful going through all this."

"Sure, it is," Dr. Sharma said, "and it'll take time for you to get over it. But you will get over it."

"He wasn't anything like Scott," Megan said firmly. She and Dr. Sharma had talked a lot about Scott, so he knew the history.

"I know it's difficult."

"Good thing Travis and I didn't have a long history together," she said. "Not like I had with Scott."

He looked at her with a raised eyebrow and they talked a little longer. Dr. Sharma gave his usual words of encouragement, and, as always, Megan was better because of it.

He reached over, gently touched her arm and said, "Hang in there, Megan. Things will work out in time. Life is like a book, it's brief, and once the pages are read, you move on to the next chapter. It's up to you how you want the next chapter to read. You have some influence on your life so make the best of it."

She knew it was up to her to be positive and try to make good decisions. Then decided not to discuss the nightmares she had about the sounds coming from the attic at the Orange Street house. It was something she could handle on her own unless things got worse.

Back in her apartment, she walked to the kitchen and picked up a box of chocolate candy from the countertop. She flopped down on the sofa and started eating one piece of chocolate at a time. One was filled with a soft sweet cherry filling, another with delicious raspberry cream, another one with coconut cream, another filling with walnuts.

After eating the entire box, her stomach started to hurt, and she was sick. She searched the bathroom and found a large bottle of liquid antacid. Megan drank it directly from the bottle, then sat down on the sofa just staring at the floor. A few minutes later, she called Ashley and told her what had happened.

"I'm sorry to hear that. Do you want me to come over and we can talk?"

"No, I'll be all right."

Twenty minutes later, Ashley stunned Megan and appeared at her front door. She had little Parker in tow, holding his hand as he trailed behind her. Megan opened the door for them to come inside and Ashley hugged her tightly. Megan's eyes were puffy and red, and she had obviously been crying. Her curly hair was a mess, sticking out all over her head. Her mascara was smeared and running down her cheeks. Parker stared at Megan for a few seconds because she didn't look like her normal self.

"Megan isn't feeling good, but she'll be better in a couple of days," Ashley told Parker.

Megan hugged Parker and gave him a toy to keep him entertained. He sat down on the carpet with his toy while Ashley sat down on the sofa next to Megan.

"What's all the white chalky stuff on your lips?" Ashley asked.

"What?" She got up and walked over to the mirror, saw her face, she was a mess. "Oh, that's the antacid I took for my stomach."

She wiped it off her lips and sat back down on the sofa. Ashley glanced down and noticed Megan was wearing two different house slippers on her feet. The slipper on her right foot was pink and the one on her left foot was pale blue.

"I know you're hurting," Ashley said, trying to comfort her.

"I don't know how I feel, Ashley. A few weeks ago, everything was fine. Suddenly it's over between Travis and me. I can't even remember what I did two days ago. My mind's been confused. Then out of nowhere, I started thinking about Scott again. It's just bringing up old feelings."

"Remember when Justin and I broke up?"

Unable to think, Megan sat there, her mind still numb. She said, "Ashley, my mind is just too foggy right now."

"Do you want to know what my mother told me?" Ashley asked.

"What?" Megan replied.

"She said, it takes time to heal and get over letting go of someone. Someday I'll meet someone else who will love me. Right now, you need to take time and focus on your own priorities and someday the right person will come into your life."

"You're right…"

Ashley put her arms around Megan and tried to provide her with some comfort. Talking to Ashley always helped, there was no denying it.

"Why do I still care about him and dislike him at the same time? Life is just the pits," Megan said.

"That's just part of it," Ashley replied.

"I think I could have loved Travis under different circumstances. He had the personality, the looks, the passion… but he just wasn't ready to be committed to one person."

Thoughts about Travis were too exhausting. She had to admit to herself it wasn't a whirlwind relationship. There was an immediate attraction, but it wasn't like fireworks went off either—not like in the movies. When they'd met, she really wanted to love someone and enjoyed the attention he gave her. He made her feel so special when he was around, but he came into her life when she was most vulnerable.

Ashley said, "In some countries parents pick who you are going to marry, hoping you'll eventually fall in love. I really don't think your parents would have ever picked Travis."

Just then the doorbell rang. Ashley opened it, and there stood Mark and Corey. They came to cheer up Megan.

Corey sat down and hugged Megan. "One day your Prince Charming will come along. He just took a wrong turn along the way."

"What?" Megan replied. She was confused by what he had just said. "This isn't a good time to be funny, Corey."

"I wasn't trying to be funny," he replied. "We brought you a box of taffy candy with different flavors. There's strawberry, chocolate, vanilla, peppermint and peanut butter. Maybe it'll make you feel better."

"Thanks, guys." She opened the box and pulled out a piece of taffy, individually wrapped. "That's nice of you. Who's going to reimburse me for the caps and fillings the candy pulls off my teeth?" Megan replied and smiled.

"It's not hard taffy," Mark said. "Just try it later when you feel like it."

Mark and Corey talked for a while and hugged her. They decided to leave knowing Megan was not up to having much conversation. Even the comfort of friends didn't spare her from feeling sad.

After everybody had gone home, Megan positioned herself on the sofa and stared at the ceiling wondering,

Why would one person stop loving or even stop liking the other and provide no explanation: not even one truthful sentence. She decided there were probably no simple answers to that question.

During the next few weeks, Ashley got Megan, Heather and one of their other friends to play tennis together. They went on two hiking trips during the day trying to get Megan's mind off of Travis.

As time passed, Megan finally got over feeling down in the dumps, but when she got on the scale, she discovered she'd gained eight pounds.

"Wow! How the hell did that happen?"

Perhaps it was just muscle? Nope. She went to the kitchen and dumped all her chocolate candy in the trash. Megan knew she needed to make better choices and was anxious to finish her classes so she could graduate. Her immediate need was to find another job that paid more money because she was still struggling to pay her bills.

On Tuesday evening after work, Megan went for a walk. It helped her relax. Just then she heard the engine of a car as it pulled up beside her next to the sidewalk. The music was blaring, and the car's tinted windows were rolled up and so dark it was hard for her to see who was inside. The driver lowered the windows. He was driving a late model, navy blue Camaro, slowly keeping pace with Megan as she walked.

"Want to go for a ride?" he asked.

"What?"

"You really look great."

"I don't even know you and I'm not getting in your car."

"Megan, it's Drew!" he said, almost shouting.

"What?" She was startled and turned to take another closer look at him. He had thick, black hair, and wore a plaid cotton shirt over a pullover black T-shirt. He took off his sunglasses.

"What are you doing here, Drew?"

"Let's go grab a coffee."

"No, I don't think so," she said unfazed by his suggestion.

"I saw you shopping last week but you didn't see me. I was thinking about you. I just want to talk to you," he said. "You know... we did have some good times together, didn't we?"

"You're crazy, you know that?"

"I've changed."

"Drew, that was in the past. You need to find yourself someone else."

"Call me if you get lonely." He was flirting with her. He slowly drove away, still smiling at her.

Somehow, he must have found out she and Travis had split up. News spreads so quickly in small towns.

She remembered Drew very well. How could she forget? He was trouble. Bad boys always seemed more interesting than the good ones. They met through a friend, and he had quickly fallen in love with her. He was handsome and buff. But for her, Drew had just filled the emptiness she experienced after Scott died. Megan hadn't seen Drew for a long time.

She was never happy with him. He was nothing like Scott. Perhaps she just liked the way Drew looked and the way he dressed. He was young, single and sexy, but she had never known how to handle him. He had irritated her at times and had a habit of saying 'whatever' whenever they didn't agree on anything.

In the few months she dated him, he would call her Meggie. She hated that name. He would laugh when she got irritated with him, and then there were the times he would ask to borrow money. It aggravated her to no end, because she didn't have much money, even if he paid it back. She wasn't his bank, and she couldn't figure out why he always ran out of money. She often thought, what kind of person would borrow money from his girlfriend? It was a sure sign of an unsuitable trait in a guy.

Ashley and Heather didn't like him. Ashley said he was nothing but trouble, and Heather told her she heard Drew smoked marijuana all the time with his friends, and that was why he was always broke.

Megan remembered the time he called her stupid and she had gotten angry with him. She thought of herself as naïve at times but never stupid. Her parents told her years ago that word should never be in her vocabulary no matter how angry she had gotten with herself or others. It was obviously something he never learned. She disliked him because of it.

The final straw was when Megan was having car problems. Drew told her to leave the keys in it and he would have someone steal the car. All she had to do was tell the police she accidentally left the keys in the car, and her insurance would pay for the stolen vehicle so she could buy another car.

Megan was shocked by his suggestion, and the following week when he pestered her about committing fraud again, she broke up with him. She didn't want to see him any more and wanted no part of it.

Megan called and told Ashley about Drew trying to hook up with her again.

"He can mess up his own life but I'm not going to let him destroy mine," Megan said. "I have no desire to be locked behind bars in a small room with only a bed, sink, and a toilet. There would be no pleasure in staring at the cold, concrete walls."

"He's not a good person," Ashley said.

"I agree," Megan replied, and scratched her head. "I can't blame anybody for my unhappiness with Drew. It was my own fault. I ignored his character flaws all because of wanting to be loved. He was a sure sign of trouble. I wonder how many other women do that?"

"Probably more than we'll ever know," Ashley replied.

"I've learned a lot over time and have gotten wiser. I try not to ignore noticeable character flaws in guys I meet. It's the part of them that they try to hide."

"Yeah, we both still have a lot to learn, Meg."

CHAPTER 20

THE NEIGHBORHOOD BARBECUE

On Saturday morning, Megan woke up feeling great, eager because Nathan would be attending the barbecue. The room felt cool and the floral scent of lavender from the fabric softener in her bedsheets was refreshing. She opened the shutters and glanced outside. It was a cloudless day, and she could feel the warmth of the sunshine streaming through the window. She took a deep breath and felt like a little girl wanting to go outside and play. The sky was blue, the leaves were green, and the sun was warm and bright. It was going to be a beautiful day for the neighborhood. Many of the neighbors were planning to attend. She just hoped Sasha and Anita weren't going to be there. Backstabbing and throat cutting were the norm with them, and she learned to avoid both. There was no goodness in it. Nobody knows the damage done.

After taking a long, hot shower, she washed her hair, letting it fall loosely to air dry into naturally flowing curls. Her chestnut brown hair was even more beautiful than usual. She spread lotion all over her natural, sun-kissed skin, giving it a golden glimmer. As far as she was concerned, paying for manicures and pedicures was a waste of time. She didn't have money to spend on those types of things. So, she smoothed the heels of her feet with a pumice stone. Then she painted her well-shaped nails a soft coral color.

She put on makeup and added soft coral lipstick to her lips for a natural glow. After taking out the clothes from her dresser, she put on a knit jersey top and tan shorts. Her friends always told her she had nice legs, so this wasn't the time to cover them with long pants or jeans in the warm summer months. She could feel the warmth of the sunshine as she walked outside.

Each person paid a small fee for the barbecue two weeks prior to the event, and they could eat whatever they wanted. The neighbors brought all the drinks, potato salad, macaroni salad, green salads, veggie trays and watermelon, and they had chips and dip, bottled water and soda. Two of the neighbors owned homes in the neighborhood with large front yards. They planned on grilling the hamburgers and hotdogs, and veggie burgers for the vegetarians.

Megan looked around and everything was arranged on folding tables with colorful tablecloths. Nearby sycamore trees were full of deep green leaves, and they shaded the area. The ground was covered with thick, green grass. A few leaves were scattered on the ground, creating a beautiful carpet which would soon be gone if the sundowner winds started to blow again.

There were several large, colorful plastic tubs filled with ice sitting on large tables with bowls and containers of cold food and potato salad. There were ice chests with bottled water, cans of soda and beer. The neighbors had a lot of folding chairs and tables for everyone to sit on. They were talking, eating, playing music and socializing. Her neighbor, Ben, was playing his guitar and singing for a small group of friends.

Megan was talking to Ashley, Heather and the other neighbors when Heather saw Nathan from a distance.

"Megan, look. There's Nathan over there talking to our neighbors."

Megan turned and watched him, and her heart pounded as she tried not to be obvious. At that moment a tall, beautiful woman walked over next to him. She stood close to him, smiling, and brushed some fallen leaves off his shoulder as he was talking. He smiled back at her. She obviously knew Nathan well.

Megan closed her eyes, took a deep breath, and slowly counted—one, two, three. She needed to calm down, but she was crushed and disappointed. After all these months with thoughts of him being single, now there was a woman standing next to Nathan—very close to him.

How foolish of her to assume he was single. There was no doubt in her mind he was in a relationship with an attractive woman. Of course, he would be. He was handsome. A lot of women were probably interested in him.

She took another deep breath and let out a sigh of disappointment. Megan leaned in low and whispered to Heather, "He's here with someone. She's standing right next to him."

The young woman suddenly ended her conversation with Nathan and started talking to someone else, then walked away toward the food table.

"Nathan's not with anyone," Heather whispered softly. "That's his younger sister. I met her earlier."

Megan paused for a moment. "Oh... thank goodness," she whispered. She let out a sigh of relief. Maybe there was hope for her after all.

"Go talk to him!" Heather said.

"I can't walk over and talk to him, Heather. I don't even know him."

"You want to get to know him, don't you?" Heather asked.

"Yes, of course I do," Megan whispered.

"Well, what do you think these get togethers are for? Just walk up behind him and pretend you accidentally bumped into him. Look, he's talking to John now."

"Heather, you're more outgoing than I am. I don't know if I can do that."

"Yes, you can," Heather whispered. "Just walk over there now." She gave her a slight push on the back.

Megan hesitated for a moment. "Okay, fine," she said and cautiously walked toward Nathan.

She could see his well-built body. He was wearing a short-sleeved, multicolored cotton shirt unbuttoned with a blue T-shirt underneath and a pair of tan Bermuda shorts. He had great legs. He was wearing a silver watch with a large face on his left wrist. It looked expensive.

Megan slowly walked over to where John and Nathan were standing. She deliberately bumped into Nathan from behind and he turned around.

"Oh, I'm sorry. I didn't see you standing there."

"No problem," Nathan replied, smiling.

Just then John said, "Hi, Megan, great to see you here! I'd like you to meet Nathan."

"Hi, Nathan," she replied.

"Hi, Megan, it's nice to officially meet you." He reached out and shook her hand.

His hand was masculine, yet warm and tender. The firmness of his handshake gave her a feeling of wanting to touch him more. Closer to him than she had ever been, she got her first good look at his face. His eyes were a beautiful light brown, his eyebrows were well defined, and his hair was thick and dark. She tried not to stare at him.

"I often see you leaving in the morning."

"You do?" She was elated when he even noticed her.

"Yes, all the time actually," he replied, staring at her and smiling.

He studied her smile intently and she glanced at his beautiful eyes for a few seconds trying not to be obvious. She had a strong attraction to him and her whole body was warm all over. He spoke gently yet his voice was deep, his accent soft and his pronunciation clear. There was a mature sense of confidence about him. And the smell of his cologne... it drove her crazy.

"You must be a busy person," Nathan said.

"Why did you say that?" she asked, smiling slightly.

"I see you coming and going several times during the week."

She was happy he had finally noticed her. It was obvious he had been watching her for some time now.

"Yes, I'm busy working but so is everybody else," she said smiling shyly.

"Aren't we all," he said, still studying her face.

"I think some people live on their own islands. We live in the same neighborhood but rarely have time to get to know people. I'm really thankful for this get together today," she said.

He leaned over close to her and whispered, "Well, perhaps we can change all of that." He had a flirtatious expression.

"Maybe so," she said, feeling excited. She loved the attention.

She was nervously fiddling in her pockets when her cotton lace-trimmed handkerchief popped out and accidentally fell to the ground. When she reached down to pick it up, he did too. Their heads were so close her hair gently brushed up against his face.

He picked up the handkerchief and handed it to her. "Your hair smells like fresh spring flowers."

"Thanks," she said, blushing. "It must be my shampoo."

Just then several other neighbors, including John, interrupted and joined the conversation. They were all making small talk getting to know each other a little better. Mrs. Johnson walked over to everybody with her new, ankle-biting, little Chihuahua. He was two years old and weighed five pounds. Every time someone tried to pet him, he growled and showed all of his teeth. Mrs. Johnson said he just needed time to get to know everybody.

Megan whispered to Nathan, "If he was an eighty-pound dog he'd probably eat us. Maybe that's why they aren't supposed to be large dogs."

"You're right. I love dogs, but Chihuahuas are a different breed, aren't they?" Nathan said and laughed.

"My Uncle James calls them ankle biters."

Megan noticed people grazing through the food on the tables. She excused herself politely from the conversation and started to walk over to the table to get some food. He glanced down at her legs as she walked away. She was famished because she hadn't eaten breakfast.

Before she walked away, John whispered to her, "Nathan likes you."

"You don't know that," she whispered softly.

But Nathan did watch her walk away. That had to mean something, didn't it?

She started to fill her plate with food. A few minutes later, he walked over to the table where she was standing. He put some food on his plate and spoke quietly, his eyes still flirting with her.

"So, Megan, do you have any hobbies or fun things you like to do?"

"I like a lot of things but mostly biking, hiking and camping. I really like mystery movies and reading novels when I have the time."

"Oh really? I love to hike, and I'm a huge fan of British mystery movies and books."

She realized here was someone who actually wanted to know what she liked to do, and she was eager to know more about him too. Everything about him seemed different from anyone else she had met. She enjoyed the attention he was giving her. He kept smiling at her and she silently tagged him as a flirt.

"Do you—" Megan started.

Suddenly, Sasha walked nearer and interrupted Megan, totally ignoring the fact Megan was standing there next to him. She couldn't believe Sasha. It was obvious to Megan she was flirting with him and practically throwing herself at him. She'd noticed her doing her rounds, taking a shot at every eligible man there. *Oh boy. She's a real problem.*

Nathan was cordial to her even after she interrupted their conversation. Then when Sasha turned and started talking to someone else, he turned his attention back to Megan. Several other neighbors walked over to the tables, started piling up their plates with food, and joined in the conversation. A couple of minutes later, Megan politely excused herself and mingled with the others, feeling frustrated. She walked over and sat down at the table where Mark and Corey were sitting. They'd arrived late but were already digging into the food.

Megan wondered if Nathan was attracted to women like Sasha. She was dressed to the nines, curved in all the right places, with a low-cut top, black, tight-fitting pants and four-inch, open-toe wedge heels. Her fingernails and toenails were painted a dark red, and she was wearing long, dangly gold earrings and a sparkly necklace.

Then Megan laughed to herself. Her feelings of jealousy evaporated as she determined Sasha obviously didn't know a neighborhood barbecue was a casual event where you didn't need to dress up. It was clear Sasha wasn't interested in talking to the women; she completely ignored Megan and every other woman in attendance.

Corey whispered to Megan, "I know a lady when I see one and Sasha is not a lady."

"Yeah, she's practically drooling over every guy here. She even came up to Corey and me, but as soon as she found out we weren't making six figures, she moved onto the next. She's a vulture," Mark said, laughing. "I know you're interested in that Nathan guy. Don't worry—if he's half the man you think he is, he won't be interested in a girl like her."

Megan smiled and hoped Mark and Corey were right.

The food was plentiful, and everyone was having fun. Already it was beginning to get dark. Nathan was busy being social with everybody, but she noticed, every once in a while, he would glance at her. He carried himself with such composure and confidence. She was truly attracted to him, and her body was on fire with a strong desire to be with him.

Candles on the tables were lit as the sun dipped behind the mountains. There was no sundowner breeze. The daytime slipped away so quickly. Kids were running around, getting ready to watch the fireworks from a distance at the local park.

Suddenly someone tapped Megan on the shoulder. She turned around and was startled. It was Travis and her face lost its color. She didn't know what to think. Megan didn't expect to see him at the barbecue—not on her street. He certainly wasn't a neighbor, and he wasn't her friend. She didn't invite him. Maybe someone else did?

"Megan, I need to talk to you."

"What are you doing here, Travis?" She stared at him mouth open.

"Let's talk."

"Not now." She looked around. "There are people here." She stood there awkwardly uncertain what to do next.

"It won't take long."

"Travis, please go away and leave me alone. I don't want to talk to you," she whispered because she didn't want anyone else to hear.

Megan didn't want him to know how upset she was after they had broken up. She was looking around hoping nobody noticed what was going on.

"There's nothing for us to talk about," she whispered again.

Her inner thoughts told her his girlfriend must have dumped him, or he got tired of her. But she wasn't going to be his rebound or his second choice when he didn't have anyone else. She valued herself more.

"Everybody deserves a second chance." Travis said.

She swallowed hard and thought, that was a matter of opinion and didn't respond.

Nathan glanced at Megan and saw Travis talking to her. Maybe he overheard their conversation. He walked toward them.

"Is there a problem?" Nathan asked.

"No," Megan said. "Travis was just leaving." She was embarrassed and wanted to crawl into a hole and disappear.

"No, I wasn't," Travis said, taking a step closer to Megan.

"Travis, you heard the lady. I think you need to leave," Nathan said, stepping between him and Megan. Travis was annoyed, opened his mouth to say something, thought better of it, then walked away.

Nathan turned and whispered, "Let me know if he bothers you again."

"I'm fine," but Megan was shaken and tried not to show it. "I need to go home anyway. I have schoolwork I need to finish."

"That's too bad… I'm sorry you have to leave," Nathan replied. "It was nice getting to know you, Megan."

"You too," she replied, flashing him the best smile she could despite the circumstances. "Bye, Nathan."

He watched her as she started to walk away. John was standing there too.

"I'll walk with you back home. I'm tired," John said. "Sorry about the old flame of yours showing up here. But it looks like Nathan had it covered."

"Yeah," Megan replied, still shaken by what had just happened. "Thanks, John."

As they walked, Megan told John how glad she was to finally be able to talk to Nathan.

"I'm glad you met him. I think he likes you, Megan," John replied.

Megan didn't say a word. They walked back in silence. John didn't say anything else because he knew she was upset over Travis showing up unexpectedly.

CHAPTER 21

THE HOSPITAL VISIT

The following weekend, Ashley and Megan took both John and Ben to join a monthly support group because they struggled living alone. They walked into the entrance of the community center and saw Nathan on his way out.

"Megan! Hi," he said smiling.

Hearing her name coming from his lips was exciting. She was elated to see him. "Hi, Nathan, what are you doing here?"

"I work here as a volunteer counselor."

"Really? That's a nice thing to do," Megan replied.

She could smell the fragrance of his cologne and detected a masculine, woody scent and loved it. It was hard to swallow, and she could feel her thudding heartbeat.

"We brought John and Ben here to see what kind of services they can get."

"I'm sure someone here will be able to help you."

He stopped talking and glanced down at his watch. "It's really nice seeing you again, but I'm running late for another appointment. See you later, okay?"

"Bye, Nathan."

She watched him leave, turned to Ashley, and whispered, "I have such a strong attraction to him. I wish I could get to know him better."

"If he's interested in you, I'm sure you will eventually get to know him," Ashley replied.

Megan knew she was on the road to recovery from her relationship with Travis. She was ready to meet someone new and was happy to see Nathan again.

The next day during work, she received a phone call. John had been admitted to the hospital and had emergency surgery for appendicitis. He had some other problems and would probably be there for a few days. The nurse said John needed her to come by the hospital.

When her workday ended Megan went to visit him. After walking into his hospital room, he sat up in his bed and smiled.

"Hey, Megan. I'm so happy to see you."

She gave him a big hug and a kiss on the check.

"What happened to you?"

"I was watching television and had this pain in my side. I called Ben and he managed to call the paramedics. They took me to the hospital. The doctor had to remove my appendix."

"Wow! How are you feeling now?"

"Much better but I still have some pain from the surgery."

"I'm glad Ben was home to help you."

"Me too," he said. "Meg, I need to ask you a favor."

"Sure, what do you need?"

"Can you take care of my dog for me while I'm here?"

"Of course, I can. What's his routine?"

"He goes outside when he wants through the patio doggie door. He needs someone to feed him, put fresh water in his bowl, and walk him at least once a day. Can you manage that?"

"Don't worry, John. I'll take good care of him. Just work on getting better, all right?"

John was thankful and handed her the keys to his apartment. His eyes were wet from tears and Megan leaned down over his bed and kissed him again.

"Don't worry, you need to rest, recover, and get out of here."

"Yeah, you're right. I really don't like hospitals," he said.

Just then the nurse walked into the room to give him his medication. Megan decided it was time to leave. She walked to the parking lot with thoughts about his little dog. How was she going to fit him into her busy schedule for the next few days or even longer?

Megan walked downstairs to John's apartment to feed the dog, then put on his leash, and brought him to her place. She decided to take him on a short walk so quickly changed clothes and took him outside. Looking forward to taking in the fresh air and stretching her legs, she decided a long walk was even better.

Out on the street people turned and smiled. Max growled at times, but the walks were always relaxing. As the sun started to set behind the mountains, the streets lights came on.

Max was a friendly, frisky little dog and well trained. She walked him around the block a few more times, but as she was walking, she heard footsteps behind her. She turned the corner, and the footsteps did the same. The sound of the footsteps got louder, she could hear the sound of a dog panting, so she stopped and turned around. It was Nathan walking his dog.

"Hi, Megan. It's a beautiful evening, isn't it?" he said.

She was happy to see him again. A warm surge of heat went through her entire body. She found it difficult to swallow.

"Hi, yes, it's gorgeous outside," Megan replied.

"I might be mistaken but your dog looks just like John's dog."

"This is John's dog," she said, laughing. "I'm dog-sitting for John while he is away from home."

He laughed too. She liked his laugh. "That's really kind of you."

"Yeah, John is actually recovering from surgery. I'm helping him out until he can go home."

"Oh, I'm sorry to hear he had an operation. I hope he's doing better."

"Yes, he's doing well," replied Megan.

"Good. Let him know I asked about him."

"Okay, deal!"

"It's nice seeing you again," he said, with a flirtatious smile. "Maybe we'll run into each other again."

"That would be good. Enjoy your evening." Megan replied, brushing her fingers through her hair and smiling at him.

"Bye," he said, and walked briskly toward his condo.

Heart on fire, Megan walked John's dog back to her apartment. She didn't want him to stay by himself while John was in the hospital, so she put his dog bed in her bedroom. Yesterday, she made a strawberry cake with white icing and had it sitting on her kitchen table. She was going to give it to John for his birthday before she found out he was in the hospital. He wouldn't be eating cake for a while, so she decided to walk over to Ashley's and gave it to her and Parker.

Megan sat down at her desk, closed her eyes for a few seconds, and tried to put it all in perspective. Nathan. Remembering his face and his tall, masculine, lean body she wondered if he could be another Travis. Then she thought about Scott again and how she was at that time. They would go biking and running. They would stop for ice cream or sit on the grass just talking about everything. She quickly focused her attention back to what she was doing and worked on her schoolwork late into the night.

CHAPTER 22

MUCH LOVED PET

During the next few days, Megan took John's little dog on long walks in the evenings when she wasn't attending class. On Friday, John called and said he had to stay in the hospital for another week. She told him not to worry; Max was well taken care of, and they were getting along great.

While walking, she saw Nathan with his dog, speaking to her two neighbors. She didn't know whether to approach them or not, but she could feel Nathan watching her. She experienced an overwhelming, warm familiar feeling of excitement whenever Nathan was around.

On Friday, John was released from the hospital earlier than expected. He thanked Megan for taking care of his dog, but she was sad to see him go. She had a real attachment to Max and told John she would take care of him in the event of an emergency or if John ever had to go out of town.

The next morning, Ashley and Megan drove to a new homeless shelter to help serve food. Megan and Ashley entered through the front door of the homeless shelter and were happy to see Nathan there working. Another volunteer told them he was often there working. He helped people who needed guidance on how to find different kinds of public assistance and medical services.

"Hi, Nathan," Megan said as she and Ashley walked by him. He was sitting at a table with two chairs and talking to a young woman.

He looked up, "Hi, Megan. It's nice to see you."

"It's good to see you too." She smiled.

"What type of volunteer work are you doing today?" he asked.

"Ashley and I are helping serve food and cleaning up the kitchen."

"That's great. This place can use all the volunteers they can get. I didn't know you were interested in helping the homeless."

"I guess there are a lot of things you don't know about me," she said, smiling.

"Well, that's true. Maybe we need to get to know each other a little better."

"Yes, that would nice." She blushed.

"Are you going to take John's dog for a walk tomorrow?" Nathan asked.

'Yes, actually. John will be out of town for a couple of days."

"Why don't we walk together and take the dogs to the park?"

"Sure!"

"Great! I'll meet you in the courtyard tomorrow about eight a.m. if it doesn't rain."

"Okay!" she replied and smiled as he walked away believing Nathan was just what a guy was supposed to be: kind, sensible and intelligent. Megan was impressed by his good manners.

Megan got up early Sunday morning and noticed the sky was dark and cloudy. It looked like rain. She got dressed, grabbed a glass of juice, ate a piece of toast, and put on her sneakers so she could take the dog for a walk. The weatherman had said chance of rain in yesterday's weather forecast. She glanced out the window and it started to rain.

Just then Ashley called. "Hey, Megan, what are you doing?"

"I'm going to take Max for a walk."

"Are you crazy or what?"

"Nathan said he wanted to walk together today, so I'm going to see if he's outside."

"That's dumb. There is no way Nathan would be out there walking his dog with all the thunder and lightning." Suddenly, there was loud thunder and a flash of light. It vibrated the ground beneath them.

Megan hesitated for a moment and looked out the window. "You're right. It's really a bad idea." She sighed with disappointment. "There might be a break in the rain later."

"Don't count on it," Ashley replied. "Want to come over later and watch a movie and eat popcorn?"

"No thanks. I have other things to do." She hoped the rain would stop soon because she was eager to see Nathan.

"Okay. I'll talk to you tomorrow."

The rain came at the worst time. It fell in torrents and occasional intervals of light showers. Megan sat down, leaned her head against the window and gazed outside watching the pouring rain. In the midst of the storm, she sat there for nearly an hour, and it started raining even harder. The rain beat on the top of the roof with such force and clatter, pouring off the gutters with a deluge of water. Deep puddles of water formed on the grass and the thunder rumbled even louder directly overhead. *There's nothing to see but rain, rain and more rain.*

Disappointed that she had missed her walk with Nathan, and with nothing else to do, she quickly got up, walked upstairs to Ashley's apartment, and rang the doorbell. Ashley opened the door and was happy to see her.

"Hey, girl, I changed my mind. Let's watch a movie."

"Great! Come on in. Me and Parker were just going to put something on. Popcorn?"

"Yes please!"

Megan spent most of the day at Ashley's apartment, enjoying the company and playing games with Parker. And although she enjoyed herself, her thoughts were about Nathan. She wondered if he thought about her too.

The next day was clear, the rain had finally finished its work of beautifying the earth. The ground, plants and trees were drying out. The smell of freshness and dampness filled the air. The sun was breaking through the thick white clouds, and some parts of the ground were soft and soggy from the previous day's rain, with a few muddy puddles.

Megan took Max for a stroll in the park. The dampness and muddy ground weren't bothering Max at all, but then he suddenly saw a cat, pulled at the leash, and started chasing it. The leash was ripped right out of her hand.

"Oh, no!" Megan started running after him through the park. "Max, come back here!" she yelled, running through the damp grass and mud puddles. "Max! Max, come back!" She scratched her hands and arms as she ran through the trees and bushes, her hair full of leaves and twigs. She couldn't hear him barking any more.

"Oh, no! What am I going to do if I can't find him?" she mumbled to herself. She panicked for a few minutes, uncertain what to do next. "John is going to kill me. He'll never speak to me again. Max, you're his baby. This is terrible! What if someone steals him? Oh man…"

She kept running through the trees but still couldn't see him or hear him barking. She ran past a set of orange and blue playground equipment still wet and shiny from the rain, but had to stop.

Feeling breathless, she said, "Oh, please God, don't let him go by the creek. Anything could happen to him if he falls in." She could hear the rushing water from the previous day's rain.

Suddenly she heard him barking in the distance. Thank goodness she could at least hear him. The cat ran up a tree and he was barking at it about one hundred feet away. She ran toward the tree as fast as she could, slipped and fell in the mud, and was soaked through and wet.

"Oh, no," she moaned, then got up from the mud, and started running again. She finally got close to Max, grabbed his leash, and pulled him away from the tree.

"Max, bad dog!" She pulled his leash again. He barked and growled, showing his teeth as he barked at the cat in the tree.

"We're going home." Megan and Max were muddy, and she was clammy, dirty and needed a shower. He started barking again. "Bad dog! You shouldn't have run off on from me like that." She pulled his leash for him to follow her. After they got far enough away, even though she was upset with him, she leaned over and gave him a big, wet hug.

This dog was a handful today. Thinking she probably looked foolish running through the park, she sighed. Just then, Nathan walked by Megan with his dog and stopped and glanced at them.

"What on earth happened to you?" he asked, looking at her soaked from head to toe.

"I'm fine," Megan said, blushing. "Max just got away from me."

She felt embarrassed because she was a mess. Her hair was damp and smelled of dirt, leaves and twigs. Her arms and hands were all scratched, and she had mud all over her shirt, pants and shoes.

"Those cuts need cleaning."

There was a little bit of blood on her arms from the scratches. Pulling the leaves and twigs out of her hair, she forced a grin. "I'll be fine… I'm on my way back home."

"Okay," he said, still staring at Megan. "Sorry we weren't able to walk yesterday because of the rain." He was disappointed.

"Yeah, me too," she said sheepishly.

"Maybe we can another time?"

His smile made her feel warm all over. She wanted to melt right into his arms.

"Yes, that would be nice."

"Do you need some help getting back home?"

She wanted him to take her home and get her warm and dry, but she wouldn't tell him that. "No, I'm fine. Thank you, anyway."

"No problem. I hope you have a better evening, Megan," he said, then started walking away with his dog.

"Me too… bye," she replied feeling both awkward and clumsy. Nathan had seen her at her worst.

When she got home, she gave the dog a bath and he enjoyed every minute of it. Afterwards, she took a long hot shower and began to relax. Her mind drifted back to Nathan and how foolish she must have looked.

CHAPTER 23

UNCLE HARRY

Hoping to get a better paying job, Megan spent several days filling out job applications. Frustration was becoming a more common word in her vocabulary. It was hard to be enthusiastic about her job when it provided no promotional opportunities or pay increases. She had attended several interviews over the last few weeks, but nobody had hired her—not yet. Unemployment was high in the area and companies wanted people with a lot of experience, something she didn't have.

Then life got even more complicated. Jennifer called with some disappointing news for Megan. She and her husband had been saving some money to buy their own home. They didn't want to renew their rental lease agreement for the Orange Street house and wanted to pay for it month-by-month.

"Will your mother agree to it?" Jennifer asked.

"I'll have to talk to my mom and get back with you."

"That's fine. Can you get back to us in a few days and let us know?"

"Sure, I can, Jennifer."

Megan absorbed it all and was worried again but decided this wasn't the time to have a pity party. Just when things appeared to be getting better there was another setback.

If Glen and Jennifer moved out of the house it could be vacant for a couple of months or more. Her mother wouldn't be able to pay the monthly mortgage payments. Things would get tough again and they'd lose the house to foreclosure.

With some encouragement from Megan, her mom eventually agreed it was best to go with the month-by-month rental agreement. It was better than having a vacant house while waiting to find another long-term renter. If Glen and Jennifer eventually found a new home to buy, then Megan could put the house up for rent again with the hope someone would rent it rather quickly.

She needed to vent because there were so many things on her mind. The situation with Bruce really troubled her too. She needed to tell someone her story, just once. In the evening, during girl talk she finally told Ashley and Heather about him.

"I need to tell you two something."

"What?" Ashley and Heather replied at the same time.

"The job with the photographer, Bruce, didn't work out. I found out he's a real creep."

"What happened, Meg?" Heather asked.

"I was really happy when Bruce called and said he had a photoshoot for me a few months ago. I thought I was going to make all this extra money to help Mom with the house payments."

"What did he do?" Ashley replied.

"I went alone to see him, something I shouldn't have done. After modeling some of the clothes, he wanted me to unbutton my blouse to show more of my breasts, you know... more cleavage."

"Did you?" Ashley asked.

"I was uncomfortable, and it was a little sleazy, but I did it because I wasn't nude or anything like that."

"So, what else happened?" Heather asked.

"He took a lot of photos, then asked me to put on a skimpy negligee even after I told him I wasn't interested. I really knew he was bad news when he tried to get me drunk and kiss me."

"Who in the hell does he think he is? I wish I could kick his you know what!" Heather shouted.

"Wow! What a criminal!" Ashley said. "He thinks it's okay to treat women like that."

"I was angry, mad, like he had this power over me just because of his job and his money. He knew it would be hard for me to get a modeling job, so he used that. Then I said to myself, this isn't worth it, so I got the hell out of there. I still feel foolish, because if Corey had been there with me none of that would have happened."

"I bet you were terrified," Heather said, and reached over and hugged her.

"I wanted to throw up after he tried to kiss me. So, I grabbed my stuff and ran out the door."

Megan was embarrassed and didn't tell them how forceful he was and that he had fallen over the coffee table.

"Well, I hate to say it, but I told you it was a bad idea," Ashley replied.

"I know. I'll never let someone trick me again. I know I'm smart and can make money doing something else. But there are a lot of male chauvinist pigs out there trying to take advantage of women."

"I'm sorry you had such a terrible experience. Chris told you to be careful."

"I know, I know. I've learned my lesson. It's time for me to move on and put the whole thing behind me. Honestly, I have never understood how some people go through their entire life being a victim; never recognizing the damage the do because of their own poor decisions."

Ashley and Heather looked at each other and changed the discussion topic to something more pleasant.

Later in the week, Megan received some good news. She got a call for a second interview for the state government position she had interviewed for three weeks ago. They preferred applicants with a degree or near completion of getting their four-year college degree. She was pretty close to finishing, so Megan had a shot.

In the evening, Megan's phone rang as she was getting out of the shower. She quickly grabbed a towel, wrapped it around herself, ran to her nightstand, and picked it up. Her mother was crying.

"Mom, what's the matter?"

She muttered a few words and started crying again. Megan couldn't understand her at all.

"Mom, stop crying and tell me—what's the matter?"

"It's about Uncle Harry in Elk Grove."

"What about Uncle Harry?"

"He passed away this morning."

"Oh, no!"

Megan tried to comfort her, but it didn't help because she started to cry as well. After the phone call, Megan was speechless and fell into her overstuffed chair, unable to focus on anything else. She stared out the window for a while and tried to organize her feelings.

She picked up her phone, called her brother Chris, told him about his passing and the grief the entire family was experiencing.

"Uncle Harry was a really nice person. I'm gonna miss him too, Meg."

"I know, me too." She started crying again.

Uncle Harry was their mother's oldest brother who had never married and had no children. He worked his way through a vocational school and managed his own plumbing business for years. Never believed in banks, said people shouldn't trust them with their money. Nobody knew if his business was prosperous or not. He lived in the same house for forty years and did all his own home maintenance and repairs. The house was a modest, well-maintained, two-bedroom house in a small town in the suburbs of Sacramento. His home, business building, plumbing supplies, and equipment was on twenty acres of land.

"Megan, he always made a point to visit the family members twice a year during the summer and during the Christmas holidays, and if he couldn't make it to Shady Grove, we would go visit him. He was funny and always liked to tell jokes and make people laugh."

"I saw Uncle Harry during Christmas dinner last year at Aunt Ruth and Uncle James' house, and he looked a bit frail. But he never told anybody about any health problems," Megan said.

"Being in the military, I haven't seen him in a long time. Mom said he had several different housekeepers over the years who would come to clean his home every week and cook his meals. Based on their appearance, mom always had the feeling some of the ladies he hired did more than just cleaning and cooking," Chris said and laughed.

"Did you know he wrote his own obituary?"

"How do you know that?" Chris asked.

"Three years ago, Uncle told me he wasn't going to leave it to chance. People would say things about him just to be polite. He wrote it to tell the world his accomplishments and the kind of person he really was like."

"Don't you think that's strange?"

"No, not really. I think it's a good thing." Megan replied. "Nobody knew much about his personal life, Chris. He never talked about a girlfriend. He was content with his life and eventually retired from working full time in his plumbing business. Still, he occasionally worked part-time just to keep busy doing something."

"Let me know, when you guys go to his memorial service."

"I will," Megan replied. "Talk to you later."

Uncle Harry's most recent housekeeper, Nina, cooked and cleaned his home. She had a pretty face and the appearance of a wannabe Dolly Parton with bleached blond hair. She often wore a red, tight-fitting dress and was a little overweight with huge breasts. She spoke with a slight German accent.

Her mother said it would be a challenge for Nina to do real housework. Whenever she bent over her breasts appeared as if they would fall out and display everything. Every time Nina walked by Uncle Harry, he would stare at her and smile all the time. Uncle Harry said Nina had recipes that had been in her family for years, passed down from one bad cook to another. But he claimed she was getting better with her cooking.

Nina had worked out the funeral and memorial arrangements after talking to Aunt Ruth many times over the phone. Unfortunately, Megan's second interview for the job was scheduled on the same day as Uncle Harry's funeral services. Megan called Edith from the human resources department and asked if the employer could reschedule her interview for another day. Edith said she had to talk to her supervisor and would call her back.

Two hours later, Edith called Megan and said she was sorry but couldn't change the day of Megan's scheduled job interview. Megan was very disappointed because it was an opportunity for her to get a better position. She told Edith she couldn't attend the interview because she was going to her uncle's funeral service. Megan was so disappointed, but family was more important than some job she may or may not have gotten.

Aunt Ruth made airline reservations for all of them to fly to Sacramento. They would rent a car and stay at the Woodland Suites Hotel. The plan was to drive fifteen miles to Elk Grove for Uncle Harry's service. Aunt Ruth reserved a suite with two bedrooms and a sleeper sofa in the living room for Megan to sleep on.

After arriving in Sacramento on Friday evening, they entered the plush hotel lobby and walked over to the reservation desk across from the gift shop. As they walked down the hallway, Megan noticed the large dining room. The whole family quickly crowded into the elevator and took it to the third floor.

Uncle James opened the door to their room. The suite was large and nicely furnished with rich dark cherry wood furniture, a built-in wet bar with a small refrigerator, and a microwave. There was an ample supply of plush white towels in the bathroom and a small basket of toiletries.

Everyone put their suitcases down and hung up their sweaters. Megan's mother and Aunt Ruth got out their toiletries and carefully placed them in the bathroom. Uncle James sat down on the overstuffed chair with the ottoman.

He immediately got comfortable and started reading his book to kill time before dinner at five p.m. in the restaurant downstairs.

During the funeral services the next day there were photos of Uncle Harry because he had already been cremated. Many of the church members and his close friends were there including his housekeeper, Nina. She had dressed conservatively in a black dress, one that didn't show much cleavage, and a wide brimmed hat.

The service was held at the Elk Grove Community Church at eleven a.m. with burial to follow at the cemetery located just two blocks beyond the church. The service wasn't dark and gloomy but pleasant with prospects of hope of a better place for Uncle Harry.

Megan's mother said Uncle Harry attended church twice a year during Easter and Christmas. He knew everyone in town because of his plumbing business. She was amused by the speed with which the small town embraced the passing of her uncle and the number of people in attendance.

After the services, the family and friends talked and grazed through lots of food covering several tables set up buffet style at the church. Nina had organized a tide of food for everyone including casseroles, fruit and cakes.

The food was served downstairs in a large dining room with kitchen facilities. There were numerous chairs and tables decorated with colorful tablecloths and small centerpiece vases with artificial flowers. The people were friendly and talkative. Megan was hugged and embraced by people she didn't know. Some of the large women hugged her too tightly, trying to express their sympathy. The air was full of conflicting fragrances from expensive perfumes that were overwhelming at times. A few older individuals hugged her a lot longer than usual. Perhaps, they missed the human touch, a gentle squeeze, and the kindness that filled the room. Megan soon got tired of the mindless chatter of people. She didn't know Uncle Harry's friends.

Megan turned and asked the person standing next to her, "How did you know my Uncle Harry?"

"Oh, I never met him. I'm a member of the church. I come to all the memorial services."

"Oh?" she said. "What's your name?"

"I'm Walter."

"Well, it's nice to meet you, Walter. Thanks for coming," she said, turning her attention to two other men standing next to Walter. "So how did you two know my Uncle Harry?"

"We didn't know him. We're Walter's friends."

"Oh…" Megan said, not knowing what to think. She got the impression attending funeral services and eating the food served afterwards were social events for some people.

"You would be alarmed to know how many people leave this earth and have nobody attend their services," Walter said.

"I wouldn't know anything about that," she replied with a half-smile.

"Apparently your uncle knew a lot of people."

"Yeah, he was a plumber. He owned his own business."

"They're always busy," he said. "Faucets drip and pipes get blocked all the time."

"That's true."

"Rumor is plumbers make more money than some doctors."

Megan raised her eyebrows. "I'm not so sure about that." She laughed.

"Trust me they do. My brother is a plumber. They charge a huge amount of money. Do you own a house?"

"No, I don't. I just call my apartment manager when I have a problem."

"Very convenient," he said.

"Yes, it is. Excuse me, I need to walk over there and join my family now."

"Okay, Megan. It was nice talking to you."

Not long after Uncle Harry's service was over, the family was told they would receive a letter in a few days from Uncle Harry's attorney notifying them about Uncle Harry's will. Megan's mother and Aunt Ruth didn't even know Uncle Harry had an attorney.

It was a long day. When the service was over Megan drove everyone back to the hotel. They planned on relaxing and going to dinner later at one of the restaurants in the hotel.

Upon arriving back home the next morning, Megan was informed Glen and Jennifer had bought a new house and were giving their thirty-day notice. Megan managed to hide her disappointment at the house being vacant again. She wasted no time putting an ad in the paper and on the internet advertising the Orange Street house for rent.

CHAPTER 24

THE ECONOMY

Food prices were rising in California because of the drought. Even water was becoming a scarce resource, and people in Megan's neighborhood had to go to church and distribution centers in Shady Grove for groceries, relying on the food donations from church members and the community.

Even Megan and Ashley didn't have much money. Getting from one payday to the next was a real challenge. There were paycheck deductions, rent, automobile expenses, groceries and medical insurance premiums. Costs for food just kept rising, and it wasn't just food. Some of the tenants received much higher gas and electricity bills than usual. Even the price of gas had increased, leaving Megan and Ashley struggling to fill up their cars.

On Thursday things changed for the better. She checked her phone and had a message with some great news. It was from Edith from human resources asking for Megan to call her. Megan hadn't heard from her since she declined the interview to attend Uncle Harry's funeral.

The next morning Megan woke up early and returned the call. Edith asked her if she was interested in an interview for a different job with the state department.

"Of course!" she replied.

For three days she thought about it. Her confidence had increased and on the day of her interview Megan dressed in her navy-blue two-piece suit and high heels, with her hair neatly tied back. She arrived at the government office thirty minutes early and was a little nervous as she was escorted to a reception area. There were several people waiting there for different reasons, but the waiting room was quiet. People were sitting looking down at their cell phones, oblivious to their surroundings, and nobody talked to the person seated next to them. She cleared her throat and sat up straight in her chair. Trying hard to remain calm, she rehearsed in her mind how to respond to the interview questions.

Fifteen minutes later, a professional looking man in a business suit opened the door and called her name.

"Hello, my name is Thomas Hendricks." He smiled and shook her hand. "I'm going to escort you to the interview room."

"Okay, thank you," Megan replied and followed him down a long hallway to a large room.

There were two men and one woman seated on the opposite side of the large conference table. Mr. Hendricks introduced the others to Megan, she sat down, and he took the lead in talking. He tried to make her feel comfortable by making small talk and asking if she had difficulty finding the building.

During the interview they took turns asking her different questions. Thirty minutes and ten questions later, Mr. Hendricks and the others at the table had finished. Then he paused for a moment.

"I have one last question to ask you," he said.

"Okay, sure," Megan replied.

"Why do you think we should hire you? Take your time and think about it."

Why should they hire me? Are they kidding or what? she thought. Was it a trick question? She needed to respond with caution and her hands were hot and clammy.

She really wanted to say, you should hire me because I have to work to survive, need food, and money to pay my rent. I need a job with a decent salary. I'm sick of these low-paying jobs. I don't want to struggle any more trying to help my mom. I also need a new car. I'm tired of my car being in the repair shop all the time. But she knew that response wouldn't be appropriate.

Megan said, "You should hire me because I feel I'm the best person for the job. I'm a fast learner, a dedicated worker and a team player. I spent a large amount of time working on my college degree which I feel has prepared me for this kind of work."

Mr. Hendricks smiled. "Thank you, Megan. We'll be in touch with our decision within the next three days."

Megan left the interview feeling good about how she responded to the questions. But she'd had good feelings about previous job interviews, so she wasn't going to get her hopes up. Still, she sincerely hoped her luck had changed for the better.

Now, she had to wait. It was the agony of not knowing and the slowness of the response that made her stomach upset. There was nothing more she could do but wait, counting the hours, starting at eight a.m. until five p.m., often looking at her watch.

Three long days went by with no phone call. It was a sure sign she hadn't got the job. The waiting was even more stressful. Feeling disappointed again, she tried to busy herself with something else—it was just another job she didn't get. But she did expect someone to let her know the outcome of her job interview whether it was good or bad news. Normally, government offices send a letter to those who weren't selected for the job thanking them for interviewing with their agency. She checked her mailbox and hadn't received a letter—not yet.

The next day at work she tried to focus on her priorities. It was almost three in the afternoon when she received a message on her cell phone from Edith in human resources asking Megan to return her call. At first, she was hesitant to make the return phone call right away, but she had to find out. She grabbed her phone and dialed Edith. It was great news—they were offering her the job. She couldn't believe it. Her face lit up with happiness.

"You'll have to go through a training program to become familiar with the job. There is a six-month probationary period to evaluate your performance before you will be hired as a permanent employee," Edith said.

"Yes, that's fine," Megan replied. She was glad the starting salary was much higher, and benefits were much better than what she was currently getting. There was also a guaranteed pay raise after one year of employment.

Megan accepted the new job. She was so happy and wanted to celebrate, so she called Ashley and Heather.

They decided to go out on the weekend and celebrate when Heather got back into town. Megan loved living in her community of friends who were like family.

She called home to tell everyone the news. Uncle James answered the phone. His hearing was getting worse, and he still refused to get a hearing aid.

"Hi, Uncle James, get Aunt Ruth."

"What?"

"Get Aunt Ruth," she shouted.

"You lost your tooth?"

"No, get Aunt Ruth!"

"What?"

"Get my mom."

"I can't understand you. I'll get Ruth."

Megan told Aunt Ruth the news about her new job. Everyone was so excited for her, especially her mother.

CHAPTER 25

SASHA

Jennifer and Glen had moved out of the Orange Street house, which meant Chris had to borrow some more money to help cover the payments. He got another loan and Megan scraped together some of her savings. Megan had known for a long time it was becoming more and more difficult trying to keep her mom's house. The mortgage companies weren't sympathetic. They were evicting people and repossessing hundreds of homes every day. She called Chris to talk about everything.

"Chris, this whole thing about mom's house is stressful again with both of us trying to help pay the mortgage. I doubt Mom's ever going to be able to work again and move back in."

"You know, we can rent the house out again, but it's only a temporary solution. She really needs to put it up for sale," Chris replied.

"I know but she doesn't want to. The good news is several people have called about renting the house and have gone over to see it. But nobody has agreed to sign a rental agreement—not yet."

"I think we should just wait and see what happens. Maybe somebody will rent it again?"

"Yeah, you're right but we can't wait too long. Anita would be happy if our mom missed a few house payments so she could have Austin buy the house. I heard a neighbor tell someone Austin is her boyfriend. That's why she helps him. I'm worried, Chris."

"I know, I know. We'll just take one day at a time. Try not to worry so much, Meg."

The Orange Street house was vacant again and Megan slipped back into thoughts about why she avoided going back there. She was afraid to go there alone but she had to clean it. Her friends were busy. They had their own obligations. So, she gathered all her cleaning supplies and went to the house by herself. She definitely wasn't looking forward to it.

Megan unlocked the front door and slowly walked into the entry way. She could feel something creepy was going to happen because her arms were cold, her stomach was churning, and her fingers tips were tingling. She stood there for a few seconds looking at the walls, the floor, the finished wooden shelves she had been so familiar with for years. The house was quiet, and she took a deep breath telling herself there was nothing to fear. Cleaning the kitchen was her priority before progressing to other parts of the house.

The first hour passed uneventfully. There were no strange noises from the attic. The second hour went by with no problems, and she was glad. Then the inevitable happened. She heard strange scratching and bumping noise coming from the attic. She tried to ignore it and turned up the music and adjusted her earbuds. Then suddenly, there was a loud bang; she was frightened and jumped. The noise was like someone banging on a metal pipe.

"What the hell was that?" she blurted as she looked up toward the ceiling.

Chills went through her entire body. Her gut feelings told her that noise wasn't from the water heater in the basement, no way. Then she noticed the hallway door with the stairs up to the locked attic was slightly open. She closed it. An hour later she walked past the door, and it was open again.

It was creepy. Megan was sure that she had closed that door. This entire situation was unnatural, like something out of a sci-fi movie. She'd had enough of this mess. Megan was angry, thinking somebody or something was playing a joke on her.

She looked upward, with wide eyes, and shouted boldly, "Is somebody up there? You need to leave. Like right now!"

Megan was hoping whoever was there would hear her and be alarmed. But there was nothing but silence. She grabbed that doorknob and closed the door again. Megan glared out of the window into the front yard, then the back yard. Didn't see anybody. She had the feeling someone or something was watching her. She didn't like being there by herself, not without Ashley, Heather or Mark. All of a sudden, she felt cold, put on her pullover sweatshirt, moved her backpack with the taser gun tucked inside nearby, and continued cleaning.

Thirty minutes later she heard the sound of footsteps in the attic, like somebody walking back and forth. It was frightening. Every time she heard footsteps, her heart rate went up. She thought it was weird. Perhaps the noise came from the house next door so Megan walked toward the window, looked outside, and could see the yard and the neighbors' house. It didn't look like they were home. There were no cars parked in their driveway and she didn't see or hear people talking. She shook her head and felt it was strange.

It was scary. She knew it wasn't her imagination. She kept telling herself it was nothing even though she knew deep down inside it was more than that. She had no plans to stay longer than she had to. Megan finished cleaning, quickly gathered all her belongings, and went home. She was determined to stay strong, accomplish the work that had to be done, and not dwell on her fears. After she arrived home, Megan poured herself a glass of wine, sat down on the sofa, and focused on relaxing.

John had to go out of town for the weekend and asked Megan if she could watch his dog. She had a weakness for animals, so she never turned him down. While walking Max around the block, she saw Nathan in the distance walking toward her with his dog. Her heart throbbed faster as he got closer. Excitement engulfed her body and wanting to talk to him, she stopped, reached into her pocket and pulled out her cell phone. All the while, pretending to be talking to someone, when he got just a few feet away, her cell phone started ringing.

Feeling embarrassed, Megan wanted to hide.

"You need to answer your phone," he said, amused by what had just happened.

She quickly turned her phone off, still blushing, "Hi, Nathan."

"Hey, how are you?" He smiled at her.

"I'm fine. It's good to see you again."

"You too," he said. "You know, I've been thinking about you, and I was wondering if you would—"

Before he could finish, Sasha walked toward both of them and interrupted their conversation. She didn't even look at Megan standing there next to Nathan—like she was totally invisible.

"Hey, Nathan. I'm having several people over for a dinner party tomorrow and I would like you to come. It starts at six-thirty," Sasha said.

"I don't know if I can make it," he replied politely.

"Don't be silly. I won't take no for an answer." Sasha flashed him a flirtatious smile. "See you tomorrow," she said, smiling at Megan as she walked away. Megan didn't like the kind of smile she had on her face, that sneer. It was almost triumphant.

Megan was upset over the entire incident and tried not to show it. Sasha was mean and rude. She was the kind of person who would throw her best friend under the bus if it would benefit her.

"Sorry about that," Nathan said. "As I was saying, maybe we should get together sometime and go hiking. There's a really good trail near Fairmont Park and a lake there with cute bronze ducklings at the entrance. I named them Gucci and Lucy."

She laughed. "Sure, and it sounds original."

Megan started to feel butterflies in her stomach again because she was interested in more than just hiking with Nathan. He aroused all of her senses.

Suddenly, her neighbor, Ben, walked up and interrupted the conversation. He had trouble seeing people but could recognize their voices most of the time.

"Hi, Ben," Megan said.

"Is that Nathan with you?"

"Yes, it's me," Nathan replied.

"Hi, Nathan. How's it going?"

"Just fine," Nathan replied.

Ben talked about the beautiful weather even though it was cooler than normal, and about the sound of the birds singing. He reached down and petted Nathan's dog and continued to talk about dogs. Just then two neighbors walked up and started talking to everyone.

She thought, *My goodness this neighborhood is like a zoo*. There were just too many interruptions. After listening to their conversation for a few minutes, she glanced down at her watch because she had to leave.

She leaned over close to Nathan and whispered, "I really have to go. Please excuse me. I'll talk to you some other time."

"Okay, I'm looking forward to it," he said with a flirty smile. Nathan watched her walk away.

The following day Megan was busy talking to Ashley and Heather and told them about the incident with Sasha.

"Sasha needs to learn how to speak politely to people," Ashley said. "Expensive clothes. money and dinner parties are how she measures her success."

"Sasha is unhappy and just envious of anybody who's successful in other ways," Heather added.

"You're probably right," Megan replied.

"Did Nathan actually ask you out for a date?"

"No, but he kind of hinted about going on one," Megan replied.

Megan wondered if Nathan was attracted to Sasha. There were men who liked women like her. John and some of the other men in the apartment complex were certainly taken by her flirtatious behavior. Of course, John was an older man and only had his dog as the center of his life, and there was no doubt Ben would welcome her attention.

That evening was Sasha's dinner party. Megan wondered if Nathan was attending the party. It suddenly crossed her mind to walk down to the courtyard and see who was ringing Sasha's doorbell.

Megan asked Ashley for advice.

"That's too obvious," Ashley said. "It's a dumb thing to do. Sasha even invited me to her dinner party, and we don't even get along. I think she did it just to upset you. I told her thanks, but I had something else planned."

"Thanks. You're truly a best friend."

"I know but you shouldn't be spying on Sasha and her friends."

"All right, well I'm glad I called and asked before I did something foolish," Megan replied.

She wondered if Nathan had any angry exes ready to disrupt any attempt for happiness. And how well did he know Sasha anyway? *Maybe he's just being cordial or perhaps he knows her romantically?* If he liked Sasha, he probably had no interest in getting to know anyone else.

Megan decided she had to know what was happening. After searching through her closet, she pulled out a pair of binoculars, wiped the lenses clean and held them to her eyes. Pushing back the drapes she peered out the window to see who was entering the courtyard. It was getting dark, and she couldn't see well. Twenty minutes passed and then she could see different people walking toward Sasha's apartment. She still didn't see Nathan. Five minutes later, there was Nathan, walking on the sidewalk toward Sasha's home. Then there was John walking through the courtyard with his dog. He glanced up and waved at Megan. She was stunned but waved back, embarrassed, not realizing people could see her.

She quickly closed the drapes and sat down on the sofa. "Oh man!" she said and leaned her head down and rubbed her forehead. She hoped Nathan didn't see her looking out the window with her binoculars. What would he think of her?

So many crazy ideas were going through her head. Hoping one day Nathan would officially ask her out for a date, she needed to stop having thoughts about Sasha's party. She decided she would invite the gang over for dinner, so she threw the binoculars in the closet, walked into the kitchen, got several things out of the pantry, and started cooking, trying to keep the dinner party across the way out of her mind.

As the days went on, Sasha continued to shun Megan whenever they walked past each other. Megan avoided talking to her because she didn't want to make a scene. Then one day Sasha mumbled something, clearly directed at Megan.

"What did you say?" Megan asked.

"I didn't say anything important. But since you asked, I'm telling you. Nathan wouldn't be interested in you."

"Oh, really?" Megan said feeling insulted.

"You're not the only one interested in him. There are a lot of women who like Nathan, and honestly? You're not his type. You're pretty but you're not that pretty," Sasha replied.

Megan rolled her eyes at her angrily. How dare Sasha talk down to her again like she was somebody insignificant! Frustrated with the way Sasha made her feel, it was difficult trying to avoid any confrontation with her in the past but enough was enough. Trying to be nice was not working. Maybe Heather was right, and Sasha was envious of all the attention Megan got from her friends and other people.

Megan thought as a young woman it was not appropriate to get physical with this snob of a person, but her lips tightened, she took a step closer, put her finger in Sasha's face and said, "Ever since I moved here, I've tried to be nice to you. I know you don't like me but that's your problem. I don't like you either. You're just rude! You should keep your mouth shut!"

Sasha reacted and her hands reached and grabbed Megan by the collar. Megan felt adrenaline rush throughout her body and pushed her. Then she grabbed Sasha's head, her fingers dug into her hair and pulled it, and she screamed. Her long hair was tangled.

Sasha pushed back, then grabbed Megan's arm and twisted it. She felt the pain but got over it.

"Don't you dare touch me again! I'll call the police!" Sasha shouted.

"Yeah, do it you snob and we'll settle this once and for all!"

Sasha picked up her handbag that had fallen on the ground and swung it at Megan. She ducked quickly and it missed her. Megan's face flushed red with anger, and she clenched her fists. Then Megan reached and grabbed her hair again.

"You're a spoiled and self-centered—"

Just then John walked up in between them and shouted, "Stop it! Stop it! What's wrong with you two?"

"She started it!" Sasha yelled.

"No, I didn't. You did!"

"You both need to go home!" John shouted forcefully. He was shocked by their behavior.

"Good idea. I'm not going to waste my time fighting with her!" Megan shouted. "I have better things to do," and she turned and started to walk away.

Surprisingly, Sasha walked over and pushed Megan. She turned around and pushed her back. Sasha stumbled, fell into the courtyard water fountain, and had gotten all wet. Megan laughed.

John didn't think it was funny and helped Sasha get out of the water. Her body was rigid, and she said nothing. They both quickly turned and walked their separate ways. John stood there stunned, looking at them, wondering what could make them be so mad at each other.

Normally, Megan wouldn't have made any sarcastic comments, but she was so angry and decided life was too short to tolerate so much crap from someone like Sasha. She wasn't going to take it any more.

CHAPTER 26

UNEXPECTED SURPRISES

A private contractor agreed on a short-term rental agreement for the Orange Street house. He and his staff were working on a government project and needed a place for the employees to work and stay overnight only during weekdays. Nobody would be there on weekends. He planned on renting furniture, so the empty house was no problem. Megan found some comfort even though it wasn't long term but was grateful—it would help pay the mortgage for a while and avoid foreclosure.

Soon after their trip to Sacramento, Aunt Ruth received a telephone call and a letter from Uncle Harry's attorney on the same day. In his will, he left his bedroom set to Megan and a key to his safety deposit box. He left his furniture and his home on three acres of land to Nina, his housekeeper. Apparently, he even had a life insurance policy and left some cash for Megan's mother and Aunt Ruth.

Surprisingly, Uncle Harry left seventeen acres of his land to her mom and Aunt Ruth as well as a deed to some land in the foothills of the mountains. Nobody knew if it was worth anything. Megan's mother said Nina deserved the house and the land in Elk Grove because she'd taken care of Uncle Harry for a long time. Aunt Ruth was not so sure about Uncle Harry's decision because she had never met Nina except at the funeral service.

Megan had been regularly reviewing her mother's finances and all her bills over the past two months. Her medical bills were still mounting and putting her into deeper debt. Megan and Chris talked to her about it and Aunt Ruth and Uncle James encouraged Megan's mother to live with them permanently.

They had many long discussions about her selling the house since it would soon be vacant again. Fortunately, the contractor's staff never complained of strange sounds. Maybe it was because most of them wore wireless earbuds, and some worked late through the night or early morning. There was always a lot of activity in the house.

Eventually, her mother decided she needed to sell the house so she wouldn't have to worry about foreclosure ever again. A huge burden was finally lifted from Megan's entire soul, and she was ready to go out and celebrate.

Megan loved the home which was once in the middle of an orange grove; the home her parents had restored and painted. She cherished the front yard and the sycamore tree they planted years ago. There were so many good memories, and Megan knew it was going to be hard to let go, but her mother needed to move on and so did she. But what she didn't like was hearing the strange noises coming from the attic.

Since the house was being put up for sale, her mom seemed more concerned about the attic than anything else.

"I'll go over and pack everything in attic," her mom said.

"How can you do that?" Megan asked. "You can hardly walk, and you keep complaining about your back."

"I know," she replied, shrugged, and glanced across the room.

Megan's mom seemed confused at times. Something wasn't right with her.

"Listen, Mom. I'll pack everything in the attic. The renters will be moving out this week, so I'll put the things from the attic in the public storage facility," Megan said.

"I have to think about it," she said, still worried.

"We have to move everything out of the house if you're selling it."

"I guess you're right," her mom replied.

Megan needed to find out what was in the attic. She was reluctant to go there but had no choice. She mumbled, "Who else would do it?" Her mother was acting so strangely and didn't appear to be her normal self. Something wasn't right. At the end of the week, she decided to call Ashley.

"Can you come over and we'll see what's in the attic? Mark and Corey are busy with work and class exams."

"How about in a couple of hours? I'm really not excited about this."

"Me neither. Don't be too late, okay?"

Ashley was late. The sun had dipped behind the horizon when they arrived at the Orange Street house. The only sounds were the loud, chirping crickets and the sound of the heavy beating of their hearts. They walked to the hallway door that led to the upstairs attic. Megan slowly opened the door at the bottom of the stairway. Ashley flipped on the light switch on the wall, but it wasn't working. Megan quickly got a flashlight. They carefully walked up the dark, narrow, creaking stairs to the locked door.

"What if there's something strange up there like ghosts or something even creepier?"

"We've been in the house for several years and I never heard anything but scratching. Well... sometimes footsteps." Megan had been reluctant to tell her everything.

Ashley was staring at Megan open-mouthed. "Scratching and footsteps!" she shouted. "You never told me about footsteps!"

"I didn't want to scare you. Can you not talk so loudly? You're making me nervous."

"You nervous! What about me?" Ashley replied.

They reluctantly opened the door. The room was dark, and the door creaked. *It's just old hinges...* All of a sudden, something ran across the floor. They both let out a bloodcurdling scream and grabbed each other.

"What was that?"

"I think it was a mouse," Megan said, feeling relieved.

"You think?" Ashley replied.

"I don't know, it's too dark!"

"I don't like mice. Are you sure it wasn't a rat?"

"Mouse or rat, what's the difference? They're both rodents."

"Rats are larger, and they have bigger teeth!" Ashley said.

"Ashley, just focus," she whispered.

Just then across the room they saw two green, glowing eyes reflecting in the light, and a hairy creature growling at them. They both screamed and ran. Megan tripped, fell and landed on top of Ashley.

"My arm!" Ashley shouted.

"What?"

"My arm!"

"Oh no! Did you break it?"

"No, you're lying on it."

"Sorry," Megan said and helped her up.

A moment later, Mrs. Atkins' cat ran past them down the stairs, meowing and hissing.

"How did he get into the attic?" Ashley shouted.

"I don't know, that's strange. Somehow, he got in and was probably trying to catch mice."

Still nervous and shaking, they took a few moments to calm down. Then Megan, with the flashlight in her hand, searched for the light switch, eventually found it, and turned it on. A dim light shone down from the attic ceiling. They carefully scanned the room slowly looking around.

"What in the world is going on here?" Megan said softly.

They were shocked; the attic was a finished room with painted walls and vintage, floral wallpaper. It was uncluttered and clean, and there were vaulted ceiling beams. It looked like it was frozen in time. There were several old bookcases filled with books that belonged to her dad. He loved to read and had purchased them from garage sales and used bookstores. There were a few storage boxes, a large trunk and two clothing racks with clean sheets covering them. Megan pulled off the sheets and there was men's clothing hanging there.

"What's all this stuff?" Ashley asked.

Megan carefully inspected the shirts, the pants and jackets.

"It's all my father's clothes. I remember this blue sweatshirt and this black leather jacket," Megan said as she gently touched each item.

Her stomach was fluttering, and her pulse started to quicken. She knew something was wrong. His pants, shirts and jackets were clean and neatly arranged. His shoes were lined up perfectly on the floor against the wall. There was an old leather sofa, a shadow of its former self, a coffee table and wing backed chair. On the opposite side of the attic was a wooden desk and chair, as well as a blue area rug, and a twin-size bed with a soft, cotton bedspread. An old lamp was on the desk with a photograph of their entire family. Megan turned on the lamp and it brightened up the entire room. There were tools neatly arranged in small, wooden crates on the floor, and a basketball, baseballs and other items. His books were neatly arranged on an old bookshelf, but the bed covers were partly on the bed and on the floor as if somebody had been sleeping in it.

"This is weird, Megan… Is he still living here?"

"Of course, not," she replied. "He died several years ago."

"I know, but your mom has everything here as if he's still alive."

"You're right." Something was wrong. She'd imagined all sorts of awful things up here, but now she had serious concerns about her mother.

"It's like he never left," Ashley replied.

"This is really weird," Megan said. "So, this is the reason why she locked the door to the attic years ago after dad passed away and never wanted us to come up here."

"Look, she even has cleaning supplies and an ironing board."

"Yeah, that's strange too."

For a time, Megan had doubted her mom was all there. The thoughts in her head told her this was not normal. But now, though she still behaved oddly, she was confident, her mom had fallen under a spell and was dealing with her problems the best she knew how.

"What're you going to do about it, Megan? Obviously, your mom needs help or something?"

"Yeah, you're right." She shrugged and glanced around. "Frankly, I don't really know what to do. She probably needs to see a therapist."

"That's for sure," Ashley replied.

"I'll call and talk to Chris about it. I think we should encourage her to go see Dr. Sharma or somebody."

"That's a good idea. Now can we get out of here? I don't like attics."

"Wait! I have to know what's in the trunk."

"But you don't have a key," Ashley replied.

Just then Megan walked over to the crate of tools and grabbed a crowbar from the floor. She and Ashley managed to break the lock and open the trunk. Megan's breath was taken away and her heart dropped. There was a pile of family photos, old papers, jewelry, letters, baby clothes and other things inside it. She carefully went through everything and soon found a small grey metal box with a lock on it. They couldn't get it open.

"There's a lot of stuff here," Ashley said while touching and inspecting each item.

"Yeah, I know. After we move everything to storage, I'll go through it all when I have time. But I'll take this metal box with me. There must be something important inside, maybe old jewelry or something."

"You're probably right. Or souvenirs," Ashley replied.

All this time, it occurred to Megan her mother's pain of losing her husband had been stored away above her bedroom in the attic. The attic was a safe place for her mother to store all her heartbreaks and disappointments. It crushed Megan. Her mother had barely spoken of him since he died.

"Maybe the noise you heard in the attic was your mom walking around ironing or cleaning."

"Yeah, you're right. There's no scary ghosts like in the movies, just my mom. Then Mrs. Atkins' cat somehow got inside the attic, and he was probably making a noise trying to catch mice. It all makes sense now."

"That's a relief," Ashley replied.

"Ashley, will you promise me not to tell anybody about all of this?" Megan was confused about the whole situation.

"I would never tell anybody. I promise."

"Thanks. Let's get out of here and go back downstairs. We'll pack everything in boxes tomorrow, then I'll ask Corey and Mark to help us move the stuff out of the attic on the weekend and donate the books to charity.

Just then they heard a strange noise at the other door to the attic from the backyard. At first, they thought the house was just settling. Then they heard the key turn in the lock. It sent chills down their spines.

"If it's somebody trying to kill us, scream as loud as you can and let's run as fast as we can to get away," Megan whispered.

Megan's heart started beating fast. Maybe somebody was playing a joke on them. Suddenly they heard a man's voice.

Ashley and Megan just stood there for a few seconds.

"Please open the door, I need help."

It sounded like her Uncle Ray.

Megan turned toward Ashley. "It's my uncle. He needs my help."

"What if he's not your uncle, Megan?" Ashley said and grabbed her arm.

"But he needs my help," she said with wide eyes.

"But what if he's pretending to be your uncle?"

Megan walked over to unlock the door and trembled with fear.

"No! No, don't open it!" Ashley shouted, was filled with terror, and ran toward the stairs.

"Come on, Megan!"

She ran down the stairs and out of the house. All Megan could hear was Ashley's footsteps running away and her screaming.

Megan was nervous. Her body was frozen in place, she couldn't move. She reached for the doorknob. Just then the door opened slowly. She quickly took several steps backwards. Adrenalin surged through her entire body. Her instincts said, *Run! Run!* But to where exactly?

All of a sudden, the man's voice shouted, "Hey, hey, it's me, your Uncle Ray!"

The man walked inside wearing a black hoodie. Megan was frightened. She couldn't see his face.

"Stop!" she shouted and pulled out the taser gun from her jacket, aimed it at him, pulled the trigger and hit his leg. He fell to the floor and couldn't move for a few seconds. He moaned and groaned and soon grabbed his leg.

"Oh, no," he grunted then pushed back his hoodie, slowly tried to get up. "Why did you do that, Megan? That really did hurt!"

"It is you, Uncle Ray! I couldn't see your face. I'm so sorry." She helped him stand up and was glad he was able to recover quickly.

His hair was covered with gray dust and his clothes were worn and loose fitting. He was nearly a foot taller. She recognized him immediately.

"I'm glad you didn't have a real gun," he said, and took a deep breath.

"What are you doing here, Uncle?" She was totally relieved he wasn't a ghost or some eerie creature from the unknown.

"I didn't have a place to stay so I came here to sleep in the attic."

"You scared the hell out of us!" She paused a few seconds, still trying to recover and catch her breath then cut the wires. "I have to take you to emergency to get the two taser darts out of your skin."

"Okay. It doesn't hurt that much any more."

"Thank goodness for that. But, Uncle, how long have you been sleeping here?" Megan asked.

"Not long. I come here when I'm out of money."

"What? You've been sleeping in the attic and didn't even tell me or Mom?"

"Yeah, sometimes I do," he replied with a blank look.

"You should have told us when you needed help. That's really creepy," Megan said.

"You're right," he said. "I didn't think about it."

"We could have mistaken you for a thief, called the cops or even shot you."

"I'm sorry. I just need to stay here for a couple of nights."

"Uncle, you can stay longer but you need to let me know you need a place to sleep. You don't have to sneak into the attic. You're family."

She knew Uncle Ray had problems and was sorry he had no place to sleep. They had tried to help him in the past, but he never stayed in one place very long.

"Okay, thanks." He smiled and it was soft and friendly.

Megan wondered if he had keys to the attic doors, but he was also good at picking locks. Before she could ask him, he said, "I have keys your mom gave to me a long time ago when she hired me to clean out the attic. She probably forgot about it. But the key gets stuck in the lock sometimes."

"Oh, okay." She didn't know what else to say.

Megan and her uncle walked downstairs and outside to find Ashley who was still trembling. She was happy to see her there waiting. She hadn't deserted her.

"It is your uncle! Thank goodness." She grabbed and hugged Megan tightly.

"Yeah, Uncle Ray was sleeping in the attic when he didn't have a place to stay."

What a relief!" Ashley replied. "At least you didn't have any ghosts in the attic." She let out a deep sigh.

"Right. I've been frightened of the attic for a long, long time."

"Me too." Ashley smiled.

Megan turned toward her uncle and asked, "Uncle Ray did you ever open the hallway door when you were here sleeping in the attic?"

"You mean the one downstairs?" He glanced at the house.

"Yes."

"Nope. I have never gone down the stairs to the hallway. I was always very quiet and stayed in the attic. I didn't want to get caught."

"Are you sure, Uncle?"

"Yeah, I wouldn't lie to you," he said.

"Really? That's really creepy," Megan replied.

"What do you mean?"

"Oh, nothing. It's nothing," she replied and shook her head.

Megan wondered if Uncle Ray didn't open the hallway door when he was here, who did? Chills went down her spine. Was there somebody or something else in the house? She couldn't tell if her uncle was lying or not but was mystified over the entire situation.

Megan decided they had enough drama for one evening. Ashley went home and Megan took her uncle to the hospital to treat his taser wounds.

The following Monday morning, Aunt Ruth called and said Uncle Harry's bedroom set would be shipped to Megan by a moving van within the next two weeks. The safety deposit box key would be sent to her registered mail so she could go to the bank in Elk Grove to open the box.

Megan told Ashley about the will. "That's just great. Now, I just have to figure out when I can fly to Elk Grove and go to the bank. Why would Uncle Harry leave a key to a safety deposit box for me?"

"Regardless, it's nice he thought about you."

"Yeah, you're right," Megan replied. "He could have secret letters telling me something about his life and how much he loved the family. Maybe he left some money in it... but it's doubtful because Mom didn't feel he had much. He was such a private person when it came to his business and his personal life."

"Your Uncle Harry was quite an unusual person," Ashley said. "Who knows?"

"That's true. I'll have to plan a trip and fly to Sacramento when I have time. Right now, I just don't have the time to fly there with work and my classes."

On Wednesday evening, the bedroom set had finally arrived, and the movers were at her front door. The antique furniture was well made of solid wood. Megan liked it because her old bedroom set was rather plain and cheaply made with wood veneer finish. The new set included a headboard for the bed and a frame, a mattress, a tall chest of drawers, a dresser and two nightstands.

"Uncle Harry had good taste in furniture," Megan said to Ashley when she came over to help her arrange the furniture.

"Maybe he bought the furniture so long ago it actually became an antique?" Ashley replied, grinning.

"You're probably right." Megan laughed.

She gave her old bed to John and her chest of drawers to Ben who really needed one. The movers arranged the pieces of furniture and put the bed together before leaving. She put bed sheets and her comforter and pillows on the bed, then placed her clothes inside the tall chest of drawers and the dresser.

There was a cover enclosing the mattress and it was a little lumpy when she laid down on it. It wasn't as comfortable as her old and soft worn mattress, but it was thoughtful of Uncle Harry to give her the furniture. It looked just fine in her bedroom.

The Orange Street house was empty again and up for sale. Megan was scared but reluctantly had to go there to check on it.

She mumbled, "I'm not looking forward to this, but I have to do it."

After pulling the keys out of her pocket, she reached to unlock the door but there was a lock on it. She looked down and examined it. "What the heck is this?"

Megan walked around to the back door and there was a lock on it too. There was a paper taped to the inside of the window. The house had been foreclosed and repossessed.

"What the?"…her voice cracked. She was upset and screamed, "No! No! How in the world could this have happened?"

Her thoughts were about her mom making the house payments using the money she and Chris had given her. There must have been a mistake. Something was wrong. She immediately called her.

"Mom, I can't believe it! The house has a foreclosure sign on it. Do you know anything about this?" Megan was so upset, she was trembling.

Her mom was silent for a few moments. "I had too many bills to pay so I didn't pay the full monthly house payments."

"What? You what?

Megan sat down on the porch in a daze, couldn't believe what her mom had just told her. Trying to come to grips with what had happened was difficult. The damage was done. She assumed her mom had been making the full payments. She and Chris had given her the money.

"I can't believe you didn't tell me or Chris. The mortgage company told you to make full monthly payments, Mom," Megan blurted.

After further discussion, her mom said she had gotten foreclosure notices in the mail. She didn't tell anybody, not even Megan's aunt and uncle.

"I didn't want to worry anybody. Anyway, my friends said there's thousands of foreclosed homes for sale and I wouldn't get anything for it."

Megan found little comfort in what she had just said.

"I bet the friend who told you that was Zoe. Right?"

"Well, yes it was."

"I told you not to listen to Zoe," Megan said, almost in tears. "Mom, she always gives you bad advice."

"Sometimes, she's right," her mom replied trying to defend her friend.

"Mom, your friend Zoe was wrong!" she snapped. "I told you before not to listen to her. She has never even owned a house and lives with her gossiping sister. They rent! It's all about the value of your house and how much equity you have in the house over the years. You could have still sold it and gotten some money."

"It wasn't all Zoe's fault," she argued. "Austin Mitchell told me I wouldn't get much money for selling it. The investment company he works for would buy it and give me more money than a realtor."

"What? You never told me you talked to him! You actually talked to him?" Megan gasped.

"Yes, he called me several times."

"Oh, my goodness! He just wanted your house. He tries to buy houses cheap and sells them at a higher price. Mom, I'm so sorry but you've been taken!"

Her mom sighed and didn't feel like arguing. "Well, it's over and done now, I can't change anything."

"Unbelievable," Megan mumbled. She was extremely upset and leaned down with her hands against her forehead. For a split second, she wanted to scream but didn't. Instead, she took a deep breath to help calm herself. Megan's jumbled thoughts made her realize she shouldn't blame her mom totally for losing the house. Zoe was not knowledgeable about foreclosures but was skillful at being convincing and Austin was a master at being a liar, a disastrous combination for her mom.

Disappointed and shocked after all they had done trying to save the house from being foreclosed, she was totally lost for words. Her mom was too naïve at times. She immediately called Chris and told him what had happened.

"What? What? Did you say what I think you said?" he asked.

"Yes," Megan replied.

"I can't believe it!" I just can't believe it!" he said. "You know what I'm going to do?"

"No, what?" She was anxious to hear what he was going to say.

"I'm going out with my friends tonight for beer and get drunk, so I don't have to think about it. It's pretty devastating, really."

"There's nothing else we can do now! Nothing!" Megan said. Her eyes suddenly watered as she cleared her throat. She wiped her cheeks with the back of her hand.

After they talked further and had gotten over the initial shock, Chris said, "Look, let's think about all of this."

"Okay, what are you thinking?" Megan asked after an awkward pause.

"The stress of keeping the Orange Street house is no longer a burden. Right?"

"True."

"Mom is in a safe place. Right?"

"Yes," she replied.

"In fact, it's a relief. You and I no longer have to worry about house payments."

"That's true, Chris, but we worked so hard to pay the mortgage and mom lost all her investment. It was our family home; out wonderful, cherished family home."

"I know but there's nothing we can do about it," he said.

Then she decided, the numbing shock of it all had to be put behind her. There was no need to worry about the strange noises that were coming from the house any more, such a relief.

"Let's look at the positive side of all of this," Chris said, trying to be sensible but still upset.

"Yes, you're right, I guess I'm feeling a little bit better already," she said.

Some relief came from the realization she had just been freed from the Orange Street house and everything that came with it. Tonight, she could do whatever she wanted. She could have dinner with her friends, watch movies, have drinks and socialize.

They talked a little longer and decided to make the best of it. In the evening, Megan had gone out with her friends because it helped put her mind at ease. After she had gotten home, a bit tipsy, Megan had fallen asleep on the bed without changing into her pajamas.

The following day, Mark raced to Megan's place, and hugged her, and they talked about her mom's house being foreclosed. He knew she was unhappy about it.

"I'm sorry about the house, but I did get some more information for you."

"I hope it's good news," Megan replied.

"Well not exactly."

"Okay, go ahead and tell me. I know it won't change anything." She turned and glanced out the window.

"You're right but I found out when the house was empty a group of boys would go there to smoke and drink."

"What does that have to do with the creepy things happening in the house?" she asked.

"Nothing, but I talked to one of the boys all grown up now. His name is Carl."

"You did?" She looked at him with a stunned expression.

"Yes. He said they had several supernatural, ghost games in the house and would ask it questions. They had stolen them from the old, boarded up Wilsons' mansion. Everybody said the mansion was haunted. He said the things they did were really spooky. They even tried to communicate with dead people. The boys were even involved with doing other illegal things."

"Really?" Megan was stunned. "My family always told me to stay away from trying to communicate with dead people, supernatural spirits, and creepy ghost games asking it all kinds of questions. You're asking for trouble."

"Yeah. They're right!" Mark replied.

"It's so weird," Megan blurted.

"Carl said after they started doing all those creepy things, they heard strange noises in the house including footsteps. Doors that were closed when they had arrived were opened, and doors that were opened were closed. Some of the kids thought it was fun, but he was reluctant to go back any more."

"That's scary. Do you think the games are in the attic?" she said, concerned that they were still in the house.

"Sure, because he said they hid them in the ceiling," Mark replied. "There were several games because they had stolen them."

"It still doesn't make sense, Mark. Nobody in our house had been using those games. We didn't even know they were there in the attic."

"I don't know about that, but somebody needs to find them, burn them or throw them in the garbage. Just get that stuff out of the house," Mark replied feeling strongly about it.

She imagined how eerie it would feel to be in the house now. What Mark had just said sent chills throughout Megan's entire body and her hands were cold.

"Mom doesn't own the house any more but I should probably tell the new owner, whoever that may be."

"That's a good idea," he blurted. "I wouldn't want to move in there unless somebody destroyed them."

"You're right. My family always told me there were guardian angels in this world who took care of people. There were also evil spirits too so don't do anything that would encourage them," Megan replied.

"What if somebody starts playing with them again?" he asked.

"That wouldn't be good at all," she said and shrugged, "but I don't believe there is anything I can do about it now."

"Probably not but think about it. I have to go. Let me know if you need anything else, Meg."

"Thanks, Mark. I appreciate it." She hugged him.

"That's what friends are for. I'll talk to you later."

Megan thought it was strange. She still couldn't figure out why all the creepy and scary things started happening within the past year. They had lived in the house for many years, with no problems.

Her inner feelings told her it just didn't make sense. It just didn't feel right. *There must be something that Mark missed in his research about the house, but what?*

CHAPTER 27

THE CAMPUS

After recovering from the shock of the Orange Street house being foreclosed, Megan put her energy into concentrating on her job and college courses. When she arrived home from work, she quickly prepared something to eat before leaving. She was in a rush, arrived on campus five minutes early, and quickly walked to the classroom. She was almost out of breath.

"I hate being late to anything," she mumbled.

This was the first day of one of the last courses she needed to graduate from college. She was usually nervous until she had the opportunity to get acquainted with the professors and know their expectations.

Megan entered the classroom, grabbed a chair and sat down at the desk near the front of the class. Sitting near the front of the classroom made it easier to participate in the class discussions. Students were moving chairs and rustling papers behind her. Several of the students were getting acquainted and talking when the professor walked into the classroom.

Megan glanced up at him for a moment while he was standing there in front of the classroom. She was stunned. Her heart started to sink to her stomach because she couldn't believe who had just walked into the classroom. It was Nathan from across the street and her heart started beating fast. She slid down in her chair and put on her old reading glasses, trying to disguise her face. His grey suede blazer and light-blue shirt fit perfectly on his tall six-foot physique and matched his navy-blue trousers, pleated, and neatly creased.

Uncertain what to do next, she let her hair down and it fell loosely covering part of her face. She felt awkward not knowing he was a college professor. Megan looked down at her book and held it up in front of her to partially hide her face. Luckily, he didn't look directly at her, so she was hoping he didn't recognize her.

He introduced himself to the students as Professor Nathan Engel, and all the while she had one hand holding her book in front of her as her other hand quickly fumbled through the college course schedule. Nathan told the students he was teaching and working on his Ph.D. degree.

There it was in clear print: N. Engel listed as the professor for the course. Megan didn't even know Nathan's last name and had no idea she was enrolling in his class. Feeling uneasy about the entire situation, she started wondering what to do next. She had a hard time listening to what he initially said to the students.

Nathan continued talking and delivered an in-depth overview of the course. He then proceeded to discuss the course syllabus in detail. He was calm and articulate. Megan was captivated by his narrative and his beautiful brown eyes, perfectly shaped nose, thin, firm mouth, and smooth cheeks. His body was sculpted with muscular perfection.

Her mind was in a whirlwind. She would search for another class to take and withdraw from this one. That's it. She had a perfect solution and it put her mind at ease. Tomorrow, she'll go to the college admissions office and enroll in another course.

When class ended, she started walking quickly toward the door. Some of the other students in front of her were in her way, slowing her down. She wanted to run out the door but knew that would be too obvious. Just then Nathan walked up from behind her.

"Hi, Megan. It's nice to see you."

She turned, looked at him, and said, "Hi," sheepishly.

"I noticed your name listed on my student class roster."

"What?" she replied.

"The list of students enrolled in my class." He was amused.

"Oh," she mumbled.

She didn't realize he had known the names of his students even before the class started. How silly of her to not have known Nathan knew she was sitting there all the time. Megan blushed at the same time grasping for words to say. But the right words just couldn't come out of her mouth.

She was tongue tied and stuttered a little, but finally managed to say something. "I think I enrolled in the wrong course. I have to check with the admissions office tomorrow."

"Oh, really," Nathan said with a confident smile and a raised eyebrow. "I was looking forward to you participating in some of the class discussions with the other students. I think you'll enjoy the class."

"Oh. I guess I won't be doing that," she said with a sheepish smile.

"That's disappointing."

"I have to go now and take care of John's dog." She was lost for words, so she turned and rushed toward the door.

"Bye," Nathan said, watching her leave.

She was wondering why she said such a foolish thing to Nathan. John hadn't asked her to take care of his dog. She was just nervous, and it was the first thing she thought of.

When she arrived home, she immediately turned on her computer and tried to find another class she could take, but she couldn't find one. After searching and searching, she discovered all of the other classes were full.

"Okay, calm down," she whispered to herself.

She had a plan. She would go to the college admissions office tomorrow to see what they could do for her. There was nothing else she could do tonight, and, besides, she was exhausted, and it was getting late. It had been a long day, and she would be able take care of everything tomorrow.

The next day after work, Megan drove to the campus and talked to Mrs. Clark in admissions.

"Megan, all the classes you need to complete your degree are full," Mrs. Clark said. "But you can go to a class and sit in the class sessions if you get permission from the professor. If another student drops out of the course, then the professor can add you to the class roster."

"I don't want to risk not getting into the class if someone didn't drop out of the course," she said.

"That certainly would be a risk," Mrs. Clark replied.

"Thanks anyway, Mrs. Clark."

"I think you've made a wise decision," Mrs. Clark replied.

Megan was eager to finish college. This was one of the last courses she needed for graduation. *What am I going to do?* Megan didn't want to stay in Nathan's class as one of his students, but she had no choice.

The next day, John asked Megan if she could take his dog for walks because he wasn't feeling well. She agreed to take him on short evening walks around the block so as to avoid running into Nathan. He normally walked his dog in the nearby park.

The following afternoon, Megan had to build up her courage to go back to her evening class. She got a tingling feeling in her stomach, nervous about it. How was she going to do this? She just had to work on not showing any attraction toward him. She planned not to look at him directly in the face unless he spoke to her, and when she wasn't being addressed, she'd look down at her textbook. Yes, that's what she'd do. She had it all figured out.

She sat in the back of the classroom. Nathan frequently called students for class discussions, but rarely did he call on her because she was hidden at the back behind her textbook. It took all of her effort to focus on the subject matter and the class discussions instead of Nathan. She found it hard to do considering he was standing there right in front of the room. Later in the evening, before the class ended, Nathan told the students he didn't want them reading their textbooks while he was lecturing. He was talking about Megan but was trying to be professional about it.

There were times when Megan would come back from class break and sit down, and he would glance at her as she settled behind her desk. She wore a business suit to work with a fitted knit top and a skirt. She didn't have enough time to change clothes before class started. Sometimes, she could feel him glancing in her direction, but he tried not to be obvious.

On Tuesday evening during class, Nathan kept asking Megan to respond to the discussion questions when nobody else would raise their hand. The class was almost over, and Megan was tired and annoyed.

He called on her again.

"I'll pass," she said.

"What?" he replied.

"I'll pass."

"You can't say 'I'll pass' when I call your name," he said firmly.

"But I'll pass anyway and not comment," she said.

"Why?"

"Because nobody else is participating in this class discussion."

There was complete silence in the classroom. She could even hear a fly buzzing against the window trying to get outside. She was uncomfortable, didn't like the silence, and could see the tense look on his face. Nathan was staring at her. He had been calling on her too much because she was such a good student. But he couldn't let her say something like that to him in front of all the students. He needed to maintain control of his class.

He looked directly at the students. "I want all of you to read the last ten pages of the textbook chapter again in addition to your next week's assignment. Next week come prepared for further discussions. Anyone who responds with, 'I'll pass' will have points taken off their grade." Then he said in a firm voice, "Megan, I would like to see you after class."

Oh, no! Now what? She imagined he was really ticked off and she was uncomfortable about it. When the class ended, Megan walked to the front of the classroom. She felt uneasy like she was in high school, again.

"Have a seat," he said and wasn't smiling like his usual self.

She sat down in the chair next to his desk. She looked down and started picking the polish off of her fingernails.

Before Nathan said anything, Megan frowned and said softly, "I'm sorry about what I said during class. I'm really tired and was annoyed with the other students not participating."

He looked directly at her. "Well, I do accept your apology."

The scent of his cologne surrounded the air and was both masculine and sexy.

Then he firmly said, "Never say 'I'll pass' again."

"What?"

"Megan, I have to treat you the same as I treat the other students."

"What do you mean?"

"You're my neighbor and, and…" Nathan was lost for words. He didn't want to tell Megan he was really attracted to her.

"Okay," she replied not waiting for him to give her an answer. She didn't know what else to say. "Can I leave now?" She was upset with him.

"Yes, of course you can," he replied with a cordial expression. She turned and quickly walked back to her desk and gathered her belongings. She quietly walked out the classroom door feeling frustrated.

"What's with him? Is he being cranky or what?" she mumbled to herself.

The next day, her mind was full of Nathan scolding her after class like she was in high school. She was a mature, responsible adult and didn't appreciate what he said to her. At least he didn't do it in front of the other students.

The following week, Megan had lunch with Ashley and Heather. She decided to bring up her concerns about Nathan.

"Ever since I've been one of Nathan's students, he's friendly but keeps his distance and still hasn't officially asked me to go out with him. Not even dog walking or hiking at Fairmont Park. It's really difficult being in his class. Everything feels so awkward."

"Really?" Ashley replied.

"The entire situation is just driving me crazy," Megan said and cleared her throat. "I'm really having a quarter-life crisis. I considered my options and decided what to do."

"So, what are you going to do?" Heather asked.

"I'll just talk to him after class next week and tell him I don't really want to be in his class, but I don't have a choice."

"Are you crazy?" Ashley said in a loud voice. "Wait a minute! Nobody in their right mind would tell a professor who you have never dated but like, and someone who grades your papers, you don't want to be in his class."

Heather said, "Calm down, Megan. I think there's some kind of policy professors can't date students. I had an old boyfriend who's a professor in San Francisco."

"Heather, you have old boyfriends everywhere," Ashley said, and smiled. Heather ignored her comment.

"I don't know anything about that," Megan replied. "Maybe that's why he hasn't asked me out after all this time. In the past, he had just mentioned it casually."

"Of course, that's why. He probably found out a while back that you're a student at the college and he can't date you. He has to keep his distance or get fired," Ashley replied.

"Well, it does make sense," Megan said.

"Take my word for it. If he's smart, he won't get involved with you as a student at the same college where he's teaching," Ashley said.

"Did you ever tell him you were a student there?" asked Heather.

"No, I didn't, and I didn't know he was a college professor."

"Well, then. He was probably as stunned as you were when he found out. Thank goodness this is one of your last college courses," Ashley said. "I think he likes you."

"Yeah, he probably has dreams about you." Heather laughed.

"Yeah, now he has an image of your long legs and body fixed in his mind." Ashley smiled.

"Okay, you two. You're not helping me at all. Let's change the topic to something else," Megan replied, blushing.

During the next few weeks, Megan attended several more classes. It was getting near the end of the school term. She became more relaxed around Nathan but still had a strong attraction toward him.

On Friday evening, she sat home relaxing when her phone buzzed on the table. She reached over and picked it up. There was a text message from Travis. Why was Travis texting her? She was trying to forget about him.

The message said, 'I miss you and think about you often. We should spend some time together.' She swallowed hard and began to struggle with her feelings for him.

She hesitated for a moment and had flashbacks and memories of him being with the other woman. She didn't know why he wanted to see her again. Maybe he had gotten tired of his old girlfriend, or she found someone else?

Megan felt she could never trust him again. She replied to his text message, 'I don't know Travis. You're the one who didn't call me. I don't understand you.'

She knew her life would be even more complicated if she got involved with him again, but she was feeling lonely, and couldn't help but text him back.

He replied, 'I know I made some mistakes and I'm really sorry. I miss you and was wondering if we could go out to dinner and talk.'

Deep down inside, she knew what he did was not a mistake. Mistakes are accidents. What he did was not an accident. It was intentional. It was bad judgement he probably regretted.

Megan had fond memories of Travis, but now she had an overwhelming attraction to Nathan too. She remembered how good he looked in his clothes on his tall, handsome body, and the way Nathan talked and the way he walked. Her head was spinning, and everything was so confusing.

Nathan hadn't even asked her out on a date. Megan thought maybe it was because she was his neighbor and his student. There was the possibility he wasn't even seriously interested in her at all. Perhaps he liked Sasha? After all, he did go to her dinner party. Why would he go to her dinner parties if he didn't like her?

Megan's mind was in a whirlwind. Maybe she'd be just another conquest for Nathan and was just deluding herself. Too many feelings were going through her head. Her future with Nathan was uncertain. They had no history together.

She sent a text message back to Travis. 'I have to think about it. I'll let you know.' She wanted him to feel what it was like to wait for an answer.

'Okay, just don't take too long,' he replied.

Life was stressful enough without Travis coming back into her life. Was he a changed person? Was their relationship just a game? She started to wonder if it was possible to be deeply attracted to two men at the same time.

Then her thoughts were about Nathan and how he often glanced at her in class. She could sense him looking in her direction and tried not to be obvious. There was a sensual, sexy look in his eyes like he was scanning all over her entire body. She got an intense feeling of heat all over like she had never experienced before.

She tried to imagine what it would be like for Nathan to embrace her, to hold her in his arms, and to kiss her passionately. She imagined it was the most wonderful kiss she had never had. *This is what it's like when a girl gets carried away*, she admitted.

CHAPTER 28

THE CALIFORNIA FREEWAYS

On Tuesday Megan and two of her co-workers had to work overtime. It was seven p.m. when she left the office and headed home. The Santa Ana winds scattered leaves everywhere, bringing a chill to the night air. Her cell phone buzzed briefly telling her the battery was dying. She picked it up and plugged it into the car charger.

After driving a few minutes on the freeway, her car started to make a strange noise. The car's motor started to slow down, and she pulled over to the side of the road. She took out her cell phone from her handbag to call for roadside assistance, but her phone's battery was dead.

The freeway exit ramp was about one mile ahead, so she got out of the car and started walking. She had high heel shoes on and found it difficult to walk. She kept stumbling on the rocks along the side of the highway. On the freeway the cars were going by fast and the car lights were bright, illuminating the entire California interstate roadways. She just wanted to hurry and get to the exit.

As she was walking a handsome guy in a silver SUV stopped. "Come on and get in. I'll give you a ride."

She studied him for a moment and was hesitant to get in his vehicle. He could be a mass murderer. Maybe he was some kind of criminal? He was handsome, but it was hard to trust handsome men. All kinds of crazy thoughts were running through her mind.

She said, "No thank you. I don't have far to walk," and kept walking.

Five minutes later, another car stopped, and a thirty-something woman asked Megan if she wanted a ride. She was dressed in all black with long jet-black hair and black lipstick and had long black, manicured fingernails, and showed a lot of cleavage. She looked like Elvira, the hostess of the old horror movies on television. Megan wondered if she was going to a costume party or if she was just weird.

Megan smiled. "No thanks. I just have to walk a little way to the exit."

Three minutes later another car stopped. It was a friendly, elderly lady with four dogs. One dog was a German shepherd, another dog was a Chihuahua mix, and the two other dogs were mixed boxers. The German shepherd barked at Megan the entire time the lady was trying to talk. The Chihuahua was showing his teeth and growling, and the two boxer dogs were drooling all over the car.

Megan was not fond of drooling dogs. The car windows were smudged with dog slobber. The car's interior was disgusting, filled with dog blankets and magazines.

"Thank you. I'll be fine. I don't have to walk far," she said to the elderly lady, trying to show she appreciated her offer.

She finally reached the freeway exit ramp and could see a gas station with a small store inside for buying drinks and snacks. Thank goodness! She began to feel better the closer she got. As she got closer and closer, she noticed the attendant was turning out the lights.

"Oh no, wait!" she shouted. She started running because she had to make a phone call to get help. It was dark and she didn't want to be on some dark street alone.

She was waving at the attendant from a distance with one hand in the air and shouting, "Don't close up! Please don't close up!" She was stumbling and running with her heels on and almost fell down. She took her shoes off and started running barefoot on the sidewalk and the pavement. The small rocks hurt her feet and they were getting dirty and gritty.

The attendant saw her running and was staring at her. He couldn't hear what she was shouting. He watched her. When she got closer, he asked, "Everything okay?"

"My car broke down, my cell phone isn't charged, and I need to call someone to come help me."

"You should really keep your phone charged," he said.

"I know, I know."

He handed her his phone through the open cashier's window. She called Heather and asked her to come and get her.

"Thanks so much," she said to the attendant.

"You're welcome."

"Can I buy a bottle of water and a chocolate candy bar?"

"Sure. Which kind of candy bar do you want?"

"Any kind of candy just as long as it's chocolate. I don't care," she said.

He handed her the bottled water and candy bar, and she paid him. He closed the cashier window, worked on putting things away, and arranged items on the shelves while Megan waited.

"Hurry up, Heather," she whispered to herself while standing outside the front door of the gas station. She didn't want to be there all by herself after the attendant left.

She sat down on the concrete curb in front of the door and started drinking from her bottle of water and eating her chocolate candy bar—comfort food. She was enjoying every bit of it. She deserved it after everything she had been through.

"I would stay but I have to leave. I'm going to another job," he said. "Are you going to be all right?"

"Yes, my friend is on her way and should be here shortly," she replied.

The gas station attendant walked to his car. Megan was apprehensive about him leaving but there wasn't anything she could do. He got in his car and soon drove away.

Her heart was thudding in her chest as she glanced into the darkness, making sure nobody was there. She was afraid.

Five minutes later a deputy sheriff's patrol car drove by the station. He quickly made a U-turn and came back, then he pulled his car near the front entrance of the station, drove up next to her and rolled down his window. She was shocked because it was Travis. She heard he was helping out because of the shortage of deputies.

"Megan, what's going on?" he asked.

"My car broke down on the freeway. I had to walk here to call for help."

"What happened to your cell phone?"

"It needs charging."

"You need to keep it charged."

"I know, I know," she said, exasperated.

"Get in my car. You can use my cell phone to call roadside service."

"No thanks," she replied.

"Don't be silly. You can't stay here all by yourself," he said in a commanding tone.

"I'm not going anywhere with you, Travis."

"Well, I'm not leaving you here alone," he said. "Anything could happen to you."

"I'd rather get kidnapped than ride with you."

"Okay, have it your way," he replied. "Let me see some form of identification."

"What? Are you kidding me?"

"You heard me."

"Don't be ridiculous! You know who I am, Travis." Megan was beyond frustrated with him.

"Do you have a driver's license?"

"What?"

"Do you have a driver's license?" he asked again.

"Of course, I have one! You know I do."

"Then let me see it," he said.

"This is crazy!" Megan responded and started looking through her handbag.

He leaned over next to her. "I could arrest you and take you to the sheriff's station for not cooperating with an officer."

"You wouldn't," she replied.

"I would," Travis said. "Just watch me. I can't leave you here all by yourself at night."

"I'm not going anywhere with you!"

Just then she looked up and saw the headlights of an approaching car pulling into the gas station. It was Heather turning into the lot.

"Megan…"

"Don't text me ever again!" she said firmly to him and ran, got into Heather's car and they soon drove away as he watched her. Megan was so glad to see her and let out a deep sigh of relief.

"You don't know how glad I am to see you, Heather." She grabbed her, put her arms around her and gave her a big hug.

"You should keep your cell phone charged."

"I know, I know. Why does everybody keep saying that!"

"You look a mess. Why are your shoes off?" Heather asked.

"It's a long story."

"I can only imagine."

"You should have seen some of the people on the freeway who offered me a ride. It was scary."

"Well, probably not as scary as some of the passengers on my flights." Heather laughed. "So, you refused help from Travis?"

"Yeah, I did. You were already coming to get me, and I really didn't want anything to do with him," Megan said. "Let me use your phone. I have to call roadside service."

"Sure." Heather handed her the phone.

Heather took Megan back to her car and they waited a few minutes for the serviceman to arrive. He towed Megan's car to her mechanic's parking lot in the business district near town.

Heather dropped Megan off in the front courtyard because she was in her bare feet and went to park the car. Megan got out of the car and started walking toward her front door. Just then Nathan startled her because he walked up behind her with his dog.

"Megan, what happened to you?" Nathan asked.

Oh no! Her hair was flyaway, her bare feet were dirty and black from walking on the pavement, her clothes were wrinkled, and she had pieces of chocolate candy all over the front of her white blouse.

"My car broke down and Heather had to pick me up," Megan replied.

"I'm sorry," Nathan said. "It looks like you need to clean up."

"Well, that's obvious," she said with a forced smile feeling embarrassed.

"Can I be of any help?"

"No. I'm fine," she replied.

"I hope you have a better day tomorrow."

"I hope so too," she said.

Nathan said bye to Megan and continued walking his dog. She was embarrassed seeing him, but she was tired, so she pushed it from her mind. She opened the door to her apartment, walked directly to the bathroom and took a long, hot bath, and almost fell asleep in the tub.

The following day, Megan received good news from the sheriff's department. The suspect in the Johnson case had a history of criminal charges and theft on his police record. He had an arrest record for slashing tires of witnesses. They didn't know whether he was responsible for her slashed tire, but Megan was sure he did.

The detective said an older man, one of her neighbors, was able to positively identify the suspect. His testimony played a major role in his conviction. The suspect had been sentenced to time in prison, and while they weren't able to recover Mrs. Johnson's stolen money and jewelry, they did find her precious diamond wedding ring at a pawn shop.

CHAPTER 29

IF WALLS COULD TALK

Megan was resting, taking a break from cleaning before starting on her homework assignment. Her phone buzzed.

"Hey, Meg. Guess what?"

"Hi, Mark. Let's not play the guessing game." She laughed. "I'd never come up with the right answer anyway."

"Yeah, that's true." He chuckled. "I've got some more information about the Orange Street house."

"You do?" She wasn't anxious to hear what he had to say but listened anyway.

"The company where Austin works bought the house and sold it for a large profit."

"That's no surprise." She frowned and her lips tightened. "My mom loved that house. She and my dad put so much love and time into renovating it."

"Yeah, I know but that's not all."

"There's more?" Megan asked with a puzzled look on her face.

"Yes. The people living there heard strange sounds at night. They wanted their money back and contemplated moving out of the house. So, Austin tried everything to get rid of the noise. He had the water heater replaced because they thought it was causing all the bubbling and popping noise. They still kept hearing things. Then a pest control inspector Austin hired discovered a couple of small animals and a few mice in the attic, so he had the guy set traps. In fact, the inspector said Austin went with him to the attic. Things were quiet for a while then the noise started again."

"Wow! That's creepy, Mark."

"Strange, huh? There was no explanation for the loud banging noise or the opened doors. Then one day the homeowners searched the attic. Guess what?

"What?" she replied.

"They found your Uncle Ray up there in his sleeping bag."

"What?" Megan was shocked. "My uncle? I told him he couldn't do that any more. I even had the locks changed."

"I know but the family claimed when nobody was home, your uncle would sometimes go downstairs, leave the doors open, and take food from their kitchen."

"Really?"

"Your Uncle Ray swore that he had never gone down the stairs and had never taken their food, but the police didn't believe him."

"Poor Uncle. He's not a violent man, just a little confused at times. What did they do to him?"

"Listen. He was arrested, released, and then went to live in a group home. They knew he needed help. Hopefully, he'll stay there for a while."

"Yes, it'll probably be good for him. I'll go see him tomorrow. Do you have the address?"

"Good idea. Yes, I'll text it to you."

"Thanks, Mark. You're a great friend. I don't know what I'd do without you."

"I know. Everybody tells me that." He laughed.

Megan was totally mystified. She didn't waste any time and went to see her uncle the following day.

Uncle Ray was glad to see her, gave her a big hug, and said he was getting good care where he was living. They talked for a long time. She learned he had been occasionally sleeping in the attic for months even when Megan and her mother lived in the house. He had found several eerie ghost games in the attic ceiling. He played with the games when he went to the house to sleep. He asked questions and someone or something answered him. He had gotten obsessed playing with them.

He was alone and was addicted to playing them, almost like a gambler in a Las Vegas casino. Then he started hearing strange noises in the house afterwards. It was creepy and scary. Her uncle said he had never gone downstairs and had never taken any food from the kitchen. Megan believed him.

Megan recalled in her mind everything that happened in the house. If it wasn't her uncle then who was actually leaving the hallway doors open and taking their food? Who was making the banging noise? Could it have been evil spirits? *Is the Orange Street house haunted?*

It all made sense now. Megan was sure Uncle Ray was contributing to whatever was happening in the attic. He was inviting ghosts into the house playing supernatural games. The games needed to be thrown away and hauled off by the garbage truck or even burned.

The following week, Megan called Austin and told him she had some information about the house that would benefit the new owners. But he told her he didn't want to hear anything from Megan or her mom.

"Your mom doesn't own the Orange Street house anymore. Have you forgotten? It's none of your business. So don't bother calling to discuss anything about it," he replied.

Megan was stunned by his response. He was rude and acted like he had been insulted. She tried to talk to him, but he hung up the phone.

As far as Megan was concerned, anything that happened with the Orange Street house was not her problem. There was nothing she could do.

Nearly one month had passed and Megan was absorbed with work and school. She didn't have many thoughts about her mom's old house anymore until Mark showed up. He knocked on her door, sat down on the sofa, leaned back and had made himself comfortable like always.

"Hey, Meg. I've being doing some more investigating and guess what?"

"All right, Mark." She laughed. "You know I don't like to guess. I wouldn't have given you the right answer. You know that."

"It' about the Orange Street house." He was serious and wasn't smiling.

"To tell you the truth, I really don't care any more." She shrugged her shoulders, glanced at the table, and picked up her soda. "My mom and I have moved on with our lives. That was in the past."

"Yeah, I agree but this is something you should know."

"Okay. Tell me anyway." Megan laughed. "You won't be happy until you do."

"You know me really well, don't you?" he said, and he smiled.

"Sure, I do. We've been friends for a long time."

"I found out the owners of the house moved out and were able to get their money back. They said the house was haunted," he blurted.

"Haunted?" Megan was stunned. "I know there were some weird things going on, but they really thought it was haunted like in those ghost movies?"

"Yes, and the investment company Austin works for is looking for a new buyer for the house but hasn't been able to find anybody," Mark said.

"That's unfortunate. But since my mom doesn't own the house, I could care less about what Austin did or didn't do." She frowned and wiped her forehead with the back of her hand.

"I don't blame you, but you need to know this. The family who was living there said they would sometimes see a ghostly figure of a boy, a teenage boy walking down the hallway at night opening the doors. It was like he was trying to find a way out of the house. They once saw the figure of a man standing in the hallway. Other times they heard footsteps in the attic, banging noise, and scratching sounds."

"That's creepy. So, all the strange noises and things happening weren't my imagination?" Megan asked.

"No, I don't think so. I went back and talked to Carl, the guy who was part of the group of teens that would go to the house to smoke, drink, and play all those creepy games. I told him that none of it made sense to me, the weird things happening in the house. There was no crime committed and nobody died there. Then he made a startling confession!"

"What? What was it, Mark?" Megan's eyes widened with anticipation.

"Way back during that time, Carl was going to meet one of the other boys at the house in the late afternoon to drink beer and just hang out. His dad told him he couldn't go out because he had gotten into a disagreement with his mom. He was being punished so he couldn't go meet the other boy. Carl's parents also told him he couldn't use the phone."

"They did?" She gasped. "What happened?"

"He was sure the other teen went to the house all by himself and was waiting for him to arrive. But Carl never went there because he was being punished."

"What was the other teenager's name?" Megan asked.

"His name was Eric."

"Okay, so what?"

"Things got worse," Mark said.

"What do you mean?" she asked.

"The boy just vanished, disappeared. Nobody had ever seen him again."

"Wow! Really sad. That's a parent's worst nightmare. I can only imagine how horrible they must have felt. What did they think happened to him?"

"Nobody knows but Carl thought it had something to do with all the ghostly games they played at the house and when they tried to communicate with dead people. Something haunting was going on. The teen was a problem and was always getting into trouble with the law. But the police thought that he just ran away from home, but his friends didn't think so."

"That's terrible," Megan replied.

"Carl said he felt guilty for not telling his parents that he was going to meet his friend at the Orange Street house. He had regretted it after all these years."

"That's unfortunate," Megan replied as she walked toward the window and glanced outside.

"Yeah. If Austin would have listened to you, they could have searched for all those creepy games hidden in the attic and trashed them. They needed to get them out of the house. No telling what else they might have found," Mark said firmly.

She turned her head and stared straight into his eyes. "What do you mean?"

"Carl said when the boy disappeared, nobody searched the attic walls. Who knows what's up there? He thinks the boy is buried in the walls or something."

"It's worse than I imagined," Megan replied.

"Carl said, maybe the ghost of the boy was making all that noise and opening the doors because something was after him and he couldn't find his way out of the house. Perhaps he's trying to tell people he was buried in the walls."

"Mark, I think Carl's imagination is getting carried away." She didn't believe him, but chills went throughout her body not knowing what the police did or didn't do when they investigated the boy's disappearance.

"Austin should have listened to what you had to tell him," Mark blurted.

"You're right but he didn't want to talk to me because my mom didn't sell the house to him. He had to wait until after it was foreclosed and put up for sale."

"I know but Austin's boss still got the house at a low price, sold it, and initially made a large profit," Mark said as he cleared his throat.

"Well, the entire situation with the house is not my problem." Megan was angry. "I wonder how many other people got caught up in their deception of trying to buy the houses for little to nothing. He deserves whatever happens to the house."

"Probably hundreds, Meg, but there's more."

"There's more?" She turned and looked straight at him again.

"Yes. I haven't finished telling you everything."

"Okay, go ahead and tell me," she replied. "Mom doesn't own the house any more but I'm curious as to what happened."

He was silent for a few moments, then said, "When the house was vacant, somehow it caught fire last week, and it actually burned most of the structure down."

"What?" Her eyes widened and she sat down on the chair. For a split second she thought he was joking. "I can't believe it! Are you serious?"

"Yes, it's true," Mark said, and his lips tightened. "Didn't you see the news?"

"No, I guess I was too busy working and studying to watch the news. I avoid driving past our old neighborhood on purpose. It still hurts a little to see it." She got up again and stared out the window for a moment.

"Yeah. The house burned down. Not much left but a shell of a house with smoldering wood, brick and ash. The police didn't find any human remains in the burned wood and ash Nobody will ever know what happened to the missing boy now."

She turned toward Mark. "That's really unfortunate. Does the teen's parents still live in town?" Megan said while frowning.

"Yes, they're still in the same house they lived in when their son disappeared."

Even though she felt bad for the boy, she refrained from expressing her feelings about the house burning down. It wasn't her mom's house any more.

She opened the window to let in a little fresh air. "What caused the fire?"

"They don't know but there's a rumor going around the neighborhood the house was haunted so it was difficult for Austin to get anyone to buy it. A few people thought he started the fire. The insurance would cover the cost of building a new house if it burned down," Mark replied.

She shook her head in disbelief. "It doesn't surprise me. Some people will go to any extreme to make a lot of money."

"You're right but there's no proof he did it or had someone do it. Not sure what's going to happen until the insurance company completes their investigation."

"I don't care what happens to the house or Austin," Megan replied, still angry with Austin for having deceived her mom and many other people.

"I know. He's not a good person."

Megan walked back to the chair and sat down. "Wouldn't it be wonderful if walls could talk? What secrets would they reveal? I wish that I could command the walls to speak to me. Tell me everything they know. Tell me the happiness, the dreams, the secrets, the heartbreak, and the ugly. Just like in a story book."

Mark was puzzled by what she had just said. "If walls could talk, we would be able to solve most of the crimes in the world but that's not gonna to happen. You're just dreaming."

She smiled. "Thanks, Mark. I appreciate everything you've done trying to find out the history of the house. I owe you one."

"Sure. Let me know when you want to go biking. You need to do something relaxing."

"Okay, I'll think about it."

"Gotta go now, I'll talk to you later." He hugged her and walked out of the door.

Megan sat down on the sofa, totally stunned by what Mark had told her. She carefully thought about everything for a long time. She didn't know if the house was haunted, if the boy had died there or was a runaway, if he was buried in the walls, or if Austin hired someone to set the house on fire. As far as she was concerned, those ghostly games should have been destroyed a long time ago. Now, the house had burned down to the ground, and there was nothing left. None of it mattered to her any more. What really mattered were the pleasant memories of living in the Orange Street house that would stay with her forever, no matter where she went or where she lived. But Megan was still concerned the police had never found the whereabouts of the missing teen.

Late that evening, Megan got undressed and lay in bed. She closed her eyes and quiet thoughts were going around and around in her mind. The whispers in her head said something was not right. Her mind was filled with images of the missing teen. His parents must be suffering not knowing what happened to him. The teen was gone, just vanished. For any parent, it was a nightmare that never ends. She wished hard for him to be found.

The next day, Megan drove to the Orange Street house and stood there on the sidewalk for a long time staring at it. She had to see it for herself and could smell the burnt wood, a mix of electrical wires, plastic and everything else that was destroyed. It was an unpleasant odor.

Eventually, her feet had gotten tired of standing. She stepped back and leaned on her car thinking, *What do you say when someone's home has burned down? I'm so sorry. How can I help you?* All the while knowing, what was left of the house would be bulldozed, the land cleared, and the ground would become freshly plowed soil. It was like the house never existed, not even a place left behind. No longer would she be able to smile, raise her hand, point to the Orange Street house, and say to others, "See over there? That's the house where I grew up. It's the house my parents once owned." A tear ran down her cheek.

CHAPTER 30

THE TRIP TO NORTHERN CALIFORNIA

Megan arranged to fly to Sacramento. She planned on driving the twenty miles to Elk Grove to open Uncle Harry's safety deposit box. Megan wondered if he left gold or his diary for her. Her mother told her not to get her hopes up.

Aunt Ruth suggested Megan stay overnight at her house. She would drive her to the airport in the morning so she wouldn't have to worry about traffic and airport parking.

Megan packed her small carryon suitcase and drove to her aunt and uncle's home. The bedroom was crowded, so Megan put her suitcase on the floor, opened it up and took out her pajamas. She was tired and went to bed with thoughts about poor Uncle Harry and how nice he had always been to her. She was planning to stay overnight in Elk Grove and come home the next morning in time to go back to work.

She woke up early and took a warm shower and quickly got dressed. Then she threw her pajamas, toothbrush, and other belongings into her suitcase.

After arriving at the local airport near Shady Grove, she decided to get something to eat. Taking her seat at one of the tables in the restaurant, she ordered breakfast and a cup of coffee. She was almost finished eating when she glanced up and saw him. There was Travis with another woman, waiting to be seated at a table. His arms were around her and they were laughing and talking. Megan sat there motionless, staring in disbelief, and trying to absorb her disappointment. She put on sunglasses and raised the newspaper up in front of her face to partially hide it. She was still angry at him for the other night.

His actions validated her thoughts of him being a player, not serious about anyone. She had the urge to walk up to him and confront him about it, but she knew it was probably not a good idea. Who knew how he might respond?

When Travis and his lady friend were seated, Megan quickly searched her wallet and left the money for her breakfast on the table. She got up and walked in the other direction out of the restaurant to her departure gate. She didn't want to be seen.

After arriving in Sacramento, Megan picked up a rental car for the drive to her hotel. She unpacked, went to get a cup of coffee, and took the newspaper with her to read, enjoying the luxury of some free time. She barely had a moment to herself when she was at home.

In Elk Grove, it was finally time to find out what was in Uncle Harry's safety deposit box. Parking in the lot, Megan took a deep breath. Her heart was pounding, her palms sweaty. What was she going to find in the box? Whatever it was, it could change her life—all her problems could finally be over. Or perhaps it was just something that wouldn't make any real difference to her life, like a letter or some personal effects. Either way, she couldn't wait any longer to find out. Taking another deep breath, she headed into the bank, trying to stay calm.

Standing in front of the safety deposit box, she took a moment to clear her head and then carefully opened it up and looked inside. Surprisingly, there was only one thing in there: a sealed envelope.

What? No treasured book or diary? No savings bonds. I wonder what's in the envelope. How mysterious. She carefully took the envelope out of the box, noticed how light it was, then put it in her handbag. For the entirety of her drive back to the hotel her head was spinning about what it could contain.

Back in her room, she sank into the soft, overstuffed armchair. Taking off her shoes, she rested her bare feet on the ottoman. She told herself she was trying to get comfortable, but really, she was just delaying opening the envelope. Prolonging the anticipation. What was she going to find inside? Slowly, she peeled it open. There was a letter inside. She carefully unfolded it and started to read it out loud.

To my dearest niece, Megan,

Family has always been most important to me, ever since my childhood. We have always been a close family, keeping our business to ourselves, and never trusting others with our secrets. It's for that reason I have never trusted banks with my money. When I became a plumber and fulfilled my lifelong ambition of opening my own business, I decided to go there and then I would never trust anybody else to look after my hard-earned cash. I've led a happy, successful life, although I won't lie, there have been times I wished I had a wife and a family of my own to take care of and leave my money to when I am gone.

If you're reading this letter then I am no longer with you, but I want you to know Nina took the very best care of me while I was sick. It's for this reason I have left my house and belongings to her, apart from the set of bedroom furniture I know you will appreciate—she is a truly selfless woman who has done everything for me.

Of all my nieces and nephews, you were the only one who came to visit me a lot, and I always loved seeing you and your mom so much. I'm not sure if you knew this, but it was me who sent you the hundred-dollar bill for your birthday every year. You've always been my favorite, Megan!

I hope you will be as happy and successful in life as I have been, Megan. I have one more surprise for you—it's in the mattress.

Lots of love,
Your favorite Uncle Harry

Megan started to cry, and tears flowed down her cheeks recalling all the kind words her Uncle Harry had written. She was really going to miss him so much; the visits during the holidays and summer months, the talks on the phone, and all the little things he said and did. She was all choked up, so it took a few minutes for her to clear her mind.

"In the mattress?" she said aloud, suddenly excited. "What could be in the mattress?"

Megan was anxious to get back to Shady Grove and didn't want to share the information from the letter with anyone until she got home. For now, she was tired and started to get ready for bed, even though she knew she wouldn't sleep.

The next morning Megan boarded her plane back to Shady Grove. Aunt Ruth picked Megan up from the airport and she told her about the letter. Megan's mother and Aunt Ruth were curious, but they were sure Uncle Harry didn't leave any big treasure behind. Megan soon arrived at work but found it impossible to concentrate. All day long she couldn't stop her thoughts about what could be on the mattress.

CHAPTER 31

TIME TO CELEBRATE

When five p.m. finally came, Megan couldn't wait to get home. All day long she wanted to leave work early but couldn't. The workday seemed as if it would never end. She drove home as quickly as she could but there was more traffic than usual. Earlier in the day she'd called Ashley and asked her to come over to her place before she picked up Parker so they could see what was in the mattress together.

Ashley was already waiting for her when she got back home, and once inside they both slid the top mattress off the bed, unzipped the mattress cover, and started looking for openings or cuts in the fabric.

After searching for a while, Ashley said, "Forget this!"

She went to the kitchen, got a box cutter from the drawer, walked back into the bedroom, and started cutting and ripping the mattress apart.

"What are you doing, Ashley? You're destroying my mattress!"

"I'm helping you! You can always buy another mattress."

"Wait! If you keep ripping it open, what'll I sleep on?"

"On the sofa if you have to," Ashley replied. She started cutting more of the mattress to see if there was something inside. "This is just too exciting!"

"Easy for you to say," Megan replied.

"You worry too much."

After a few minutes of cutting and feeling around inside the mattress, Ashley suddenly withdrew her hand with a loud gasp and a shocked expression.

"What? What is it?" Megan asked, concerned. She was hoping there wasn't anything weird inside the mattress.

"You're not gonna believe this..." Ashley put her hand back inside the mattress. She smiled and withdrew it, clutching an inch high stack of one hundred-dollar bills bound together.

"What the..." Megan's mouth gaped open in shock.

They counted one hundred of them neatly wrapped.

"Wow!" Ashley replied.

"I can't believe it," Megan said, her eyes glowing with excitement.

"Let's see if there's more money!"

"Good idea."

This time Megan started digging around inside the mattress and found another stack of hundred-dollar bills. They started throwing the cotton from the mattress all over the bedroom and laughing, shredding the mattress even more. There was so much money they didn't even know how much was there.

"No wonder the furniture movers were complaining the mattress was bulky and heavy when they delivered it," Megan said and started laughing.

The bedroom was a disaster zone, but Megan didn't care. They were screaming, jumping, and laughing all the time, throwing around the money and the mattress stuffing.

"And to think I was considering giving the mattress away and buying another one. No wonder it's so uncomfortable!" Megan laughed.

"Thank goodness you didn't!" Ashley shouted.

"Imagine what I can do with all this money!"

"Where do you think your uncle got the money? Do you think it's drug money?" Ashley asked, suddenly serious.

"Of course not! Uncle Harry liked to gamble. Maybe he won some of the money? You know what this means, right? I can pay back Chris the money he sent Mom to pay the mortgage and help all of you out with some extra cash."

"I couldn't ask you to do that, Meg. But this is amazing!"

"I can help Mom, Aunt Ruth, and Uncle James!"

"I know! I know!" Ashley said, laughing and jumping up and down. "Isn't this great, Megan?"

"I can have a new storage shed built for Aunt and Uncle," Megan said.

"Yes!" Ashley shouted.

"And I can hire a dog trainer to train Nosey not to pee on my things. I can help you, Mark and Corey. I can buy Heather something nice."

Ashley smiled. "Yeah, but she already has everything."

They were still throwing the cotton from the mattress up in the air and all over the floor, laughing and shouting. They turned on their music and started dancing around like the Bollywood dancers in India, doing the steps they learned from watching *Slumdog Millionaire*.

Megan said loudly, "Who would have ever known Uncle Harry was putting all his money in a mattress instead of the bank. Let's call everyone and tell them what we found."

"Yes, let's do that!" Ashley said.

They called Heather but she didn't pick up, so they sent her a text message asking her to call back.

"Megan, call your mom, aunt and uncle!" Ashley shouted.

Megan called and Uncle James picked up the phone.

"Hi, Uncle James. We're rich!" Megan shouted.

"What!"

"We're rich?"

"You're sick?"

"No, we're rich?"

"You want Mitch?"

"No, we're rich."

"Mitch doesn't live here."

Just then Ashley grabbed the phone out of Megan's hand and shouted in a loud but slow voice, "Get! Aunt! Ruth!"

"Okay," he said.

They told Megan's mother and Aunt Ruth about the money in the mattress, and they couldn't believe it. They spent all night celebrating, putting the money in a suitcase trying to determine how much they had in total. The money was all of Uncle Harry's life savings over the years. They eventually found out everything hidden in the mattress totaled two hundred and fifty thousand dollars.

Megan had read about people stuffing money in mattresses, but she never gave much thought to it. She knew it was a dumb thing to do. What if the house caught on fire and the mattress burned up? What if she had given the mattress away? It made more sense to Megan to put money in the bank, but there were people out there who didn't trust banks, including her Uncle Harry.

Regardless, it had all worked out for her. She wasn't a millionaire but had more money than she ever had in her life.

Megan was busy the entire week. She sat down to relax and turned on the TV. Thirty minutes later her phone buzzed, and it was Mark.

"Are you watching the news? His voice was anxious.

"No, not really. Should I be?"

"Turn it on, you'll be shocked."

"Mark, I'm watching a movie." She sighed, was a bit annoyed, but after three seconds of silence said, "Okay, give me a minute."

She turned to the news channel and couldn't believe what the reporter had said. Her mouth dropped open.

"Did you hear that?" Mark blurted.

"I did." She was stunned as she stood there in front of the television.

"Yeah. Austin Mitchell was arrested for setting the Orange Street House on fire and for concealing a body. The police had been investigating him for a long time according to the detective who is one of my adjunct instructors at the college."

"Wow! That doesn't surprise me!" Megan replied.

"Yeah, they unearthed a body buried in the ground next to the house when they were digging through the rubble and ashes. The police used specially trained canines to help look for human remains. They identified the teeth and other DNA as being from the missing teen who was Carl's friend," Mark said and cleared his throat.

"A body? I'm watching the TV now. Wait a minute, let me make sure I fully understand all of this." Megan flopped down on the sofa still listening and said, "Austin admitted he went there to look at the vacant house several years ago. It was before he started working for the investment company."

"That was before your parents bought the house," Mark added.

"You're right."

"Austin told the police he went to inspect the house, the boy was there smoking marijuana and drinking, and saw him. He claimed the teen ran because he wasn't supposed to be there and fell down the stairs and died. Austin said the boy was drunk," Mark explained.

"Yes, I hear it too. Austin thought they would blame him for his death because he was once charged with assault and battery years ago. So, he panicked and buried him in the backyard near the steps so the neighbors couldn't see what he was doing. He concealed the teen's backpack and sweatshirt inside the wall in the attic. He removed part of the wall, sealed it up, and wallpapered over it," Megan replied. "But why would he do that if he was innocent?"

"I don't know but rumor is he isn't a good person, has a history of swindling a lot of people out of money, and has a shady past. Maybe his background is a lot more suspicious than we think. Maybe he murdered the boy."

"That's a horrible thought." Megan shuddered. "We know one thing for sure."

"What's that?" Mark asked.

"Austin has no empathy. It's eerie to think that boy was buried there all this time and he had known it," Megan said loudly.

"Yeah, you're right. I saw an earlier news report on TV today. The police said the house remained vacant for a long time until your dad and mom bought it. Austin found out from Anita your mom was having difficulty paying the monthly house payments. He wanted to buy it for the company he worked for so he could remove the body and bury it someplace else."

"That's probably why he got upset when my mom didn't make the full house payments and the mortgage company repossessed the house."

"Yes, that's true," Mark responded. "Another employee from the same company handled the purchase of your mom's house after it had been foreclosed. It was immediately put up for sale. Austin didn't have a chance to move the body, take the boy's belongings out of the attic wall, and repair it because people were coming and going looking at the house all the time.

"The people who bought the house were unhappy because they heard noise in the attic and heard the house was haunted, wanted their money back and moved out. Austin was worried so he volunteered to work on trying to resolve the noise issue, but it didn't help."

"Yes, I get it now. So, Austin's solution to the problem was to burn the house down, not realizing the police investigators would find the body and DNA to trace it back to the missing boy." Megan shook her head.

"You're right."

"He's something else," Megan replied feeling angry.

"Carl told me this morning the police detectives finished their investigation into the death of his missing friend Eric. They had recently interrogated Carl, and some of the other people who knew the teen, and the teen's parents.

"Did they think there was foul play?" Megan asked, as she pushed her hair away from her face.

"Well, the experts know why the teen died. He had a fatal injury to his head that could have come from a fall down the stairs or from a blow to the head. The forensic evidence was not conclusive as to how it happened."

"So, there wasn't any evidence to charge Austin with homicide or murder?" Megan asked.

"No, there wasn't any. It was a tragic end for the teen and sad for his parents to find out about their son years later. But do you know what was really strange?"

"What?" she said not knowing what to expect.

"Carl said, not even once did Austin apologize to the family for the death of their son or ever say he was sorry it happened. Carl thinks there was more to it than Austin confessed. Maybe he's a serial killer."

"My dear God. That's a terrible thought. Carl has a dramatic imagination. Nobody will ever know what really happened," Megan responded. "But he'll be going to prison for a long time for setting the Orange Street house on fire and for concealing the body. He's not a good person at all. Shady Grove is better off without him."

"I totally agree," Mark said and nodded his head approvingly.

"There's one more thing."

"What?" Mark replied.

"There's actually something good thing that came out of all this?"

"What's that?" he asked and swallowed hard.

"Austin is going to prison and the boy's parents now know the truth about what happened to their son."

"That's true. Think about all those years of them not knowing. They deserved an explanation. Now, they don't have to worry any more. I'm sure Carl is glad to know the truth too," Mark replied and sighed.

Megan walked to the kitchen with her cell phone and poured herself a glass of iced tea. She sat down next to the table still thinking about everything.

"You know what, Mark?

"What?"

"I do think houses can talk to people. That house was trying to tell me the teen was buried there," Megan said, "and something or someone was trying to uncover the secrets of the Orange Street house. Maybe it was an angel trying to bring closure to the boy's family."

"You're right. Strange things happen sometimes for a reason. All those years the parents didn't know if their son ran away, was kidnapped, or died mysteriously. Now, they have their son to grieve over and bury properly in a place they choose," Mark replied.

"The Orange Street house had secrets, just too many secrets. My mom was trying to keep the house for a long time, but it was time to move on," Megan added.

"Looks that way," Mark agreed. "The original owner's grandson died from the flu, and his parents moved out, and the house was vacant for a long time before it was sold to your parents. Strange things happened when the house was empty. A body was buried in the backyard. Your uncle was hiding in the attic, sleeping there, and playing with those creepy games

"Yeah, bizarre, isn't it?"

"What about the strange noise, opened doors, the eerie sound of footsteps, and the people who bought the house saying they had seen a teen ghost?" Mark asked.

"I don't know, Mark. I can't explain any of that stuff. I know people have their own ideas about ghosts and haunted houses. It is all so creepy, but I know the house was trying to tell me the truth. The truth is what really matters. How did this seemingly ordinary house become so bloody complicated anyway?" Megan asked, as she rubbed the back of her neck.

"That's a difficult question to answer," he replied.

"Well, I know one thing for sure."

"What's that?" Mark asked.

"I'm glad the house is no longer standing and is a pile of burnt wood and ash. There's more to life than trying to hold on to a house. Life can be full of disappointments, but it can also be full of sunshine. My life is full of more sunny days than rainy ones and I am grateful because of it."

"I totally agree with you, Megan. Let's try to keep it that way."

On Thursday, she got up early and her mind was going around and around thinking about everything. In the late afternoon, she was sitting in Dr. Sharma's office waiting for him to end his conversation on the phone with another patient, all the while feeling safe with him. He was more knowledgeable and understanding than her brother, Chris. They always talked about a lot of things, and he helped her to think about her options before she made her own decisions.

After he hung up the phone, she told him everything that had happened, about the Orange Street house and how it had been burned down, and Austin was arrested. He calmly listened to everything. Then they talked about her nightmares.

"Megan, we discussed this before about your nightmares being the result of fear and worries."

"Yes. I know Dr. Sharma. I was always having the same dream of being locked out of the house in the cold and I could see a dim light shining from the attic window. It took me a long time to figure out what my nightmares meant."

"Do you want to tell me about it? he said and leaned back in his chair.

"Yes, of course. I was afraid because of all the losses in my life; the loss of my dad, then the loss of Scott, Mrs. Emerson losing her home, some of the other neighbors losing their homes to foreclosure, my mom losing her job and us moving out of the house. We were threatened with being homeless and being cold and hungry. My nightmares felt so real, and I would wake up sweating. I was afraid of the unknown in the attic with all the strange sounds and creepy things that happened. The dim light shining in the attic represented the unknown."

"It's common for people to be afraid of a lot of things, including the unknown, Megan. We talked about it many times."

"Yes, we did, and it all made sense. Not knowing what was in the attic was frightening to me in addition to my losses. I watched a lot of scary movies with my brother about creatures from outer space and ghosts in the attic when I was growing up so that just added to my fears. I don't know if there were ghosts or not, but I do know the truth was finally revealed about the missing teenager."

"Yes, that was tragic and sad for the parents. You have gone through a lot over the years, learned a lot, have matured, and made many good decisions on your own. I'm proud of your progress. Let's hope the nightmares go away completely now," Dr. Sharma added.

"Thanks, Dr. Sharma. You've helped me a lot."

"I'm glad," he said, and smiled.

"But I don't think I'll be coming here as often any more."

"You won't?" he asked and studied her facial expressions for a moment.

"No."

"Well, that's your choice. You know that I'm always here if you need me."

"Thanks," she said. "I can always call your receptionist, if I ever need another appointment, right?"

"Yes, of course, Megan. That's fine."

She got up and thanked him, hugged him goodbye, and walked out the door. He watched her leave feeling good he had been able to help her when things were difficult but was hoping he would see her again, if she needed help. She was like the daughter he and his wife wished they could have had even though they were happy with their twin boys.

CHAPTER 32

GIRL TALK

On Monday at 5:30 p.m., Megan walked through the courtyard to her apartment. Feeling happy about her new wealth, she had already made plans now she'd inherited Uncle Harry's fortune. She had never had that much money in her entire life. It was going to be a wonderful day. Just then, she heard someone walking behind her. She glanced over her shoulder and saw Sasha.

"Hi, Megan."

"Hi, Sasha." Megan wondered if Sasha was finally trying to be friendly.

"I had a great dinner party last weekend with friends and Nathan came."

"That's nice."

"Everyone had a good time," Sasha said, being spiteful.

"Well, good for you." Megan was annoyed.

"I wouldn't get my hopes up too high if I were you," she said snobbishly. Her words cut through Megan like a knife.

"I don't know what you're talking about," Megan replied.

As she walked away, Megan noticed traces of bluish color visible on the side of Sasha's face. It appeared as if someone had slapped her.

Later in the day, Megan called Ashley. "Sasha should be in charge of an annual flirt festival. It's probably the only thing she'd be good at doing."

"Just ignore her," Ashley responded.

"I know I should but it's really hard because she is so... rude."

The same evening, Heather came home from a flight from New York. She asked both Megan and Ashley out to dinner. While they were at the restaurant, Heather said, "I heard some rumors about Sasha."

"What rumors? Ashley asked.

"Sasha used to be a wild party woman. She is just an unhappy person and doesn't have any real talents in life other than buying designer clothes and being rude."

"Seriously," Ashley muttered.

"What's more, Sasha was married to a man twenty years older. She likes to drink and spends most of her money shopping for clothes. After he died his two adult children inherited most of his money. They didn't want Sasha to get anything. They consider her to be a gold digger. She hired an attorney and had to fight them in court. She got some of the money anyway."

"I guess it's her problem. That's the life she chose for herself," Megan replied. "I don't like talking about her. Let's change the subject."

"Okay, fine with me," Heather said, realizing Megan was getting irritated.

They continued to talk about other things. Heather told both of them about her new love. His name was Roberto. He was from Madrid, Spain and looked a bit like a young Antonio Banderas. She told them about how romantic he was and how they planned on taking a trip to Spain together. He volunteered to be her personal tour guide, and she was going to meet his family.

Heather was always meeting someone new and usually ended the romance after a few months, but this time she said it was different. Megan and Ashley were happy for her, although Megan wished she could meet somebody too.

Ashley talked about her brother's friend, Steve, who she'd had a crush on for several years. They started to date a couple of months ago, but Ashley wanted to keep it a secret for a while. Steve had the same interests as Ashley and was a social worker, helping at the homeless shelters when he had the time. In fact, this week they were going to work at the homeless shelter together near his home and then going to see his parents in Sycamore Park just a few miles away.

"That's great, Ashley. And I'm happy for you, Heather."

"I know you hate this question, but how's your love life, Megan?" Heather asked.

"Don't ask. I'm not sure," Megan replied.

"Why?"

"I ran into Sasha the other day. I think she has an infatuation with Nathan. Maybe he likes her."

"Have you ever seen Nathan and Sasha together alone?" Heather asked.

"No, not really, but why would he go to her dinner parties?" Megan asked.

"I don't know for sure, but I think Sasha is probably a little envious of you."

"Why?"

'Why? Megan, you're pretty and smart. That's a good combination. You got promoted to a good job and will be graduating soon with a degree. All she has are her precious dinner parties and fancy designer clothes. And now you're rich!" she said, laughing. Megan still wasn't used to having all that money, so she didn't know what to say.

"Thanks a lot, but I'm not rich and you two are my friends. You see me differently than other people."

"I don't think so," Heather replied. "Just give it some time and things can change."

"Nathan isn't making any moves on me. I'm really attracted to him and find it difficult being around him."

"I think that part is difficult because he's your professor. He's got to be careful," Ashley said. "We've been over this!"

Megan wanted to tell Ashley and Heather that Travis had texted her again, but she didn't. Heather changed the subject, and they ordered dinner. They discussed how they would solve all the problems in the world in one evening.

The next morning at eleven a.m. an employee from the homeless shelter called Megan. The volunteer scheduled to work at the front desk was sick, so Megan was asked to cover for her. She showed up and had been there about an hour when Nathan walked in through the front entrance. She was happy to see him. Megan was wearing a skirt Heather bought her as a gift. It was a long, ankle length, multi-color crinkle skirt made in India with an elastic waist band. The wheels on her office chair legs rolled over the bottom part of her skirt, but she didn't notice.

"Hi, Nathan," she said, smiling as she stood up.

Just then the bottom of her skirt got caught under the bottom wheel of her chair, and as she stood up her skirt was pulled down to her knees.

"Hi, Megan," he replied.

Nathan stood there smiling and glancing at her hot pink panties with white lace trim, and her long, slender legs beneath. She could see Nathan's eyes sliding down her entire body. He was scanning her all over. He had a sensuous look about him.

Oh my goodness. This is the most embarrassing moment of my entire life! Blushing, she awkwardly reached down and grabbed her skirt, pulling it up.

To his credit, Nathan acted as if nothing had happened. He looked at her with a smile of amusement and raised one eyebrow. She stood there not knowing what to say. Suddenly, he stopped smiling and glanced down at his watch.

"Nice to see you, Megan. I'll see you later. I don't want to be late."

He walked toward the small office to talk to someone who was waiting to see him.

She tried to rationalize what had just happened. *He's seen me in shorts already, so this was like him seeing me in a bikini, she thought. It's totally fine.* The only problem was she didn't wear bikinis. How embarrassing. She cringed.

She left the shelter before Nathan finished his volunteer work. Megan couldn't stop her thoughts of how embarrassed she was, so she tried to calm down. She arrived home, picked up the phone and called Ashley, and told her what happened. Ashley started laughing. Megan swore never to wear the skirt again.

The next day, Megan went to the mailbox to get her mail. Sasha was across the street talking to Nathan and, for a moment, she was jealous of the attention he was giving her. Just then John appeared.

"I guess Nathan must have an interest in Sasha," Megan said.

"Oh, no I don't think so," John replied.

"Why not?"

"Because Nathan told me last week Sasha is his cousin. His second cousin."

"What?" Megan said, stunned by the news.

"She'd probably like to be kissing cousins," John added, "but he said that's never going to happen. He said she likes to flirt with anybody who gives her some kind of attention."

"What? Are you serious?" Megan asked, in total disbelief but elated at the same time.

"Of course, I am. He said Sasha was kind of wild, but she has always been that way even when she was younger," John replied.

"Oh, well that explains everything." She smiled and wanted to laugh but didn't because she didn't want John to think she was odd.

"Explains what?"

"Oh, nothing, John. I'll talk to you later."

She let out a sigh of relief as she walked back to her apartment, feeling much happier. She couldn't believe she had spent a lot of time worrying about Sasha and Nathan. She fixed herself a bowl of chocolate ice cream and binge-watched her favorite movies on television, feeling satisfied and more content than ever.

Megan had a busy week at the office. On Thursday evening, on her way to her weekly evening class, she found that she still had butterflies in her stomach just knowing she was going to be in the same room as Nathan. As she was walking toward the classroom, Travis was standing outside next to the door.

"What are you doing here, Travis?"

"I want to talk to you, Megan. You haven't called me."

"This isn't a good time. I have to go to class," she said nervously, unsure of his intentions.

Just then Nathan walked from the front of the class to the door. "Can I help you?" he asked.

"No. I'm talking to Megan," Travis replied.

"Are you attending a class here on campus?" he asked firmly with a stern look on his face.

"No, I'm just here to see Megan,"

"Then you have to leave," Nathan said in a firm, irritated voice.

"I told you I just want to talk to Megan for a couple of minutes."

"If you don't leave, I'll have to call the campus security," he said loudly.

"You do understand I work for the sheriff's department, right?" Travis said.

"Yes, but you're not campus security," Nathan said sternly, "and you're not attending this class."

"Okay, okay," he said, clearly irritated. "I'm going, but this isn't over." He turned and walked away, glaring at Nathan.

"What's going on, Megan?" Nathan asked.

"He's just an old boyfriend," Megan replied, embarrassed not knowing what else to say.

Nathan seemed aggravated. "Well, I don't think he's the right person for you. Why would you pick someone like him?"

She was stunned with what Nathan had just said to her. He was so blunt and appeared upset. Did he like her?

"I'm not involved with him any more," she replied.

"Thank goodness," he said with a frown. "You deserve someone better."

Nathan turned and walked to the front of the classroom. He started shuffling his papers. She could see he was upset. Megan walked to her desk, sat down on her chair, and opened her textbook. She dared not to look up at him.

A few minutes later the students were all seated, and class started. She focused on the lecture and the class discussions. Nathan was not as talkative as he normally was during class. He asked the students to form small discussion groups and didn't spend a large amount of time lecturing.

After class was over, Megan walked toward the door. She saw Nathan watching her as she was leaving but he didn't say anything. Then suddenly he rushed toward the door and said, "I need to talk to you, Megan."

"About what?"

"Please, have a seat next to my desk."

What did I do now? she thought.

"Okay." They both walked back to the front of the classroom and sat down. All the other students had left.

"You really don't need to be seeing Travis."

"What?"

"People like him aren't committed to anyone. He likes to date different women," Nathan said.

"How do you know that?" she asked with a shocked and embarrassed expression.

"I know it because he previously dated my sister, and she ended their relationship."

"What?" Megan said. She was stunned and didn't know what to say.

"Travis is not interested in a serious relationship," Nathan continued. "He even had a fling with Sasha."

Megan was lost for words and her face blushed red. "Well... we... we weren't in a serious relationship," she stuttered.

"That's good," Nathan said. "He's not right for you."

"I know that." She still didn't know what else to say. It was so embarrassing. "Thanks for the advice. I know you're trying to help."

"I'm serious, Megan. Think about it."

"Okay, I will." She forced a weak smile and got up and slowly walked toward the door. He watched her.

"Bye, Megan. See you next week."

"Okay, good night," she said and walked out of the door.

Megan had driven home still feeling upset. She rehearsed in her head everything Nathan had said. She decided to call Travis when she got home. She sat on the sofa for a few minutes rehearsing what she was going to say, then grabbed her phone.

"Hi, Travis. It's Megan."

"I was wondering when you were going to call me."

"Travis, I have something to tell you."

"What is it?" he asked.

"It's not a good idea for me to see you again."

"Megan. Just give me another chance. I'll make it up to you."

Megan knew she couldn't trust him. She just couldn't ignore the things he had put her through.

"I don't understand you. I don't feel I could ever trust you. I really need to go."

"Well, I do want to see you again. Call me if you change your mind."

"Goodbye, Travis." She quickly hung up the phone.

She didn't tell him she saw him shopping with another women, holding her hand or that she saw him again at the airport restaurant with someone else. There were too many things about Travis she didn't know. What bothered her even more was he never told her the truth and never said he was sorry.

She replayed everything about Travis in her mind, then decided that chapter in her life was over. He was history now. She grabbed her cell phone, deleted his photos, and put the soft cashmere sweater, gold necklace and bracelet he had given her in a donation box for charity.

Megan's thoughts were about Nathan. She spent an hour just lying there in bed and came to the realization that maybe Nathan was the person she was really meant to be with after all. The only problem was, Nathan was her professor, and she was in his class. He hadn't even asked for her phone number.

The next day, Megan had a lot of things to do. She started cleaning her apartment and saw the locked metal box in the back of her closet. She had totally forgotten about it. She reached for it and carefully put it on the bed, forced open the lock, and started looking through it.

There was a stack of letters tied together with a blue ribbon, and photos of her mom with a man in a military uniform who wasn't Megan's father. There were photos she had never seen before. *Who is this guy?* Their faces were close to the camera. She was smiling and he was looking at her adoringly. She was totally inquisitive. Inside was her mom's diary with a black leather cover.

Reluctant to read it at first, she put the diary back in the box. She wondered if she'd wake up the past by reading it. Should she read something so private? Would it be betraying her mother's privacy?

With the diary in her hands, she studied the soft leather cover for a few minutes but couldn't resist opening it up. *It wouldn't hurt to read through a few pages*, she thought. *There's no harm in doing that.* She scanned through the pages and felt guilty about reading it, but truthfully, not guilty enough then continued to read several more.

Apparently, her mom had dated a young man in the Navy stationed in San Diego. The letters were the ones he had written to her when he was away on the ship. He eventually left and went overseas to Europe and the letters stopped coming. She was pregnant and the last thing she wanted was to have a baby to take care of all by herself. She had no idea where he was and had no way of telling him. She wasn't even sure if he would care once he found out. She was young and didn't know what to do. It was a small town and people talked a lot. Then she wrote about Megan's father who was seven years older, marrying him, and about the birth of Chris. Megan's father and other relatives showered her with baby gifts when they found out she was going to have a boy. If her father and mother had disagreements, she was never aware of it. Life seemed to be normal.

Megan was stunned. She sat there on her bed gasping for a moment with so many things going through her mind. Her thoughts focused on Chris. Her mom had a secret—one she had kept for years. She began to wonder if her father had known it. *Did he know she was pregnant when they got married? Which man did she really love? Does the other man even know he has a son?* Should she ask her mom about it, or should she tell Chris?

Megan needed to talk to someone, but she couldn't tell Aunt Ruth. Her aunt always said blood was thicker than water, meaning loyalty to the family, the bloodline is greater than loyalty to anyone else. She poured herself a glass of wine, and drank quickly, trying to calm herself. Her mind was bombarded because this wasn't about her, it was about her brother. What about his bloodline? No person should be denied their birth right. His dad lived in another world; a world Chris was totally excluded from.

She wondered what Chris's dad's world was like and how he would feel if he knew about Chris.

So many things were going through her mind—confusing things. She poured herself another glass of wine. How was Chris going to feel when he found out? She had read stories about ancestry and DNA testing where a lot of secrets were uncovered, some happy stories, and some painful. Some people were in denial and others wanted everything to be forgotten.

There was no one else Megan wanted to talk to but Dr. Sharma. He'd help her decide what to do. She was convinced some people have three types of lives: a public one, a private life and a secret one. When her mom was growing up, there must have been a lot of people with secrets. But she didn't want to be one of those people. She needed to speak with him, now.

CHAPTER 33

ABOUT DREAMS

On Monday just after seven p.m., Megan made a to-do list and then took a couple of days off work. She had called to make an appointment to see Dr. Sharma about her mom, but he was on his once every two years vacation. He had gone to India to visit his relatives for a month. She sat there on the sofa wondering what to do. Her heart was pounding, and she felt a pain in her stomach. Was she having a panic attack? She didn't think so, just probably nerves. Megan was lost for words to describe how she really felt. She could call his cell phone, but he might get upset with her. After all, he was entitled to his vacation with nobody bothering him, so Megan had no choice but to wait for his return. Waiting was going to be so difficult.

Chris had to pay back the money he had borrowed, so Megan sent him money to pay off the loans he had gotten to help pay the mortgage and money for his savings account. He was glad to get it and told her he and his military buddies planned on celebrating during the weekend. Megan paid her mom's medical bills and her mom kept thanking her, even though she said there was no need. Megan and her mom never spoke of the Orange Street house foreclosure again.

During the week she ran some errands and hired a dog trainer for her aunt and uncle's dogs. Aunt Ruth didn't see the need for it—she didn't think her dogs were a problem. Uncle James was satisfied with Susie just sitting on his lap most of the day. Aunt Ruth said she would try the training for three weeks to see if it made a difference in their behavior.

She suggested Uncle James buy hearing aids. He agreed, only after she spent time convincing him, so Megan grabbed her phone and scheduled an appointment for his hearing tests.

Aunt Ruth took a painting she inherited from Uncle Harry to an art appraiser and discovered it was worth $5,000. She hung it in her living room. She had never had a painting worth that much money in her entire life. Her mom and aunt put the seventeen acres of land up for sale. They were going to make some money from it, even a small fortune if it sold for as much as the realtor said it would.

Megan put most of the money from Uncle Harry in her savings account. The following week Megan took her mother and Aunt Ruth shopping. On the weekend, she took Ashley and little Parker shopping for new clothes, and she bought Heather a gift for being such a good friend. The next day, she took Ben and John shopping so they could fill up their kitchen cupboards with food. She bought Ben some audiobooks so he could listen to some good stories.

She helped Uncle Ray and even gave Mark and Corey money to help pay some of their expenses. It was a good feeling helping family and friends, and for the first time in her life she was a provider. Megan had accomplished a lot during the past week, and she finally started working on her class assignments during the evening.

On Thursday, she rushed to her last class of the term. Each student had to give a presentation in front of the classroom and turn in a final paper. Several students had already given their presentations. After an hour, Nathan called on Megan. She was a little nervous but was well prepared and got through it with no problem.

When all the students were finished, Nathan dismissed the students early. Megan let out a deep sigh of relief. This seemed like the longest course she had ever taken because of Nathan. Not only was he her professor, but he was also the man she had the strongest attraction to. She was glad to be graduating in two weeks.

Everybody was talking and laughing as they left the classroom. Nathan stood by the door, smiling and saying goodbye to everyone.

Megan was anticipating saying goodbye to Nathan. She experienced familiar feelings of excitement and warmth all over. She liked him and even liked the way he glanced at her during class. She enjoyed getting attention from him.

As she got closer, he said softly, "Megan, I'd like to talk to you. Would you wait a couple of minutes?" Some of the students were still walking out of the classroom door.

"Okay," she replied, not knowing what to expect.

He turned and smiled at her. "I really enjoyed having you in my class, Megan."

"You did?" she replied, smiling at him sheepishly.

"You were an excellent student."

She let out a sigh of relief. "Thanks, Professor Engel. You're an excellent teacher. I learned a lot in your course."

"Thanks," he said and smiled. "I would've never known it with your face hidden behind your textbook most of the time."

"Well, yes. I guess I did do that a lot."

"Can you call me Nathan?"

"Okay," she said with a shy expression on her face.

"I'd like for you to have this note I wrote, and I do hope to see you again." He handed her a folded-up piece of paper.

"Thanks, Professor Engel. I mean... Nathan."

Excitement and sensuous warmth flooded through her entire body. She put the paper in her pocket.

"Have a good night!" she said. She didn't know what else to say; she was lost for words.

"Bye. See you soon, Megan." He smiled and watched her walk out the classroom door.

Hope to see you again. Was he joking or what? Of course, she would like to see him.

He was older than she was, but he was handsome and considerate which aroused her emotions. She thought about what it would be like to feel his arms around her. She'd be graduating soon, which meant she wouldn't see much of him unless she ran into him walking his dog in the neighborhood or volunteering at one of the homeless shelters. Happiness engulfed her as she walked toward the parking lot.

After getting into the car, she screamed and shouted, "I can't believe it! He likes me. He really does like me." Her heart was pounding a million miles an hour and she was breathless with excitement, just like a young schoolgirl.

She drove home not knowing what to expect in the days to come but was anxious to read the note that was in her pocket. Her heart was racing with the thoughts of true romance and longing to be with Nathan from the first time she'd laid eyes on him.

Megan decided not to read the note, not tonight. She wanted the feeling to last a few more hours—the anticipation of it all. Tomorrow, she'd read it. She wanted to go to bed with thoughts about all the pleasant things she remembered about Nathan, and revel in a full twenty-four hours of feeling wonderful. So, she placed the note on top of her bedroom dresser. Not sure if she could sleep or not, she poured herself a glass of wine.

What if there was a fire and the note burned up? If that happened, she would never know what he had written to her. She picked up the sterling silver jewelry box Uncle Harry had given to her as a little girl and put her watch in it like she did every night. She decided to put the note in her jewelry box too. *What if someone broke in and stole my jewelry box? But that's silly... who would want my jewelry box? There's nothing expensive in it but my watch.* She laughed.

It had been a long exhausting day and it was time for bed. She poured herself another glass of wine then took a long, hot bath to relax, before putting on her pink and silky negligee. She pulled the covers over her shoulders and quickly fell asleep.

The next morning, she woke up feeling refreshed but nervous, anticipating what might be in the note. She sat on her sofa slowly sipping on a cup of hot coffee then carefully unfolded the note from Nathan and read it.

Dear Megan, I was attracted to you the first time I saw you. You're a charming and intelligent young woman. The more I know you, the more I want to know you. Here's my phone number. Please call me. I look forward to seeing you again.

A rush of excitement went through her entire body. He wanted to get to know her. She couldn't believe it and decided to wait until after graduation day in two weeks to call him. After all, he was her professor. Megan didn't want to cause any problems and jeopardize his job. In two weeks, she'd no longer be a student and it wouldn't be a problem if they started going out together. She believed in the saying 'absence makes the heart grow fonder,' so

Nathan would just have to wait two long weeks before she called him.

When graduation day arrived, Megan was so excited. Her mother, Aunt Ruth, Uncle James and her brother Chris were there, as well as Ashley, little Parker and Heather. Mark and Corey planned on graduating next year, so took photos of her and everybody else. Her neighbors John and Ben waved at her from a distance. Even Mrs. Johnson was there with her little Chihuahua stuffed in her oversized handbag with only his head showing.

Nathan was busy talking to the students and other professors. He had his professor's cap, sash and gown on. He kept glancing in Megan's direction with his eyes flirting with her as he was talking. He was so handsome. It was an occasion she would never forget. He and Megan kept exchanging looks. Her heart was beating faster, and a warm sensuous feeling radiated through her entire body every time he glanced at her.

After the graduation ceremony was over, she walked over to Nathan and asked if Mark could take pictures of them together.

"Of course. I'd love that," he said.

She could feel her face blushing warmly, not knowing how to react to his smile. He put his arms around her holding her tightly while Mark took several photos. She enjoyed being next to him and didn't want the feeling to end.

"Bye, Professor Engel, thank you," she said.

"Nathan," he said and smiled with a sexy and flirtatious look on his face.

She looked at him sheepishly, said goodbye, and slowly walked away. She could feel his eyes watching her from behind.

Megan's family, relatives, close friends and neighbors attended her graduation party at Aunt Ruth and Uncle James' home. They had a lot of food, desserts and drinks. People were inside the house and sitting in the backyard talking and laughing. Music was playing in the background.

Late in the evening when she arrived home, she was totally exhausted. She played music while lying on her bed. It had been a long but beautiful graduation day. She had grown to be more confident and secure. Wonderful thoughts were going through her mind, and she had eventually fallen asleep, dreaming sweet dreams.

The next morning, Megan woke up and fixed a cup of coffee. She sipped it for a few minutes trying to work up courage to call Nathan. Her mouth was dry, her palms were sweaty. Hoping she wouldn't make a fool of herself, she took a long, deep breath and dialed his number.

"Hi, Nathan, this is Megan."

"Hello," he said.

"I'm glad you gave me your phone number."

"If I didn't, getting to know you would be a missed opportunity."

"You sound so academic," she said and laughed. "I certainly wouldn't want that to happen. But you were a very tough instructor."

"Really? In what way?"

"You really gave us a lot of assignments to work on during the term."

"I knew my students could handle everything. I had a really good class, and you were my best student."

"Thanks… that's a really nice compliment. But I bet you tell a lot of girls that."

"No, I really don't."

"To tell you the truth, I found it difficult to concentrate having such a handsome, knowledgeable professor like you," Megan said.

"Well, that's certainly a compliment," he said with a laugh.

"It's true… is that okay?" she asked. There was silence for a moment, and then he finally replied.

"Megan, I'd really like to get to know you better. Would you like to go out to dinner with me on Saturday?"

"Yes, I would," she replied.

"That's great, how about me picking you up at six?"

"That's fine. Would you like to know my apartment number?"

"I already know where you live." He laughed. "I know more about you than you think."

"You do?" She smiled and a burst of excitement ran through her entire body.

"Then I'll see you on Saturday."

"Okay, bye, Nathan."

One thing was certain in her mind, she was on fire, on fire for Nathan. She now knew Travis was not the right person for her. Nathan, the stranger across the street, was the one for her—he had been from the first time she had seen him. He was the one for her even when she was going through her life full of challenges.

CHAPTER 34

ANOTHER STORY

The phone rang early in the morning. Megan had been rubbing her eyes from a sound sleep and grabbed it from the table.

"Good morning, Megan."

"Hi, Mom."

"Guess what? I have some really good news."

"What's up?" Megan replied still wiping her eyes.

"The seventeen acres your uncle left us sold this week to a nice couple. They really liked it. They told us they plan on building a house on it."

"What? Are you kidding me?" Not waiting for a response, she said, "That's great, Mom!"

A burden had been lifted from Megan's entire soul and she jumped up out of bed. Her mom said that she had already told Chris and he was going out with his friends to celebrate.

"I have some more good news."

"What is it?"

"Your aunt and uncle are going to remodel their home and make it larger. Then there will be plenty of room for all of us. They have enough land to do it."

"Is that what you really want?"

"Yes, it's something we can afford. I'll have my own space and be near family."

"That's good, Mom. I'm happy for you. Let me know if there's anything I can do to help financially."

"Thanks, but we have enough money for it."

As Megan walked to the kitchen, her thoughts flashed back on the memories of happiness, struggles, fears and burdens of the past. There were good memories she cherished that didn't belong exclusively to the Orange Street house any more but would go with her wherever she lived. Tears of joy ran down her cheeks as she prepared breakfast.

It had taken a while before Megan had eventually convinced her mom to see Dr. Sharma about missing her dad and keeping all of his things in the attic. She never said anything about reading her diary and letters but told her everything in the attic had been moved to the storage facility. It was a half-truth, but Megan found it easier to not tell her everything, not knowing how she would feel. Dr. Sharma said her mom needed to work things out during her sessions with him first. It wasn't Megan's responsibility to tell Chris about what she found in her mom's diary. Megan didn't know the whole story because the story wasn't hers to tell.

The therapy sessions helped her mother a lot in handling the death of Megan's father and soon she was back to working part-time. Megan wasn't sure what her mom was going to do about her secret but was hoping things would work themselves out eventually. There was another story to be told, one only her mother knew. But if her mom never told Chris, then Megan told herself that she would tell her that she had found her diary. She would have no choice. Chris had a right to know.

She was amazed when, just a short time later, Chris called from Texas. Dr. Sharma had worked a miracle with her mother.

"Hey, Megan, we need to talk."

"About what?"

"Mom told me everything."

"What?"

"Did you know our dad was not my biological dad?"

She was silent for a moment. "I'm sorry, Chris. I wanted to tell you when I found out, but I was hoping that she would do it."

"I know. She told me everything and about going to counseling. I was shocked but I don't hold it against her."

"I was wondering how you were going to react to everything," Megan said.

"She was young and single at the time and didn't know what else to do."

"You're not angry?"

"I don't know how I feel right now, a bit confused but not angry. I had a few beers last night and thought about everything for a long time. Our dad is the only father I've known all my life."

"Are you okay?" she asked. Her heart was beating slowly and steadily.

"Yeah. I'm gonna take the ancestry test and see if I can locate my biological dad and any relatives I may have. He may not even be alive."

Megan thought about the idea a person's life could be turned upside down from some spit on a cotton swab. It could have such a major impact. The results may not be what most people expected when looking for their ancestry.

"If that's your decision, I think I would do the same."

"I had to think about it for a while." Chris said.

"But be prepared that he may or may not be happy to see you," Megan replied. "I've read some good stories and a few shocking ones about people finding a parent."

"I realize that, but who knows what will happen because he never knew I existed."

"Hmmm… that's true."

They talked a little longer. Megan was glad to know that her mom had told him the truth after all those years of neither of them not knowing.

"It's your bloodline, Chris. But it won't change who you are and the wonderful person you've become."

"I know but it's something I want to do."

It was a long week and Saturday finally arrived. Nathan walked over to Megan's apartment, gave her a beautiful bouquet of red roses, and they drove to one of the finest restaurants in town. He spoke calmly and his eyes were flirting as he looked at her. They talked about everything, and she couldn't stop laughing.

"What's your family really like Nathan?"

"They're loving and fun to be around. My parents did the best they knew in raising me and my sisters. They always pushed education, so I guess that's why I ended up teaching college. My two sisters used to get into sibling rivalry when they were younger, but now they get along a lot better. I've always been the big brother, so they looked up to me."

She told him about her goals in life, and her views on politics and world events. Megan was comfortable being around him. He told her how much he was attracted to her and hoped they could spend more time together.

The following weekend they got up early and toured the Los Angeles Getty Museum. Afterwards, they had lunch at a small, colorful Mexican restaurant. She enjoyed getting to know him better. They sat down at a table and talked aimlessly, held hands across table, and discussed the endless possibilities of the things they could do together.

Nathan ordered spicy, hot Mexican food. The server brought tortilla chips as a starter, and she dipped her tortilla chips into the salsa and took a bite. It burned her lips, and she turned red, started coughing, grabbed her glass of water and took several sips to cool her tongue and wash it down.

Nathan started laughing. "You know you don't have to eat it if it's too hot. You've already impressed me."

He motioned the server to come over to the table and ordered mild salsa for Megan to eat with her tortilla chips.

"Thanks," she said, wiping her forehead with a napkin. "I really prefer something a little milder."

He took a deep breath and gazed into Megan's eyes. "I really enjoy being with you, Megan, but I think it's nice for two people to be friends first before they become serious about each other."

She was comfortable with that because she totally agreed with him. Even though she longed to be in his arms, she didn't want to rush into anything with Nathan.

They soon finished lunch and strolled down the street looking in the small shops along the way. Nathan grabbed her hand and held it as they walked together. He told her about how he had spent most of his time teaching and going to college. He had little time for dating. Most of the people he hung around with were guys doing the same thing.

After they arrived at her place, she unlocked the front door. He stepped forward closing the gap between their bodies, put his arms around her and kissed her lips. Her entire body was on fire. For a moment, neither of them moved. He released her and looked into her eyes and stroked her hair. Then he pulled her even closer than before and kissed her even more passionately. When he released her from his embrace, it was like being Cinderella in a beautiful dream.

"Want to go out again next week?" he asked.

"Of course, I do. I thought you would never ask," she replied and then smiled.

"Good. I'll call you tomorrow."

Megan enjoyed being with Nathan. Over the next two months, they went on several more dates, but Megan was reluctant to introduce Nathan to her family because of her disappointment with Travis. Finally, she decided it was time for him to meet the family. She invited him to dinner on Sunday. Her mother was looking forward to meeting Nathan because Megan had told her so many nice things about him. He liked Mexican food, so her mother and Aunt Ruth fixed him his favorite meal.

The evening dinner was great. Nathan spent time talking to Uncle James with his new hearing aids and they got along really well. After dinner, they talked for an hour and finally said their goodbyes.

The next day Ashley called Megan.

"You're never at home any more. You're always with Nathan!"

"I know but you don't have to guess where I am any more," she said and laughed. "Things have certainly changed in both of our lives."

"That's for sure," Ashley replied.

"You're always with Steve. How are things going between you two?"

"Really good. I'm happy and he really likes Parker."

"I'm glad for you, Ashley. You deserve someone nice."

"Let me know when you want to go shopping."

"Sounds good. See you later!" Megan replied.

On Friday, Megan got a call from her brother Chris. He had finally found his father's family. She didn't know if she should be happy to hear the news or not. So, she refrained from saying how glad she was for him.

Then he said, "I found out my father passed away five years ago."

"He's not alive? I'm sorry to hear that," Megan replied, feeling disappointed. She thought if it had been five years sooner, just five years, he would have gotten to know his son. That fate was not meant to be.

"Yes, I wanted to meet him and find out what he was like, and make up my own opinion about him but that will never happen.

I do have a half-sister and brother. The good news is they would like to meet me and so would the other family members. They were happy to know that I'm part of their family too."

"That's great, Chris. I'm glad for you."

"Me too. I didn't know how they would react to everything. It will be exciting and emotional for me."

"You'll be fine. Let me know how things go," she said with a big smile.

"Will do, love you."

Megan was glad to know that Chris would find out more about his father and the other siblings. After all, they were his bloodline. He needed to know about his ancestry.

The weekend was going to be warm and sunny, so Megan and Nathan went on a spontaneous trip. They grabbed two sleeping bags, a tent, the dog and some camping gear, and drove to the mountains in Idyllwild. After finding a beautiful camp site, they set up their tent near a creek. They filled their backpacks with food and water, hiked through the woods, and climbed a small hill. The mountain itself was a beautiful place with pine trees, rocks and pebbles, deer and squirrels.

It was time for lunch, so they decided to eat in the shade of an old pine tree. They dropped their backpacks and sat on some large rocks. They were sweating and got out their water first, gave some to his dog, and started to eat their sandwiches. They stared at the landscape that was like a picture painting.

"I used to go hiking a lot as a young child with my parents and sisters."

"You did?" she said smiling.

"Yes, I grew up in Shady Grove and don't like large cities. I lived in Los Angeles for a while, but it wasn't for me."

"I know what you mean, I feel the same way," Megan replied.

"The sun is going down, so we need to hike back to our camp site. It's going to take another hour."

"Sounds like a good idea."

Back at the campsite, they shared their hiking experiences with the other campers. They grilled hotdogs for dinner on the open fire and ate canned beans. It started to get cool, so they bundled up in their sleeping bags and talked most of the night in the small tent. They talked about everything, and it seemed as though they had known each other forever. They talked about the past and their lives today. Then they finally went to sleep all bundled up nice and warm with Nathan's dog lying between them.

In the morning, Nathan got up early and started cooking breakfast for her. He handed her a plate of scrambled eggs, pancakes and a cup of hot coffee.

"For some reason food tastes so much better in the woods."

"Yeah, isn't that weird?" Megan said, chuckling to herself.

"Did you sleep well last night?"

"I did! Your dog kept me warm." She laughed. "I love being close to nature."

During the morning they went walking on some more hiking trails. In the afternoon, they packed up everything and drove back home.

Nathan called Megan during the week and invited her to his place on the weekend. They grilled two steaks over the charcoal grill and ate them by candlelight with two glasses full of red sparkling wine. They talked about Megan's past experiences and his past too. She told him about her best friend Scott but was careful not to mention

Travis. Nathan still really disliked him. She didn't blame him.

Nathan said it took several years to get all his degrees and finish college. He had been in a committed relationship with his best friend's sister, but she soon had other interests and moved to San Francisco. It took him a long time to get over her leaving, and for a long time he took a dim view of women and went on occasional dates but didn't get serious with anyone. A while back he had been seeing a young divorcee for two years, but it hadn't worked out. She had one kid. The child's father was causing problems and it impacted Nathan's relationship with her. Nathan said he'd like to have his own kids someday but wanted to plan for it.

After drinking a glass of red wine, they relaxed and listened to soft music. "The touch of your hands feels so nice," Megan said.

He smiled. "You feel good too." One look at him and she was like putty in his hands.

As music echoed in the background, Nathan lowered his mouth to hers and she knew she was right about her feelings for him. There was fire there, and heat, and they poured into her, his response searing through her.

Megan was lost in the moment and enjoyed being held tightly in his arms. Who was there to know, to care, but the two of them in the dark of the night? It was her and him. It had seemed like a long time since she had been with anyone she truly adored and understood. Everything was different with Nathan. She could trust him. He was kind, and he was honest about his feelings for her. She enjoyed his soft touch and her blood pounded in her veins nearly as hard as the rain falling on a tin roof.

Nathan devoured her mouth and he seemed to be as hungry for her as she was for him. Unreserved fire and passion met her, incredibly. His tongue plunged between her lips, tasted her, found her tongue. The warm wet sweetness of her mouth made him respond with hot passion. His hands drove into her lush brown hair, grabbed handfuls of it and crushed her mouth to his as his strong fingers slid into her hair to push his mouth down against hers.

Her body seemed to melt against his. She moved herself so he could feel the fullness of her, the supple length of her body against him. Blindly, he turned to drive her back against him. She needed that body hard against hers, and wanted her firm, full breasts against his chest as he wedged a thigh between hers. The need to touch, be touched, to take and give, nearly overwhelmed her. Hunger for him surged inside her and the night was long and beautiful as they showed their love for each other.

The next morning Megan woke up feeling wonderful, totally refreshed like the fragrance of colorful spring flowers. She knew the week was going to be busy and could hardly wait for the weekend so she could be with Nathan again.

On Sunday at the park, they talked and played with his dog for more than an hour, endlessly tossing the ball. The dog chased Megan through obstacle courses, then she and Nathan took turns playing tug of war with his dog. Afterwards, in the afternoon, Megan went home and took a shower. Running around with the dog had worn her out. Nathan invited her back over to his condo to watch a movie, so later in the evening they sat down on the sofa to enjoy each other's company.

"You smell wonderful," he said. "What kind of perfume do you have on?"

"I don't remember. It's something Heather bought me when she was in Spain."

She leaned next to him, he grabbed her hand, and kissed the back of it.

"I've never had anyone kiss the back of my hand before. I really like it."

"Are you serious?"

"Yes, of course I am." She smiled sheepishly.

"Well, in that case I'll have to do it more often."

He started kissing her hands, her arms and then her neck, and slowly worked up to kissing her lips. He made her body temperature go up, hot like a flaming fire.

"Are you going to stop so we can watch the movie?" she asked reluctantly.

"I'll just keep going until you want me to stop," he said. "I want you, Megan. More than you'll ever know." They spent a long and wonderful evening together.

During the next few weeks, they were both busy at their jobs. Nathan would call her when he had time, and she would call him. They got to know each other's likes and dislikes more and more. They had gotten closer and closer, knew which foods each liked and favorite sports, colors, movies, books and music. The relationship progressed to a higher level, not going around in circles.

Megan thought about how much she loved being with Nathan. They shopped in the mall and walked into all the different stores. She could see the way people looked at them, thinking, *What a beautiful couple*. He was so loving, smart and considerate. She felt beautiful, loved and happy, happier than she had ever been.

One day, when Megan was cleaning, she accidentally pulled out the rolled-up map she and Scott had made from her closet. It was still wrapped with a yellow ribbon. Nathan looked at it and said he would make her dreams a reality. They would go on day trips, the ones she never got to go on with Scott. She was so excited.

When the weather got warmer, they went to the beach. She pulled off her T-shirt and shorts and exposed her beautiful two-piece bikini that she had bought last week.

"Wow! You look great." He studied her from head to toe and smiled.

"Thanks." She blushed.

She pulled her hair back and away from her face with a hair tie. They both started running into the water and splashing each other. An hour later, they laid down on their colorful, plush beach towels, and dried off. His body was cool, smooth and firm all over.

"Can I rub lotion on you?" she asked.

"Of course, you can."

She reached for the bottle of lotion and warmed it up in her hands. She put lotion all over his back and made circular movements with her hands as she rubbed it on his skin. She rubbed his back and arms in slow steady circles.

"That really feels good. I could stay here all day with you doing that. Your hands are so soft and smooth."

"I'm glad you like it," she replied. "You have a firm, masculine body."

"I do?" he said, smiling all the while.

"And you have big feet. You know what they say about men with big feet?"

"No, what?"

"They have really big... shoes."

He laughed. "That's not what you were really going to say," he said playfully. "It's your turn now. Let me put some lotion on you."

"Okay."

He rubbed her back and arms slowly with lotion. The touch from his hands was so warm and so good. She enjoyed every minute of it. After a few minutes, he started rubbing lotion on her legs from her thighs all the way down to her feet. She was trying hard not to get aroused because he awakened all her senses. The touch of his hands was calming but exciting at the same time.

Then he reached and pulled her up next to him. He was a little nervous.

"Megan, I knew you were the one for me the first time I met you." His smile conveyed complete satisfaction.

"Did you really?" she said.

"Yes. I've read books about love at first sight but never believed it happened to people in real life. But with you everything is different. You're beautiful. Other women just don't compare to you."

"Wow... you're so sweet, Nathan." She was blushing because she was so happy.

"I want to ask you something," he said, looking at her seriously for a moment.

"What?" she replied curious about what's he was going to say.

"Well, I've been thinking... you have your own apartment and I have my spacious new condo, yet we spend all our time together."

"Yes..."

"Why don't we just have one place to call home?" He was smiling now, but it was a shy smile.

"Nathan... what are you asking?" She was smiling too.

She felt like a surge of electricity had gone through her entire body. He grabbed her hand, and it was warm and gentle.

"Megan, will you marry me?"

"What?" She wanted to hear him say it again.

"I said, will you marry me?"

There was a moment of silence. "Yes, yes, of course I will!" she shouted.

She grabbed and hugged him. He put his arms around her and held her tightly for a long time. So, close to her she could hardly breathe.

"I love you, Megan."

"I love you too, Nathan," she said, as tears of joy were running down her cheeks.

"Give me your hand."

He held her hand gently and showed her a beautiful, sparkling diamond ring, put it on her finger, and kissed her again.

Megan was confident her whole life was going to be different now that she and Nathan were together. They'd have their own place to call home. Most importantly, he chose to love her, and she chose to love him. Nathan was her Prince Charming, and she was his princess from Shady Grove. This was the life she was here for—not the yesterdays but the todays.

After arriving home in the evening, Megan sat down on the sofa feeling happy thinking about Nathan and the wonderful time they had spent together. Dressed in her silky pajamas, she sipped on a cup of hot tea, clicked on TV, and the nightly news came on. Suddenly, a reporter flashed a breaking news story.

The Shady Grove police discovered another body unearthed from the property behind the burned down Orange Street house. Megan suddenly gasped, was shocked and stood up, her eyes widened, her jaw dropped as the color drained from her face. She was thinking, *Was Carl right after all? Is Austin Mitchell really a serial killer?* She quickly picked up her phone and called Mark.